SOMETHING THERE

Rebecca had taken her eyes away from her father only for an instant. When she turned back to him now, there seemed to be a pastel aura behind him, lavender and pink and buttercup yellow. Even with the shadows that shot through it, the lowering slant as if of light from a deep hole, it would not have been sinister except that it was clearly in pursuit of her father, who was clearly fleeing.

Rebecca was well aware of the visual distortions that the shiny waxed white floors, white walls, and fluorescent lights could generate. But this was more organized than that, more definite, and gave the impression of having intent, mischievous if not malevolent. It didn't fade as she stared at it, squinted, shielded her eyes, but swirled and seemed on the brink of coalescing into a recognizable form, which Rebecca, suddenly, did not want to recognize.

THE TIDES

MELANIE TEM

LEISURE BOOKS NEW YORK CITY

A LEISURE BOOK®

August 1999

Published by

Dorchester Publishing Co., Inc.
276 Fifth Avenue
New York, NY 10001

ISBN 0-8439-4574-5

The name "Leisure Books" and the stylized "L" with design are trademarks of Dorchester Publishing Co., Inc.

Printed in the United States of America.

This is for my father, John Kubachko, 1912-93,
himself until the end.
Thanks, Daddy.

And for Steve, who knows who he is.

ACKNOWLEDGMENTS

My thanks to:

my agent, Richard Curtis, for his ongoing support, guidance, and inspiration;

my husband and first-line editor *par excellence,* Steve Rasnic Tem;

Roberta Robertson, for the story that inspired the title;

and the residents and staff of Westland Manor Nursing Center and Everett Court Community.

Chapter 1

'Faye?'

That first evening when Faye came into his room – uninvited, unless he'd finally given off some terrible, mysterious summons as he'd been so afraid of doing twenty-eight years ago when she'd left him and the baby; unwelcome, except that his heart leaped in just that ancient and immediate way – Marshall stared and roared her name.

'*Faye!*'

Funny how he knew precisely, without even pausing to figure it, how long it had been since Faye had vanished, and what her relationship had been to him and their child, and what she'd left behind. He'd never heard from her again, but he'd imagined he would, with trepidation and shameful hope kept himself alert for signs. Funny how clearly he could picture her: piquant face, alabaster skin, the longest nails he'd ever seen on a woman shaped and polished into beautiful claws, clothes always thoughtfully chosen and arranged to appear carefree. He could hear her voice as if she were calling him now, which she was, crooning to him, singing; the sweetness of her voice, speaking and singing, had often both belied and brought out the nasty things she said, the raunchy things she sang.

He could smell her flowery fragrance. He could taste and feel her as though she were in his arms, as though her clawed fingers were at his throat.

She was endangering their daughter. 'I've got my own life to live,' she'd flung at him more than once, screamed or sung at the baby. At least once she'd raised her hand; he'd stepped in just in time, and the blow, incompletely deflected, had shocked him when she'd slapped his forearm and spun away, not crying, not apologizing. Singing.

Funny how clear and present all that was. And often these days, Marshall couldn't remember what he'd had for breakfast, couldn't keep straight in his mind who anyone was to him. Often he had the sense that who he was, the person he'd have thought he'd come to know over the span of his lifetime – how long? seventy years? – was permeable and changeable. Perhaps it always had been thus. Perhaps he never *had* known for certain who he was.

He held onto the knowledge of his own name – Marshall Emig – repeating it as though that told him something, but really it didn't. Often he was frightened, sad. Sometimes, though, he merely let what would happen happen, and then he would come back into this reality or some other with the sense of having accrued new memories he couldn't quite place.

But he remembered Faye.

Faye was here now.

'Oh. Faye.'

If Billie had been there – his wife; his companion; in his life infinitely longer than Faye had been, except that Faye had never really left his life although he'd tried to make her – she'd have understood right away, and she'd have been as upset as he was to see Faye. So for her sake – and

2

because of the guilt, for his own – he was glad Billie was gone somewhere when it happened. He was always unsettled when Billie wasn't there, always had been and lately it was worse. He used to be able to disguise how dependent he was on Billie for security and stability, but he didn't think he was so good at that anymore.

Maybe that was why Faye had reappeared. Because his mind kept pulling itself loose from the moorings he and Billie together had painstakingly constructed. Because he couldn't be counted on to remember who he was.

Faye – the memory of Faye; the dread of Faye; the insinuation and memory and, yes (he didn't understand it himself, could scarcely tolerate it) his *love* of Faye that had always been between them – had hurt Billie too much over the years. He had always done everything in his power to protect Billie from Faye, but he knew that sometimes it hadn't been enough. This time he would do whatever it took.

Rebecca was there with him. Becky, his daughter – although it was hard for Marshall to believe in any solid way, to remember that he believed, that this slight blonde young woman with the crowded eyes was the same person as the child whose raising had so consumed him for so many years. Years which now, looking back, considering them as a portion, a fraction of his life, seemed so few, so quick.

Was she, in fact, the same person as the girl-child he'd raised? Was he himself the same person as when he'd been little else but her daddy? Was he the same person as when he himself had been a child – so long ago, a span of time beyond human comprehension, like the age of the universe (yet with an immediacy like the burst of flavor from a capsule punctured by the teeth). Was he the same person as when he'd been with Faye? Was this *really* Rebecca? What did '*really* Rebecca' mean?

Always given to moody rumination, Marshall could now wander among these thoughts and bits of thoughts for hours, days, periods of time without demarcation. The reality that stretched outward from himself, to which his physical senses provided access and from which they collected data his brain was supposed to process, was showing itself to be considerably less engaging than the reality that stretched inward, behind his eyes and ears and tongue, under his mind, the back of his head expanding, the root of his brain. Many people inhabited the vast bowl-shaped space there, sometimes firm and dry, sometimes shimmering as if with tides.

A boy in a steel town on the yellow-hazed bank of the Monongahela River: no sensation of growing up there, of passing through, but of *being* there, *being* that boy. Going last night and again tonight and again tomorrow night down the steep hill to the Club to retrieve Pop, then back up the hill, Pop staggering and singing, home.

A young man friends with another young man named Windy Curtis, wrestling each other, lifting weights together, shyly double dating. Windy Curtis always smelled of fish no matter how much cologne he used, and he used a lot. Marshall's nose wrinkled and his head ached from it. The time as Windy's pal, perhaps three years, was the only spell of comradeship Marshall had ever known, and it was as present as it ever had been, though taking place this time in that space behind the boundary through which he looked out on the world as if through the windshield of an enormous and fully loaded truck, Windy as three-dimensional as ever. And Marshall was no longer the boy, the son; he no longer lived in the yellow town. Windy's friend was who he was. The two of them did everything together.

Faye's lover. God, he was Faye's lover, consumingly, but she, somehow, was not his. Faye's husband. And then she was gone.

Rebecca's father. Billie's husband. Clerk and then manager of retail clothing stores, work he didn't find especially rewarding but didn't mind, incorporated into his experience of himself because it was part of how to be father of Rebecca, husband of Billie, one of the many men Faye had taken over and passed through. Marshall Emig.

Not infrequently he did not recognize his daughter when she entered his field of vision. Sometimes he knew she was someone who mattered, but he didn't have a name for what she was to him. Sometimes she was an utter stranger. Both these perceptions had truth to them, as did his equally frequent and equally substantiated apprehensions that she was his daughter.

He knew her name perfectly well, of course, and could recount episodes out of their shared histories. Sometimes – and Marshall thought these moments were increasingly precious as his mind became more and more confused – he absolutely basked in their father-daughter love.

Maybe it was a trick. Maybe they were tricking him. Maybe the assumption that you could recognize anybody, that a person had a core identity which remained constant and discernible over time and place and circumstance, was a ruse. Or, at best, a construct which he was not required to accept anymore – was, in fact, incapable of accepting as the tidal spaces opened up behind the face the outer world saw.

Somebody was always watching him. If it wasn't his wife or his daughter, it was somebody. Every once in a while he got away, and the sense of freedom when he wasn't under their gaze could be exhilarating, until he considered what it meant about his life that he felt freed when what he really was was lost; what it said about him that just being out on the sidewalk or among trees by himself made him feel freed; pretty pitiful, when you thought about it.

That evening he'd been haphazardly plotting to escape, but he couldn't really keep his mind on it and he doubted he would have done it, even if Faye hadn't shown up. Where would he go? (Sometimes he knew, but he couldn't have said, as if the imagined destination didn't have a name.) Faye being here should have made him want even more to escape. Instead, it made him want to stay. Did Billie know that? He would never tell Billie. It would terrify her. It would break her heart.

When Faye whizzed in as if she owned the place, scarves flying and prettily gauzing her face, Rebecca was on duty with him. If he had done one thing right with Rebecca it had been to keep from her any knowledge of Faye. She didn't recognize the name he shouted. She didn't even recognize that it *was* a name. Marshall, her father, was glad of that. But Marshall was afraid of facing Faye alone. He never had been any match for her. If she hadn't left him, he never would have had the strength to leave her, even though he'd known at the time and knew even more clearly looking back that staying with her would have killed him and probably would have killed their child. 'Faye!' he bellowed again, or maybe it was just the one time reverberating in his mind the way words spoken or thought often did now.

Rebecca looked up in alarm from the papers spread out on the little table. What was she doing there, anyway?

Then she got to her feet – wearily, he thought, concerned – and came toward him. 'Dad? What's wrong?'

Faye wasn't exactly gone, but she wasn't exactly there anymore, either. Gauze from her scarves remained, around the lights, around the face of the young blonde woman leaning too close over him. He pulled back, raised his hand. In her eyes he saw Faye.

Now she had one hand on each arm of his chair, trapping him there as if her body were a lid and he in a box. She wasn't very big. He knew her from somewhere. He'd have to push up against her in order to free himself, maybe hit her, even knock her down, maybe hurt her. Maybe hurt Faye, once and for all; it wouldn't be the first time he'd wanted to hurt her, but it would be the first time he'd followed through, and the thought gave him energy and direction.

He readied himself. (He knew her from somewhere. She was somebody important to him. She was his daughter. She was Becky.)

When she said, 'There's nothing to be afraid of, Dad,' he believed her, but he couldn't allow her to put him in a cage like that. 'Come on,' Rebecca said to him, smiling. She'd always had such a pretty smile, more guarded than her mother's, less brilliant and easy, which was a good indication of her character but made him yearn for her mother as a young woman every time she smiled at him. She put her hand on his arm, but she'd straightened up now and he didn't feel so trapped, and he would never hurt her.

Now he was paralyzed, imprisoned in his chair by the knowledge that he had been prepared to hurt her, had been designing ways to hurt her for his own benefit. The need to protect his child, the drive to do what was best for her no matter what the cost to him, he had always considered one of the most primitive of instincts. He had, in fact, sacrificed a significant share of his own happiness in order not to hurt her. It was not that he begrudged her that; that's what fathers were supposed to do. But could it be that there were instincts even more primal that would rise out of the mush of his mind now like nightcrawlers out of rain-soaked soil? Something was wrong with his mind. He stared at his daughter in horror.

'Come on, Dad,' she said gently.

Marshall was certain she had said that before, she had just said that. Why was she repeating herself? He had heard her the first time. He had not understood what she wanted; he still didn't understand what she wanted, but repeating herself wasn't going to help; the problem was that she wasn't being clear. He scowled.

Rebecca stood up, away from him (relief, but also a feeling of abandonment, of imminent abandonment: would she really leave him alone? How would he survive alone?). 'Let's go for a walk. You can help me make rounds.'

He had no idea what she was talking about, and he did not care for her patronizing tone. Nonetheless, Marshall acquiesced, happy to sacrifice his own happiness for his child's. He knew how to do that. She took his arm and walked close beside him, as if they were a young couple out for a stroll in the spring sunshine. Was it spring? Marshall thought it was spring. Was it evening?

Marshall was proud to have such a pretty young lady on his arm, his own lovely daughter Rebecca for all the world to see. For Faye to see.

As they made their way out of the room into a hall, where bluish-white fluorescent lights rippled and dazzled off white floors and white walls, Marshall had the sensation of gauze trailing across his face, touching just the thinnest layer of his skin and flesh, and it was light enough to tickle and tease, rough enough to hurt. He flinched away. He smelled a flowery odor that was naggingly familiar and evocative. But he didn't say anything. The human heart requires secrets; Faye had taught him that.

Rebecca spat, 'Look at that,' and stopped short.

Marshall looked, saw innumerable things that could have accounted for her distress – holes in the linoleum that turned out to be only darker squares that turned out to be holes after all; doorways that listed; a man with his zipper open.

Rebecca had let go of him to take a pen and notebook out of her pocket. She scribbled something on what he could see was a list covering most of the page. He couldn't make out what she wrote, and he was curious, a bit wary; was she writing something about him? When she reached for the handrail and flipped it halfway off the wall he saw that all its screws on one end were missing, and the bracket clattered onto the floor. He bent to pick it up, hefted it in his hands. 'I'll fix it for you,' he offered.

He saw her start to refuse. Then she looked at him. 'That'd be great, Dad. Do you think you could?'

'I expect I could manage a job of this magnitude,' he advised her with studied irony, and to his gratification she smiled. She had a pretty smile, if she could just let herself go. But maybe it was a good thing she didn't.

She put her notebook and pen away and took his arm again, hugging it to her. They made their way along a corridor whose length, breadth, direction, and function he found inscrutable. They were in a hospital, he thought, and then fleetingly remembered: This was a nursing home. The phrase appalled him, then slid away.

Behind and above them, where neither of them noticed – and producing such a slight distortion in light, sound, and air quality that Rebecca wouldn't have thought much of it anyway, though Marshall would – Faye followed them. She'd just got here, and she still found the sheer novelty of it energizing, but she hadn't come all this way, gone to all this trouble, just for the buzz. She liked this place. There were opportunities everywhere. There'd be plenty to keep her amused while she waited for her chance at the real prize. But patience had never been Faye's strong suit. She wouldn't just sit on her hands.

Marshall was shocked that there were so many people out here, and uneasily he wondered if he was supposed to know any of them. Actually, not a few of them did look familiar, but one of the reasons he'd always had trouble with names was that the world's population (what he'd seen of it, which wasn't much; keenly he regretted not having traveled more, knew he never would now, thought maybe he would, maybe he would go to Greece, he'd always wanted to go to Greece, he would talk to Billie about it when she got back, there was no reason they couldn't go to Greece, they had plenty of money and plenty of time) was made up of *types*. Physical types. Psychological types. Marshall had made something of a study of the world's types. Consequently, he had difficulty distinguishing one individual from another, and often didn't see much point in doing so.

There, sitting in a chair against the wall with her purse upright in her lap, was one of the small, frail old-lady type; his mother had been like that, and his daughter Becky would be, too, when she was old. He missed Becky. He hadn't seen her for a long time. He wondered where she was. He gave a courtly little bow to the small old lady.

Coming down the hall was a drunk. Marshall detested all drunks. This was the happy-drunk type. Jovial, beaming like an imbecile, the guy would have been red-faced if he hadn't been a Negro. He smelled like a brewery, glad-handing you and slurring his words. Marshall knew the type and kept his face stony when the drunk approached, but the young woman on his arm – his daughter; his daughter Rebecca – stopped and was friendly. She oughtn't to do that. That wasn't the way to handle drunks. Marshall made his arm stiff and leaned away from his daughter and the drunk, hoping she'd sense and correctly interpret his disapproval. When they were out of earshot he would sit her down and give her some fatherly advice about drunks (happy drunks, fawning drunks, were the most insidious, whatever their race).

Among the nurses and aides in white uniforms were several types. The homosexual. The nervous young girl. The brazen young girl. The middle-aged female smoker with gravelly voice, nicotine-stained fingertips exaggerated by long painted nails, and smoky breath.

Marshall was certain he had never known the names of any of these people. Throughout his life he hadn't taken much interest in more than a few people – his wife Billie, his daughter Rebecca, co-workers as long as they were working with him. (Faye.) Childhood friends; suddenly he was wondering what Winslow Curtis was doing these days. Good old Windy. He stopped and asked of the woman beside him (he couldn't quite place her, but she was somebody close to him so it made sense to ask), 'Did you know Windy Curtis? What's become of him?'

'No, Dad,' she said patiently. Her patience alarmed

him. 'You knew Windy before I was born. He died twenty-five years ago or more, of a heart attack.'

Shock riffled through him, along with a dismaying feeling of *déjà vu*, as though he'd experienced that same shock and vertigo at the news of his friend's death more than a few times before. He must have swayed a little because she put her other hand on his shoulder. 'Oh,' Marshall said, struck as if freshly by the inevitability of both death and mourning. 'Oh. That's too bad. I'll miss him.'

'You had good times together, didn't you?'

How did she know that? Did she know Windy? Warily, Marshall nodded. 'We traveled across country together.' (With Faye. Both of us with Faye, although Faye and Windy had never openly admitted it.) Maybe he shouldn't have said that. Maybe he'd given away secret and potentially damaging information about himself (and about Faye, although he couldn't quite see how).

'During the Depression, when you were just out of high school and couldn't find work.'

Suspicion now rang in his ears. 'That's right,' he said curtly, and would say no more about Winslow Curtis, whom he would visit as soon as he could get out of this place. (Or about Faye.)

'Look, Dad,' Rebecca urged. She was trying to distract him. Marshall recognized the ploy. She was trying to force him to turn left. He'd have had no objection to turning left, but he was not about to be forced and certainly not by his own daughter, so he resisted. The pressure on his arm and shoulder subsided. 'They're painting a mural.'

Despite himself, he turned left, stopped, and looked. Maybe half a dozen people were painting a wall. The glad-handing drunk. A tiny, dark, intense woman of a type he had not encountered often – some sort of foreigner. Another one of the bent old-lady type – this one frail although she wasn't especially small.

Marshall squinted. It made him uncomfortable to see all these people painting on the wall like misbehaving children. If there was any coherence to the painting, it escaped him. Swatches and globs of random colors, and shapes that bore no resemblance to anything in the real world.

The drunk was painting the background. 'That's Gordon,' Rebecca told her father, as if he cared what the guy's name was. 'I guess he's painted before.'

'Sure have, Princess,' the drunk guy boomed, and Marshall, mistrusting his familiar tone, tried to put himself between Rebecca and the man and found he could not; in the attempt he nearly lost his balance and someone, the blonde young woman holding onto his arm, prevented him from doing so. He did not appreciate that. He would bide his time. The drunk, face flushed under the dark jowly skin, was still talking, too loudly, too familiarly. 'Houses, fences, one time a barn with a big high peak, none of the other fellows would go up the ladder. I know what I'm doing.'

The north wall of the lounge was now a bright satisfying white, with smudges and streaks only here and there. 'Well,' said Rebecca wryly, 'I guess we can't change our minds now, can we?'

A tall woman in a uniform, a stern-nurse type, shrugged and turned her attention back to the spiral notebook in her hand. 'Maybe it won't look so bad.'

A woman with a Southern accent said comfortingly, 'At least it's a cheap way to redecorate the lounge.'

The tiny dark foreign woman was painting stars. She

sat crosslegged in one corner, her nose inches away from Gordon's white wall, and used the brush from a child's paint-by-number set to make dozens of dots and rays. The stars were in a formation like a fan: the yellow ones at the wide end were faint and fuzzy, the middle ones were green and blue and purple and round, and at the tip was one bright red star perhaps two inches in diameter with twelve distinct points and the suggestion of three-dimensionality.

The woman appeared to be talking to herself. When Rebecca raised her voice slightly to say, 'Those are terrific stars, Petra,' she scooted herself around so that the stars were hidden by her small taut body from the view of Rebecca and Marshall, and Marshall heard her muttering curses no lady ought to know.

A stocky old man in a red flannel shirt and suspenders, smelling as his type always did of sweet pipe-smoke, was making shapes. Lumps. Black hills. He chortled in curmudgeonly glee. 'I don't know what they are, little lady. Hell, I'm ninety-two years old. I don't have to know. You figure it out, you tell me.' His swelling black brush-strokes filled the bottom quadrant of the mural opposite Petra and as high as he could reach from his wheelchair.

Another of the frail old ladies came down the hall, laboriously, leaning hard to the left and holding onto the handrail with both hands. Rebecca let go of her father's arm to get the old lady a chair. Marshall stood swaying in space until she came back to him, saying (he thought she was not speaking to him, but he couldn't be sure), 'Beatrice, I'm glad you decided to join us.'

The woman apparently named Beatrice smiled pleasantly and didn't say anything.

Completely at a loss as to what was going on, Marshall cast about for clues. Circles of light – reflections, he thought, but maybe not – were broken up in the wavy waxed white floor. Sounds were hollow and crowded, sliding into one another or separating out. 'Would you like to paint, Dad?' Marshall didn't know who was speaking, what the speaker was alluding to, whom she was addressing. Her father, presumably.

Marshall. Honey.

Faye. He knew who that was, but he couldn't be expected to know what she wanted. He never had known what she wanted. Heart pounding painfully, looking around for her, desperately hoping he'd find her again and desperately hoping he would not. 'Leave me alone,' he told her.

'Okay,' Rebecca agreed. 'We'll just watch for a while.'

A very tall wiry man walked up behind Petra, positioned his feet shoulder-width apart, and dropped his hand heavily onto her head. Still painting stars, she ignored him. He stared at the wall. 'Stupid,' he announced in a loud surly voice. 'This is fucking dumb.' Marshall winced and considered telling the guy to watch his mouth, there were ladies present, but couldn't quite put the words in the best order and then forgot.

Someone handed the tall man a wide paintbrush. 'We need something at the top, Bob. You're the only one who can reach it.'

Face stormy, Bob regarded the brush. At his feet Petra worked steadily, her undertone of furious Spanish rising and falling like an unmelodic song. 'This is fucking dumb,' he said again, but he finally took the brush.

Quietly, Beatrice moved her chair up to the wall and picked up a brush. The old woman's strokes were firm, her face set. In bright blue paint and thin lines a cluster of faces emerged, not quite realistic but utterly believable.

The grin of one was ragged and desperate; the eyes of another were haunted.

When she finished the faces Beatrice cocked her head even farther to the left and regarded them critically, made a few minuscule adjustments. Then she painstakingly cleaned her brush, found a can of green paint, and proceeded to set the faces one after another on leafless stems, each of them bending sharply one way or the other.

'You've painted before, too,' Rebecca observed.

'When I was a girl,' Beatrice admitted, 'I used to do portraits. That was a long time ago, don't you know.'

'I am Jesus Christ! They're crucifying me! I am Jesus Christ! They're crucifying me! Ohh! Ohh!'

Marshall swiveled his head slowly toward the shrieking. Though this was no more peculiar or disturbing than many other things in the world, it did claim his attention for longer than most. Briefly, he thought it might be Faye (she was somewhere close by; he was afraid of her), but then he chided himself. Faye loved making a spectacle of herself, but she would never be ugly like this, scrawny legs splayed and hair unkempt as the batting from a split pillow.

But this person somehow reminded him of Faye, and he did not dare be reminded of Faye. He closed his eyes and put his hands over his ears. But without clear external visual or auditory stimuli, his own thoughts grew alarmingly louder, brighter, and more tangled, so he took his hands away and opened his eyes wide.

'It's okay, Dad,' Rebecca said, meaning to reassure. 'Abby, I really don't think Myra can—'

'She has a right to express herself, too,' said the young lank-haired aide pushing Myra's wheelchair. Myra's eyes were opening in slits and her voice was lowering as she saw the bold colors on the wall in front of her.

Bob stretched as high as he could and daubed an approximate circle at the juncture of wall and ceiling. It splattered upward, leaving a trail of tiny orange flecks. Rebecca grimaced. The woman with the Southern accent chuckled softly. 'Hadn't planned on repainting the ceiling, huh, boss?'

'There,' Bob shouted. 'There's your fucking stupid sun son-of-a-bitch,' and threw down the brush and stomped out of the building.

'Myra,' said Abby, taking pains to enunciate. 'Here's a brush and some red paint and a big white space in front of you. Paint something. Show us what you're feeling.'

'I am Cleopatra, Queen of Egypt,' Myra said conversationally.

'Well, here, Cleo.' Abby put the dripping brush into Myra's hand and closed her own fingers around it. 'I'll help.'

Myra looked at her with clear, wide blue eyes. 'You just take your hand away from me, girlie. You just stand there and listen and maybe you'll learn something.' Abby hesitated, then obediently backed away, grinning. Myra leaned so far forward that her long body was bent almost double like a closed safety pin over the restraint, and made a vertical red slash on the wall. Then, her tongue protruding a little and her other hand raised in a loose fist, she made another slash horizontally across the first, forming a rough and dramatic red cross.

She sat back, dropped the brush full of paint into her lap, and sank into her chair as if she had abruptly fallen asleep. 'My God,' breathed the woman with the Southern accent. 'Here comes Paul.'

Two aides propelled a spastic young man toward the

group in the lounge. His chuffing noises might have signified excitement and might have signified distress and might have signified nothing in particular. Bulging eyes fixed on the mural, he grinned and drooled.

Rebecca stooped to ready the largest brush with yellow paint. Paul by now could hardly contain himself. He was whooping and twisting in the grasp of the aides, and one of them barely stopped him from shoving the laden brush into his mouth.

With one loud purposeful grunt he raised his brush back and fell with it against the wall. As he sank to the floor, his arm traced a jagged arc and a yellow streak like a bolt of lightning appeared across the mural. Abby and another aide caught him on the way down and eased him to a sitting position on the paint cloth; he was laughing in his odd breathless way, obviously not hurt and holding the brush aloft.

Many in the group applauded. To be polite, to avoid drawing attention to himself, Marshall clapped, too, although he saw nothing worth such praise. Rebecca hugged the young man. 'Perfect, Paul! That's perfect!'

Paul might have said, 'Yeah!'

Faye whispered to Marshall, 'We can do better than that, you and me,' and very softly blew into his ear.

Mortified to discover himself hardening for her, and to feel the extent of his terror, he cried out (he did not mean to say her name again, but nothing else would show his desire and his fear; maybe he didn't say her name). His daughter reached to hug him, and he held on. 'It *is* fun, isn't it, Dad? I'm glad you're here!'

Sometime later (or earlier, or in a different time sequence, or outside time altogether, or in memory, or in a kind of foretelling), Marshall found himself poised in front of a mostly white wall. A wide paintbrush was in his hand, dripping white paint onto the thigh of his charcoal trousers.

Faye encircled his hand in both her small, soft, long-nailed ones and laughed, in that delighted and malicious way that had always made him want to run from her at the same time that he would have done almost anything to cause her to laugh like that again, to smile at him like that, to show him he could still please her. 'Aren't we a team, Marshall, honey? Aren't we something?'

Faye raised his arm high above his head, higher than he could reach without standing precariously on tiptoe and bracing the heel of his other hand against the wall, which was sticky. A jagged yellow streak descended into – or, depending on your perspective, rose out of – the thick waves of white paint like the branch or the root of a tree, maybe dead, being covered or marooned by the rising or falling tide. He shouldn't be doing this.

Faye squealed, 'Ooo, this is *fun!*' and shoved his arm up.

He tried to stop, but she was quicker and much more wilful than he was, and the yellow zigzag disappeared under thick, rivuleted white.

'Marshall, what in the world are you doing?' It was Billie. He knew right away that it was his wife Billie, and he was very glad she had come, but he also felt guilty, although he had forgotten what it was he had done wrong. 'Oh, for heaven's sake, look at your clothes!'

He looked, saw his good charcoal trousers, a burgundy shirt he thought must be new, and respectable black shoes, but no socks. Why was he not wearing socks? Marshall felt himself flush with shame. No wonder Billie was embarrassed. He suspected he embarrassed her a good deal these days, but he never seemed to be aware of it until it was too late. 'I'm sorry,' he said.

'Becky, for heaven's sake, just look at your father!'

'Is he okay?'

'Look at his trousers. Look at his brand-new shirt. A brand-new shirt, first time he's worn it.'

'How did he get into the paint? I thought Lisa put it all away in the cabinets in the activity room.'

'Why wasn't anybody watching him? That's why I had to put him here, because I couldn't watch him twenty-four hours a day, but I could watch him better than this.'

'Dad! You painted over the mural!'

Uncomprehending, Marshall stared. Then, to get away from all of them, Billie and Rebecca and Faye, he retreated a step. The back of his shirt and the seat of his trousers clung to the wet paint on the wall.

Chapter 2

As an early autumn sunset stretched and thinned the blue-gray light, Rebecca walked toward The Tides. She'd been at a meeting across town and could well have gone home afterward, but it was too early; there was nothing at home that wouldn't wait, including Kurt, and The Tides compelled her.

She'd parked her car in a lot several blocks over, so she could approach her nursing home on foot, see what it looked like from a distance, experience the feel of it as it gradually came closer, larger, more detailed. Her nursing home. Her facility. Even after three months as administrator of The Tides, she still thrilled to the phrase she finally had a right to use: my place.

People outside the business, to most of whom nursing homes were nothing but warehouses where the elderly and sick with nobody to take care of them went to die, didn't understand that. When she'd met Kurt she'd already been hooked, a geriatric social worker with ideas about revolutionizing the field, and once she'd started studying for her administrator's exam she'd hardly been able or willing to think of anything else. She'd tried to tell him stories about the residents to make him see how fascinating they were, but all he could see were their illnesses and disabilities and losses, as if there was nothing else to them, and he'd just shudder or laugh and give some variation of the standard response: 'God, those places are *depressing*! And they *stink*! I don't know how you can stand it.' Kurt worked with children, where he said there was hope.

Rebecca's parents wouldn't understand, either; she didn't even try to explain her excitement and pleasure to them. 'I don't understand you,' her mother had been saying all Rebecca's life, sometimes in admiration, sometimes in pity, sometimes out of some sort of fear. Billie Emig was spending a lot of time at The Tides since Rebecca's father had been admitted, but she made it plain that she loathed the necessity of having her husband there, and defended herself against the joy and tragedy and fun of the place as she'd always defended herself, by feeling both guilty and superior. And Rebecca didn't think her father had ever been much interested in anything, except, at times, her; senility hadn't changed that.

A lot of people in the business also didn't share her involvement, not to say obsession. They just worked there. Or they were investors, and maybe the rumors of greed and corruption at the ownership level were true. Dan Murphy, her boss, never objected to her plans for getting away from the medical model and creating a community at The Tides; he never acknowledged them, either. 'Census, babe,' was his refrain. 'The name of the game is census. Keep those beds full and everybody's fucking happy. Including me.'

She knew the assumption inside the company and out was that she and Dan Murphy were sleeping together, or at least that he had lecherous designs, and she still worried that this compromised her position. But, by reputation, he'd slept with nurses' aides as well as Directors of Nursing, with housekeeping new-hires as well as Health Department surveyors who'd been around for decades.

He seemed to her less a predator or barterer than an opportunist, and she wondered about even that, for he was hardly, in any ordinary sense, an attractive man. Abrasive and impatient, crude, not easy to be around, certainly not easy to work for, he had eyes small enough, in a fleshy face, to be called beady, a reedy voice with almost no affect, clumpy orangish hair, a squat body that surely would make no heads turn.

What would it be like to have an affair with Dan Murphy? she wondered, but the fantasy wouldn't stick.

When he walked the halls of The Tides, many people didn't know who he was. But in a few deceptively casual minutes he would have learned which handrails were loose, what was causing the odor at the end of Wing 1, which rooms didn't have clean towels, which residents were ready for discharge, which staff were fucking up on the job and which were going above and beyond. Sometimes he would tell the administrator these things and sometimes he would keep them to himself until they could be used to greatest advantage.

She wanted to learn how to do that. She wanted to be that sure of something.

Rebecca didn't mind the business aspects of running a nursing home, and was confident that, once hospital discharge planners and doctors became familiar with the innovative programs she intended to develop at The Tides, she could, in fact, fill the empty beds and keep them full. She'd already started trying out some of her ideas for humanizing the institution, such as the mural on the lounge wall – Lisa had managed to persuade all the painters but the surly Bob Morley to redo their work after Rebecca's father had painted over it, and Bob's sun had been high enough to escape most of the whitewash anyway.

Walking along Hammond Street toward Elm, Rebecca laughed wryly to herself. But thinking of her father, open-mouthed and utterly baffled as though he didn't know the incriminating brush in his hand was still oozing globs of white paint, while her mother castigated him and Rebecca and the rest of the staff and fate in general for the ruination of his clothes, thinking of her own outrage that her inaugural project had been sabotaged by her father, who hadn't meant to, she felt sorrow and an odd sense of profound vertigo, but it wasn't as hard as it should have been to set them aside, to set her father aside.

As she turned onto Elm Street and started down the hill, she caught her first glimpse of The Tides, a thin darker line across the *faux* horizon created by the lower empty field behind it, and a proprietary satisfaction pumped through her like air into an otherwise formless balloon. She found herself thinking that maybe, because of The Tides, she'd have some idea who she was by the time she was thirty.

The Tides was a long, low, blond brick building with a flat roof – which, because of its lack of a slope, leaked – and a covered concrete porch along the front face that extended almost seamlessly into the parking lot. It sat on the east edge of a vacant bowl-shaped space, huge by the standards of the suburb surrounding it. Here, when the facility was built, had been the lake which had given it its somewhat fanciful name; Rebecca couldn't quite believe that this body of water had ever really had tides.

She also found it hard to imagine how anyone could have been so foolish as to build a nursing home on the shore of a lake, however shallow, however placid. Indeed, the lake hadn't lasted long. She didn't know whether the Health Department had insisted it be drained and filled in, for obvious health and safety reasons, or whether someone in the complex of ownership and management had made an independent commonsense decision, but Dan Murphy had told her the land behind the facility had been empty since before he'd owned it, which was seventeen years. After snow or rain, there was sometimes standing water, which she didn't much like, but most of the time the weedy bowl just collected trash; she didn't like that, either, but it didn't seem to require the immediate intervention that so many other aspects of The Tides' physical plant did.

The open space was vast when you considered that it was in the middle of a dense urban area, and it surprised her that Dan or his predecessors hadn't sold it or found some other way to turn it to a profit. Probably close to an acre, it sloped gently from the back of the facility for fifty yards or so, then dipped steeply. The weeds and trash were thick, but there were no trees, nothing to break its sinking profile, and the lights of the surrounding buildings could seem very distant if you stood at the back door of the dining room, say, and looked out across it at night.

Rebecca was thinking, again, that there was potential in that space, if she could just come up with the right thing to do with it. A garden, maybe; she'd like to have fresh produce for the kitchen, and surely there were residents who'd have both the physical energy and the knowledge to grow vegetables. Or maybe they could raise animals of some kind, like chickens – not that she knew anything about chickens. Or goats. Could you have goats in the city? Something glinted wet in the middle distance of the vacant space as she came closer to it; something streaked and shimmered, the suggestion of blue and violet and silvery gray. She cursed. There'd been no significant precipitation for weeks; why should there be water?

As she crossed Ahern Street and came up on the west edge of The Tides property, it looked as if the bottom foot or so of the wide depression was under water. The closer she got, the more water there seemed to be; at one point, the back wall of the building rippled, vaguely distorted as though the lake that had not been there for decades were rising up it now.

It was her facility, and her responsibility to investigate. What could be risky, anyway, about trying to find out where this seepage was coming from? But she was afraid.

She moved her right foot off the sidewalk and onto rough ground, which slanted downward away from her. Swiveling to the right, she brought her left foot around, and nearly lost her balance as the ground seemed to shift and the angle of it to steepen. Gravity and momentum, or some other force, drew her rapidly downhill, though for some reason she did her best to resist, and in scant seconds she was at the bottom of the bowl, where she'd never been before, out of breath and tingling as if she'd fallen, grasping in vain for something tall and sturdy enough to break her descent.

Her tactile sense told her that it was perfectly dry down here; there was no hint of moisture against exposed flesh or trickling through shoes or fabric. But things looked wet. The outlines of grasses and low thorny bushes were smeared. Crumpled newspapers and plastic grocery bags looked to have been melted, dissolved at the edges, in some cases even run together to form some strange amalgam. A brown beer bottle here and there, a green plastic two-liter soda bottle, a fat clear bottle with a smudged red label that had once held wine all glistened, sparkled, rendered pretty by the wavery refractions of what looked like but was not water.

Disoriented, chilled, and frightened, Rebecca thought to clamber out of the depression, which was deeper and wider, steeper-sided, than she'd have imagined, and hurry into her facility by one of the back doors; she hoped she had her key and that it would work in the new lock. Instead, she slid farther down, so that the line of The Tides was barely visible above the lake-bed rim.

Her feet seemed wider, rounder under her, her shoes soft-sided and unable to hold their shape. She couldn't quite make out separate fingers on the hand she held up before her face, and the veins and dancing tendons in the back of her hand colored haloes across the skin. The sounds in her head were gauzy. There was the smell of roses, unlikely on a September evening, but inescapable, and when she pivoted to look for the source of the fragrance, which it seemed imperative to locate, she slipped and fell into her own shadow, which shouldn't have been there at all in the half-light but which accepted and then absorbed her impression.

Sitting up, struggling to her knees and then to her feet, not wet but feeling smudged and hazy, Rebecca suddenly had a flash of a memory she'd never had before. A rainbow drawn across her cheek. A rainbow ribbon slid across her cheek and then tied into her hair. The smell of roses, which only now, with a shock, did she recognize as roses. The elongated, smeary shock of somebody important leaving and never coming back. Water closing over her face, rainbow water, and then sliding away.

Somebody called her without quite using her name.

Chapter 3

'Faye!'

Rebecca jumped and looked up from the staffing report. A cloud must have passed rapidly over the sun, for the square of indirect light from the window beside her father's bed was almost lavender for a moment, and the even less direct light inside the room, under the glare of the fluorescents, took on a decidedly purple cast before it returned to normal. Usually, outside light, temperature, weather were of so little relevance inside the facility that Rebecca could go for hours without noticing, and it would be a bit of a shock to emerge after work and find snow in the air, or a sunset.

The long, perforated sheets of the staffing report tumbled over the edge of her father's bedside table, which she should have known wouldn't be a big enough work surface. Heavy and slick, they threatened to slide off onto the floor. If she lost her place it would take forever to find it again among all the rows of numbers, columns of names, charts of symbols. This was the dozenth weekly staffing report she'd done, and it still took her most of a day, partly because of the complexity and tedium of the task itself, partly because she resented having to do it at all, and largely because it was so hard to keep her mind on it among all the interruptions, most of them welcome.

Even when she came in in the middle of the night to do it, there were myriad things more interesting than staffing reports to claim her attention. Of primary concern to her at the moment was the persistent problem of staff sleeping on the job. She seemed to be the only one who objected to this; more than a few people had informed her, defensively or indignantly or indulgently or with a shrug, that the night shift at every facility napped. But it infuriated her, and she derived a certain short-lived perverse pleasure at three o'clock in the morning from sneaking into the staff lounge, where on some nights there'd be aides and even the nurse dozing in practically every chair, and shouting, 'Staff meeting!'

Now, righting the stack of slippery papers with her fist, she regarded her father. He was still staring at nothing. Thinking of her experience the other night in the twilit empty lake bed behind the facility, she repeated to herself sternly that it *was* nothing he was staring at, just as it had been nothing that had so shaken and disoriented her then. The only strong emotion his face registered was curiosity, not fear or rage or anything else explosive that required her intervention, professional or filial.

Such intense curiosity on her father's face, though, was a curiosity in itself. He'd always taken pains to hold himself aloof. His interest in the world – in her – had always been of a removed, intellectual sort, without much passion.

Until, Rebecca had lately come to realize, the dementia had started; passion of many sorts – brief unsustained bursts, often free-floating – had in fact been one of the early symptoms, unrecognized at first but cumulative. She didn't know what to make of her father's emotional lability. Geriatric theory would have her write it off as symptomatic of chemical and physical alterations in his brain, signifying nothing but the advancing dementia. But, somehow, that explanation didn't seem to her quite sufficient.

Clearly he wasn't at the moment aware of her. Like finding no reflection in a mirror, this set off an unpleasant shiver, and she had the childish impulse to do something outrageous to claim his attention – jump up and down and make faces; shatter some object or break some rule. Say, 'I love you, Daddy.'

No matter what she did, his obliviousness to her was likely to be replaced without warning by equally discomfiting scrutiny. This had always been true; she squirmed remembering the sudden searchlight-glare of his attention when she'd been a child and, worse, a teenager – as if, all of a sudden, he hadn't exactly known who she was, or had known too well.

While he was ignoring her, though, she had the opportunity to observe this man who was her father and was, always had been, such a stranger. There'd been periods in her life when she'd watched and listened to him intently, and periods when she'd gone out of her way to avoid being with him at all and especially alone, for fear of what she might find out and of what she might not. There'd been long stretches – junior year abroad in Spain, grad school on the East Coast – when thoughts of her father and mother had hardly entered her mind at all. Now professional and personal obligation made it virtually impossible to stay away.

She hadn't thought it was a good idea for him to be placed at the nursing home she administered, but she hadn't been able to articulate why. 'I'm just starting a new job,' she'd tried to argue with her mother. 'A whole career. This is my first facility. I've been waiting a long time for this. I don't want to have to think about my father, too.'

Her mother's face had gone stony. 'I know he's a lot of trouble, but he's your father. And he'll be less of a bother if he's right nearby. If he's in your nursing home, you can make sure they take good care of him.'

'I'm not sure I know how—' Rebecca had started to protest.

'It's not as if we're moving *in* with you. You'll still have your personal life.' Unspoken: *Such as it is*. She'd added – slyly, which wasn't like her, 'You and Kurt,' and Rebecca had been surprised that her mother even remembered his name.

'Mom, this isn't a good idea,' she'd said helplessly, her doomed last shot.

'All right, Rebecca. All right. I'll find someplace else for him.' Her mother had turned her back, and Rebecca, as always, had panicked and acquiesced.

Now her father was staring straight at her, the whiskered corners of his mouth twitching in an uncertain smile. Rebecca had the impression that he didn't know exactly who she was, which wouldn't be the first time. Still expecting to be hurt or offended by that, she was surprised to find herself smiling back at him with the same kind of diffuse affection she imagined him to be feeling.

Both her parents had kept themselves from her. Her mother still did. Rebecca couldn't have said how she knew that; she hadn't in any sense been neglected, and she had no doubt that they loved her. But there'd always been distance between them and her, the sense of a secret, of something profoundly hidden. Or maybe not; maybe that was nothing but a romantic construct to soften the reality that they just had never been very close.

Not that she'd always minded. Not that she even entirely minded now. Sometimes, in fact, she'd wished for even greater distance. A certain lightness resulted from being disconnected from one's parents without ever actually having been estranged.

There was, in fact, a certain gratifying lightness in not being very connected to anybody. She and Kurt had been together for over a year, and, while she'd have said – did say – they loved each other, she wouldn't have said they were close. He'd moved in with her because his lease had expired, she owned a house, and it was a convenient and practical arrangement for them both. They divided household chores and expenses. They shared a bed. They decidedly did not share a life.

Her father roused himself and commanded, 'Get out of here. Leave me alone.' He didn't seem to be talking to her, although he might be. She chose to assume he was not, and to stay.

He'd been a bulky man, and he still was much taller and larger-framed than she was, as was her mother; Rebecca remembered waiting for her growth spurt, and she'd been well away from home before she'd decided she was always going to be a smaller person than either of her parents. There'd been times when she'd chafed at the physical difference, imbued it with a power differential that made her alternately rebellious and overly eager to please. There'd been times when she'd welcomed it because it set her apart from them, gave physical form to the separateness she already felt. By now, she scarcely thought about it, except as a genetic oddity.

Just in the last few months, her father's bulk had noticeably diminished, so that he seemed smaller, not frail yet, though that would likely come, but somehow occupying less defined space, less volume. His body seemed, like his mind, to be slipping out of reach, even nudging the basic boundaries of what was normal and predictable for a human being. When she looked at him, listened to him, there was no longer, for instance, the expectation of symmetry; no part of him could precisely be termed deformed, but nothing really matched anything else, either, and there was the generalized impression of something being awry. Sometimes he walked and sat and stood a trifle clumsily, as though the layers of the physical world and his body in it were not exactly familiar to him anymore, no longer quite aligned.

Rebecca had seen that in other people at the beginning stages of dementia. She'd been taught, in fact, to regard all such changes, subtle at first and then picking up speed – physical awkwardness, emotional lability, inattentiveness and forgetfulness and mental blankness that came and went – as symptoms that, taken together, were diagnostic in that they comprised a syndrome that could be defined and named. Not treated, though. Not reversed or interrupted or even slowed.

She'd also been taught that reorientation was the treatment approach of choice. In long-term care facilities and other institutions, the environment tended to be featureless and self-referential, contributing to the confusion of minds that already wandered. So in more enlightened facilities, activity directors and social workers gave painstaking instruction in Reality Orientation. Rebecca had led many an awkwardly chipper discussion constructed around the date, the day of the week, what was on the menu for lunch, what the weather was like outside, who the President of the United States was. Signs were posted: '*Today is . . .*' Nursing home wings were color-coded. Staff was cued to slip references to time, place, and person into their routine conversations with patients.

All this reality orientation had never seemed to have much long-term effect. Nobody emerged clear-headed from dementia or was able to reorganize drifting thoughts. But for a few minutes, a few hours after each class, a few people did seem to be more aware of their own identities. She guessed that was a benefit.

Assuming that 'identity' was a constant and 'reality' a concept with truth beyond the convenience of common agreement. When she'd started working in gerontology, Rebecca wouldn't have entertained any notion to the contrary; what was real and the basic outlines of person, place, and time – the composite factor labelled on medical charts 'orientation × 3' – had been static and clear. Now, increasingly and unwillingly, she wondered.

Her father had subsided again. His bald head glistened under the fluorescent lights Rebecca wished she could afford to replace throughout the facility with incandescent bulbs. The literature reported that the flickering and harshness of fluorescent lights seemed to contribute to the disorientation of patients with dementia, as well as to the hyperactivity of schoolchildren, but nursing-care facilities used them for the same budgetary reasons schools did.

Now her father seemed to be struggling to get up from his chair, at the same time apparently struggling to push himself deeper into it, staring wide-eyed at thin air and croaking something incomprehensible. Probably it was an actual word that meant something to him; it might even have meant something to her if she'd had a context for it, but a single syllable and out of the blue, it was nothing more than a nonsensical bray. Several of the residents did that, and Rebecca was put in mind of the speech of a baby just before its native language emerges in recognizable form – more directed and organized than babbling, but not quite words. From her own father, it both irritated and chilled her.

'Faye!' Dad was flailing now, though in a peculiarly languid way, his hands undulating as if caressing shapes in the air, his thin forearms and sharp elbows fluttering. Rebecca found herself looking for the haloes she'd noticed around her own hands the other night, but saw nothing like that. The expression on his face might have been fear, or might have been just confusion; Rebecca had been trying to read the expressions on her father's face all her life, off and on, and the more senile he became the closer she seemed to get to being able to do so. That bothered her, to be gaining something from his affliction. Right now she would swear he was, among other things, leering.

He was determined to get up. He was awfully unsteady. Sooner or later he would probably have to be restrained. She hated the thought of it. Her mother was already complaining that the staff – in other words, Rebecca – wasn't doing enough to keep him safe. He could fall. He could wander off and be hit by a car, or fall down that hill in back and break a hip. He could have eaten the paint. 'If he could take care of himself he wouldn't be in such a place,' she kept saying. 'If I could take care of him at home, I would. You know I would.'

His eyes were bulging now, and he was drooling.

Hastily Rebecca folded up the report and slipped it into her briefcase. It obviously wasn't going to be feasible for her to get any work done while she kept her father company; she'd have to talk to her mother about it, a prospect which made her stomach ache with dread.

She went to him, took his hands. 'Dad, what's wrong?' He couldn't tell her. He was looking over her head. He used her hands as leverage to stand up and then sit down again. She sat beside him and put on a classical tape. The piano and violin music agitated her, but it wasn't long before her father was sitting calmly, not asleep but not fully conscious, either. The innumerable things she had to attend to scrolled through her head, and she could hardly sit still. After a few minutes she kissed his cheek, which seemed a terribly impertinent thing to do, and told him, 'I have to go back to work, Dad. I'll leave your door open and somebody will be in to check on you. Here's your call light in case you need anything.' With an obvious effort he brought his gaze to her face, but it slipped away again, and she knew the concept of a call light was beyond him, so she was, in effect, proposing to leave him unattended and alone.

Impatient though she was, it was hard to tear herself away from him. She sat beside him for longer than she should have and watched him. Then she wasn't watching him anymore but she still sat there, lethargic, hands in her lap, her thoughts and gaze on nothing in particular, oddly reluctant to get back to work. Her father sat relaxed in his chair with a small smile on his lips, and neither of them had anything to say for a while – a unit of time that was, for Rebecca, calibrated into minutes whose passage she could virtually hear; for Marshall, they didn't pass at all but blended into one long smear.

Her mind was racing. His was, too, but more as though underwater than on hard ground. In and out of his mind and back in again flowed images from his own past and present: being tied in a chair; being immersed in the layered sensation of being lost in a place he had been for a long time; being hurt. Images came to him, too, with no personal attachment, as if his were not the life that contained them, even as if they hadn't been lived at all but stored, set aside, imbued with a different sort of reality than being lived would have given them.

Rebecca worried at the endless list of things she had to do, many of them things she hadn't gotten done yesterday though she'd been here till after ten at night; she wouldn't get them done today either. The worry, though, softened into some other kind of mental process, swirling with her father's. Not memory, exactly. Before memory.

A car in a deep woods, overgrown, vines through the windows although all the glass was intact. Multicolored vines, soft and flowing, like scarves. Himself stumbling toward it; herself at the same time skirting around. The bulk of it brown as sunlight on treetrunks, golden as delicately tanned flesh.

Not a car. A body. Not a person. Something else.

Being summoned.

Answering, approaching, and discovering it was nothing, a hillock covered with vines that weren't multicolored at all, not a pink or lavender among them, only green and gold. A curious torpor, disappointment and sweet relief.

As soon as Rebecca forced herself to stir, energy and anxiety returned. As soon as she was on her feet and moving toward the door, had her hand on the knob – which should be a lever so people with limited hand motion could use it (she took time to fish the spiral notebook and pen out of her pocket and add a note about doorknobs to the list) – as soon as she was out in the hall, the feeling of being tugged on was strong, the threat of engulfment acute, and also the anticipation that here at The Tides, maybe, she would discover who she was without even having time or inclination to think about it. She was the person who had this never-ending list of things to do. She was the one in charge.

She could have started her rounds right here. Instead, needing to get away from her father, she hurried along the corridor to the lounge in the middle, where the restored mural – not quite the same as the first one, but exuberant and expressive in its own right – caught the morning light and lifted her spirits just as it was supposed to. There was a pink spot on it that hadn't been there before, a small sunburst pattern near the floor. Rebecca liked the idea that somebody had been inspired.

As she went outside, it occurred to her that the door ought to be re-hung so that it opened inward, to make it harder for wanderers like her father to get out. On the other hand, maybe this knob also ought to be replaced with a lever or a bar for conflicting safety reasons: so that, in the event of a fire, residents with limited mobility could get out. She'd have to check the regs. It would be easier if she could just call the Health Department and ask for advice, but Dan had warned her not to do that for fear of triggering a visit or a full-fledged survey, and The Tides wasn't ready for that.

'The Health Department is not your friend, babe,' Dan had told her, laughing a little, all but patting her head. 'Trust me.' Rebecca wasn't entirely sure she believed that;

Dan had had a running battle with the Health Department for years, which made him something less than objective on the subject. Theoretically, they were all on the side of good patient care. But she wouldn't call about doorknobs.

She went out the back door, thinking to check the condition of the grounds behind the facility first. A scraggly privet hedge – later in the spring she'd get somebody to come look at it – marked off a haphazard boundary that served no purpose, since the nursing-home property extended through the empty and partially filled-in lake bed to a street considerably more than a block away. Surprised and displeased by her own unwillingness to venture out that far – it was, after all, broad daylight now, and nothing sinister had happened to her there anyway; she'd just slipped, and dusk had made things look and sound odd – she pushed through the hedge, noting that a few of its scratchy branches were dangerously at eye level.

She made her way around the end of the building where it abutted Elm Street, wondering whether it was the property-owner's responsibility to fix the buckled sidewalk, or the city's, and went out onto the front porch. She'd start at the parking lot, the way visitors, surveyors, and prospective residents and their families would experience the facility. It was easier to breathe outside than in. Rebecca harbored a fantasy that The Tides could someday be air-conditioned, though such a major construction project was quite out of reach now. At this time of year the building was only stuffy, but when she first got here last summer, it had been stifling.

Rebecca walked to the far east side of the crowded

parking lot and turned to look at her facility. A rush of pride made her catch her breath. It looked nice. It looked, if not inviting, at least not hostile or depressing. She could do good things here. She could make her mark.

There were a few pieces of trash along the curb. She picked them up, made a note in her notebook, and started deliberately along the front sidewalk, determined to notice every detail. Not noticing, though, the distortion of air around her, like a double image or the negative of a shadow.

The three people on the porch all noticed it, but none of them reacted. They were all used to seeing and hearing things that couldn't be explained. They didn't react to the bright sun in their eyes, either, didn't squint or turn away or look down. It was as if the sun didn't hurt their eyes, or as if it didn't matter that it hurt.

Petra Carrasco, in fact, didn't give a damn about the glare. Very little mattered to her, or everything mattered so much that she couldn't stand it – Bob's presence beside her on the chair and the thought of him inside her, his sudden and total and tragic absence from her life when he stepped to the edge of the porch to flick ash from his cigarette, her husband's violent death real or imagined, wished for and dreaded, reconstructed in her mind over and over, the warmth of the sun, the nest of red ants she knew had lodged in her rectum, the glare of the sun in her eyes. Petra was crazy. She had been crazy most of her life. She knew she was crazy, and it didn't matter, and it had mattered most of her life so much she couldn't stand it.

There was somebody else in her head. A new voice, one she'd never heard before. Petra cursed out loud. None of the others even looked at her, except Rebecca, who glanced up sharply and was embarrassed to find herself embarrassed and wishing she could think of some morally justifiable way to get Petra to be crazy somewhere other than the front porch.

Petra would screw or blow or jerk off any man in the place for cigarettes, and she always had enough takers to supplement nicely the one pack a day her doctor said she could have. When she went with her husband for the weekend she could still sometimes earn a few dollars, a few pennies, a few beers on the street. Her husband loved her and he beat her for doing other men; he beat her and he loved her because even now, crazy and sick and getting old – however old she was: forty or fifty or sixty – even now with the fiery red ants she delighted in telling people about busy inside her rectum, she could still earn more money than he could.

She loved him desperately, though sometimes she forgot who he was. For a long time they wouldn't let her see him because of the things he did to her; then she had thought she would die, had tried to make herself die, was often convinced she was already dead without him. When she took the Thorazine – they put it in orange juice or burritos so she wouldn't know it was there, and sometimes she didn't – it made her crazy, and when she didn't take it she was a different kind of crazy but crazy still.

Petra opened her blouse to Bob, who didn't seem to notice, although he did notice, furiously. The voice inside her head, a woman's voice brushing like gauze against the inside of Petra's skull, softening, tickling, murmured nice things that Petra couldn't quite make out. Bob got up off the swing again and picked a pine bough and brought it back for her like a bouquet.

Gordon Marek was asleep. Awake. Asleep. He'd been

up and down all night. All his life he'd been used to sleeping about three hours, being awake three hours, sleeping another three hours. At the other nursing home they'd made him take a pill so he'd sleep all night and they'd rolled up his bed during the day to keep him out of it. It had worked, they'd established a normal sleeping pattern for him, and he'd felt awful. Here he could listen to the all-night jazz station, sitting on his bed with earphones on, snapping his fingers in approximate time to the music. Several times a night he'd leave his earphones on his bed with music seeping tinnily out of them and go quietly out the side door, against all fire and safety regulations propping it open with his shoe. He'd brush away dirt or snow or pine needles and lift the hidden bottle to his lips, sitting on his haunches under the stars, until the booze hit.

Now his puppy slept warm and round in his lap. A bottle with half an inch of Ripple in it teetered between his feet. Ripple or Thunderbird or Annie Greensprings by now, by the fifteenth of the month when he was back to counting pennies in the bathroom and making booze runs for twenty-five cents commission each from the poor suckers who couldn't get out to get their own. Or wouldn't, wouldn't take the chance. His check from the welfare came on the fifth and then he could do it like it was meant to be done, man; heavy sweet purple port wine, the first long swig going down like an alto sax in his head, the next like the thrum of a big ol' bass, man, the natter and search of drums. Twenty-nine dollars from the welfare every month, and on the sixth and seventh he didn't have to do no favors for nobody. But often he did anyhow: a six-pack for the Mexican dude, a sampler Jim Beam the old guy in the wheelchair could hide under the sheet they used to tie him in. It was a rare twenty-nine dollars that Gordon spent entirely on himself. Since he got the puppy, a lot of it went for dog treats.

But now it was the middle of the month, a long time till the next check. Gordon sat back a little, rocking and bouncing on the L-shaped metal supports of the chair, and dozed in his purple haze, which was already beginning to fade from his eight o'clock trek to the liquor store. The puppy rearranged itself in his lap and fell back asleep, too.

All of a sudden Gordon wanted to dance. All of a sudden he was dancing. His feet in their tennis shoes with flopping soles moved on the concrete in a sliding two-step he'd never learned, and his squat body swayed gracefully. Groggily nonplussed, he opened his eyes and looked around to see who was making him do these things, but he was looking outward, which was the wrong direction.

After a few minutes, Gordon sank back into his torpor, which was rather a pleasant state to be in. He stopped moving and his awareness was swaddled again in thoughts of drink. He knew the lady who ran the liquor store was afraid of him and felt sorry for him, both, because he lived in a nursing home. He'd heard her indignant, embarrassed conversations on the phone. 'He's up here again. I feel sorry for him and all that, but you better come and get him and you better keep him out of my place. This is a place of business.'

And it used to be they'd do that. He'd sit on the curb in the sun or the shade, depending on the season, and chug as much of his bottle as he could before they got there. They always poured out whatever was left, a sad little puddle disappearing down the gutter. But by then he could usually be pretty well flying, stumbling, singing

'Stormy Weather' and at least he didn't have to walk the two blocks home.

Things had changed. Lately he could tell from his end of the conversation that somebody at the nursing home was telling the liquor-store lady to treat him like any other customer. That new little broad, probably, that new little boss-lady with the round face and boobs no bigger than a handful and white-blonde hair; he'd known her before and he called her Princess. He felt sorry for the liquor-store lady, and he knew she hated to do it, but lately she'd been refusing to serve him if he got too rowdy, and twice she'd even called the cops, who'd put him in the slammer overnight and then next morning he'd had to get himself home, stone cold sober and slow on his feet, and that was a damn sight farther than two blocks. The new little boss-lady must have been talking to the cops about him, too. It took him so long to get home he was worried about his dog, but somebody else had fed and watered it and changed its papers, and Gordon didn't much like that, either. It was *his* dog. He'd always wanted a dog.

He looked head-on at the sun, waited impassively for the pink haze to clear from his eyes. Not yet noon. He'd be damn near sober before he could risk another trip to the liquor store. The thought of being sober had always scared and sickened him, while he was married and had kids and then through the years in back wards and under flophouse beds and in various other forms of the loony bin.

Gordon made himself laugh. Then, to give himself something to laugh at, he tilted sideways in his chair so the metal popped in and out with a *pong*. He laughed again. He stopped himself from falling with an unsteady hand on the concrete, and that struck him as funny, too, but it wouldn't much longer. He needed a drink. The puppy woke up and tried to scramble down, but Gordon wouldn't let it.

For no reason apparent to anybody else, Bob growled, 'Fuckin' *shit*!' and hit the brick building with his fist. His knuckles split. The blood caught Petra's attention, and she muttered softly, the content unintelligible but with clear lascivious intent.

'Easy,' Gordon said. 'Easy. You're scarin' my dog.'

But the fat black-and-white puppy slept contentedly on his lap again, and he thought maybe he could wait a while longer to make the trip to the liquor store, or maybe he could take it with him. Its pink tongue came out of its mouth now and then to lick his hand, and when that happened Gordon held his breath. The puppy's tongue was almost exactly the same color as his palm. That struck him as practically a miracle. He couldn't remember ever loving anything as much as he loved this dog. He must have loved his wife, his boys. He knew rather than remembered that he had lived with them off and on for years, since he was sixteen and met Ava and got her pregnant till he'd left to work construction in Alaska nine, ten years later. He'd been a cabinetmaker, he'd paid the bills, he must have loved them, though they baffled him. He remembered fondly that they had always baffled him. He didn't think he'd ever understood one single thing any of them said or did. As long as they'd lived together, he had never allowed his wife to work. Wasn't right for a man to let his wife work.

Ada, her name was, not Ava. His sons' names were murked by the wine. He hadn't thought of their names in a long time, which was fine, like the sun in his eyes. If it hurt, it didn't matter. He had the uneasy feeling that he might remember one or both of his boys' names any minute now.

'Faye,' came into his mind. Gordon frowned. He was almost sure that wasn't anybody's name he knew.

This dog of his didn't have a name. Gordon had tried Spot because of the circle on top of its head and Blackie because it was mostly black and Rex because that was a good dog's name but nothing had stuck. 'My Dog' was proper name enough the way he said it in his mind, and it never went far enough away to have to call.

The puppy yawned without opening its eyes and stretched to its full tiny length, soft curved belly arching, front and back paws lolling on either side of Gordon's wide knee. Looking down at it, stroking a black ear with one brown forefinger, Gordon thought comfortably that there would never be any reason for him to move from this place, this creaking chair in the sunshine with his dog asleep in his lap.

Bob Morley paced. He scowled and balled his fists and muttered under his breath. He'd spent the last sixteen years of his life in this hellhole. He thought it and said it like a badge. His first thirty years had been in places no different.

All his life they'd said he was slow, and he knew it was true. Things came to him slowly – ideas, impressions, the sure knowledge that somebody was making fun of him – and then they left him slowly.

He slammed his fist into the wrought-iron porch railing, making it hum, making his whole arm ache. Behind him Petra said something and he wanted to slam her, too, wanted to shut her up once and for all, wanted to take her in his arms.

The woman was nuts, and a whore besides. He knew

these things about her slowly, and they didn't matter any more than the sun in his face. He saw envy in the faces of the other men. No one had ever envied him before. She came when he called. She did things to him that nobody had ever done before, things he liked. It had taken him a while, but he was used to her now. Nobody else came when he called, nobody touched him but this crazy woman.

Somebody touched him. Bob winced and looked down. His dick was bulging through the front of his pants, and he could see that nobody was touching him, but he could feel that somebody was.

Rage filled his throat. Somebody was making a fool of him, but he couldn't quite tell how. He looked around for Petra. She was clear on the other end of the porch. Fingers stroked his dick until they slid off the tip of it, and then the sensation was gone but his dick was still hard.

Ashamed of himself, Bob picked a pine bough for Petra. He made a point of cursing the needles, cursing her with her blouse open as she stuck the branch into her hair. She smiled.

When Beatrice Quinn was hit by the red Volkswagen speeding off west Sixth Avenue down the Elm Street hill, she was on her way home again. The morning sun was directly in her eyes. She had been months getting her bearings. First she'd set her sights on the nurses' station and then on the big glass front doors, learning the way, counting the steps from her room and back. Often she would end up needing the admonishing young hands under her elbows, the indignity and relief of a wheelchair, and then she would stay in bed for days afterward, dozing and weeping, eating only when she remembered that she had to keep her strength up for going home. Her granddaughter Mary Alice visited her every Sunday.

She had gone home at least twice before. Once in November, the worst winter in thirty years, and sometime during her first weekend the furnace had gone out. Mary Alice had found her wrapped in quilts in the rocking chair, with three old irons plugged in around her feet. Beatrice never did see what all the fuss was about. She had called a furnace company listed in the yellow pages and told them to come out first thing Monday morning; she was not about to pay double-time for them to work on a weekend. But then she did come down with the pneumonia and had to go back to The Tides, where they did take good care of her.

The other time, right after Easter, she was home two weeks and then she fell down the basement steps. Mary Alice found her on the cement floor. Once they got her on her feet she was perfectly fine, nothing broken in the fall, and could just as well have stayed home. But Mary Alice worried; Beatrice let herself be talked into coming back to The Tides again so Mary Alice wouldn't worry.

It was all foolishness. She would do it right this time.

'Your granddaughter's right! You're a crazy old woman!' bellowed Dexter McCord from his wheelchair in the middle of the hall. Dexter was hard-of-hearing, and sometimes he shouted. Beatrice was a little afraid of him, and she worried because he didn't take care of himself, didn't take care of his sugar.

'Where you off to, honey?' the young nurse asked absently.

On her way out the side door, which wasn't fitted with an alarm and wouldn't be as likely to call attention as the front door would – and besides, she didn't like going past those three who always sat out there; they were probably perfectly nice people, but they made her nervous – Beatrice stopped. The brown paper bags she hugged held all of her Tides possessions – sugar packets hoarded from the kitchen, bits of paper and string, flowers Dexter had brought her from the yard last summer. 'Just out for a walk,' she said sweetly, conversationally. 'Just out for my morning constitutional, don't you know.' This nurse hadn't been here long enough to remember her other trips home; Beatrice gambled that she wouldn't have read the chart enough to be suspicious.

'Well, you be careful now.' The nurse, younger than her granddaughter Mary Alice, patted her shoulder and went off with her cartful of pills.

The morning sun was directly in her eyes, and Beatrice never saw the speeding red Volkswagen. She never heard it, either, for she was saying a rosary. The rhythm of the rosary and Beatrice's determination to go home kept everything else out of her mind, including the gauzy whisper that tried but failed to penetrate.

The driver saw her. The Volkswagen skidded from the top of the hill and was almost to a stop by the time it hit her, but still the impact was enough to send her sprawling. One of the sacks burst, and papers and flowers and several pairs of white cotton underwear fluttered across the neighbor's yard.

The sounds of the accident didn't reach the shower room, where two aides were struggling to give Myra Larsen a shower. 'You'd think we were trying to kill her!' Abby shouted over the old woman's shrieks and the din of water against tiles. 'Why does she hate it so much?' Arthritic fingers tangled in Abby's hair and left red scratches across her cheek. 'Myra, cut it out! We just want to get you clean!' Myra Larsen had never taken a shower in her life, and the sound of the water against her flesh assaulted her.

In a quiet room at the end of the hall, Viviana Pierce was trying her best to die. She and Mrs Quinn had sat companionably at the same table in the dining room, but she didn't know about the accident either.

Viviana was more than ready to die. Some time ago she had put her teeth into a cup on her bedside stand and refused – gently – to eat or drink. She had tried it before, but always she had weakened. Ice cream or orange juice or a little homemade soup became just too tempting, and then she'd be back to eating again. This time she wouldn't weaken. Her family was with her. It was peaceful in her room. There was a nice breeze. In and out of her doorway, in and out of her window, a frothy pastel figure floated, but Viviana didn't invite it in, for, especially now, she knew who she was.

In the sunny activity room, where a group was fixing toys for the children at the State Home and Training School, someone asked Colleen, the Activity Director, 'Where's Mrs Quinn? She knows all about these doll-clothes.'

In the kitchen, steamy and much too small, Roslyn Curry, the head cook, distractedly peeled potatoes into a huge bucket and thought about the astonishing fact that she was in love with another woman.

The car came to a stop a few hundred feet down the hill, and its occupants jumped out. 'Jesus Christ!' cried the driver. 'It's a little old lady!'

'Probably from that place.' The passenger gestured toward The Tides. 'Why the hell don't they watch these people? They wouldn't be in a nursing home if they could take care of themselves.'

'Is she hurt? How bad is she hurt?'

'Don't move her.'

'Here comes the ambulance.'

The ambulance wailed down the Elm Street hill and two attendants leaped out with a stretcher between them. Rebecca stood helplessly among residents and staff at the curb, while inside the facility phones continued to ring and buzzers to buzz. Dexter McCord strained to see over the rosebushes and roared, 'I told you she was a senile old woman! I told you she was fixing to leave! I told you!'

When the ambulance pulled away, Abby went to gather up the papers and underwear scattered into the depression where the lake used to be, though neither Abby nor Beatrice knew about the lake or its improbable tides. The sacks split, so she had to carry Beatrice's personal things exposed in her arms. Before long somebody came to get Dexter for dinner, pulling him backward in his chair without letting him know where they were going, so as not to get him upset.

'She should have been restrained,' the Director of Nursing declared.

Rebecca brushed tears out of her eyes and shook her head. 'I still don't think so, Diane.'

'Then she should have been in a locked facility. We certainly can't take her back when she's discharged from the hospital. If she's ever discharged.'

'That doesn't seem right,' Rebecca faltered, suddenly unsure of herself. 'She's been here a long time. Years. This is her home.'

Someone inside the building called for Diane and she hurried away without saying anything else to Rebecca. Rebecca stood at the curb for a few more minutes, at loose ends, near tears, mind skittering. Then with a sigh she turned to go inside, too, back to the recalcitrant budget.

Faye followed. Faye, who had never been patient, irritably biding her time.

Chapter 4

Faye had come back for Rebecca.

After all this time, after Marshall had thought he could finally stop worrying that Faye would steal Becky, she was back, and Becky was in fully as much jeopardy as when she'd been a child. Old as he was, his mind not right, he was still her father and it was still up to him to save her.

He meant to get up. He lost his balance and collapsed back into the chair. Panting, he sat there crooked for a while, one hand trapped awkwardly under him, and tried to decide what course of action would be advisable.

It had actually happened only once before, when Rebecca was three years old. Marshall remembered it clearly, fiercely, and recurrently; he also remembered, though with less consistency, that his memory was often untrustworthy, but he knew this was not one of those times. He couldn't get himself straightened in the chair, and his hand twisted under his hip was starting to ache, but he sat there the way he was and remembered again:

Walking in the woods with Becky. Wands of sunlight between trees; the trunks of trees long thin brown wands. Marshall kept a close eye on his little girl. She could trip and fall. She could eat something poisonous. She could wander off and get lost.

For all his surreptitious searching of her face and manner – and, he knew, Billie's searching, Billie's stalwart resolve not to search – the child bore little specific resemblance to anybody. Sometimes she seemed light on her feet, sprite-like, like Faye, and when she was playful in a particular thoughtless way his heart would seize, but then there'd come a sudden glow of what he was sure was precocious awareness of others, and he'd think with relief how like Billie she was. If his daughter took after him, he wouldn't know it; he never encountered his recorded voice or photographed image without a rude little shock, and certainly he didn't have much feel for what sort of man he was. Indeed his time with Faye had convincingly demonstrated that he could be whatever he was expected to be, which was why it was so crucial for him to stay with someone like Billie, who expected him to be strong, steady, a reliable husband, a good father.

Rebecca ran on ahead. He called to her; she answered. A squirrel chittered from a nearby branch, but he couldn't locate it to show her. She was at his side. 'There's a lady over there.'

'A lady? Where?'

'Over there.' She pointed. 'In a car. She said she'd give me a ride. Can I?'

'No! Becky!' Marshall reached for her and slid out of the chair. His left wrist, numb from being bent under him, didn't support his weight, and he collapsed face down onto the cold tile.

After a few minutes of considering the fact that he was on the floor in his room in a nursing home, where theoretically there were nurses to help him if he could let them know he needed help, Marshall turned his gaze and saw the call light button on its thick white cord clipped to the side of the bed. Proudly, he knew immediately what it was and how to use it. It was, though, out of reach from this position; to prove it to himself, he stretched out his arm. The button was too high and about a foot beyond the tips of his fingers. He would have to move.

He maneuvered until both palms were flat on the floor under his shoulders, and then pushed up. This lifted the top part of his torso a few inches off the floor, but his muscles trembled and gave out and he collapsed again. Perhaps he fell asleep. Some time later he tried again, and this time managed to get up onto his hands and knees and move cumbersomely forward. He could reach the call button now. He didn't quite remember why he needed to call someone, but the conviction that doing so was important had stayed with him, and he exerted all the force he could muster to depress the red button with his thumb. A light went on above the bed, and a beeping started.

Stopped.

Confused, swaying, dizzy, Marshall forced himself to push the button again, again setting off both a light and an unpleasant repetitive sound. Someone would come now, and they would know why; he didn't have to try to keep it in his mind any longer. He let himself lie down on the floor.

'No, Marshall,' Faye said, gently scolding. The call light and bell went off again, and this time the cord was unfastened from the bed and lifted well out of reach, out of consciousness. 'Don't call anybody else. I'm right here. Let me take care of you. I'll take good care of you.'

In the staff lounge, Abby slid her dinner tray across the sticky table and dropped into a chair. 'God, this is horrible. Doesn't anybody clean up their own mess around here?'

Nobody answered. Rebecca's embarrassment and guilt were muted only because she was so tired and preoccupied. She was, of course, responsible for everything that happened in this facility, including the indisputable fact that the staff lounge was always a mess. Not getting to her feet until she had to, she started stacking dishes and trash onto her tray.

'I didn't mean you.' Blushing, Abby got up and moved the trash can closer to the table so she could push litter directly into it. But it was already overflowing, and napkins and pop cans bounced onto the floor.

'Sit down and eat your dinner,' Rebecca admonished her. 'You only have half an hour. I'll get housekeeping in here after you guys are off break.'

Abby sighed, sat down, and unwrapped her silverware, which clattered against the plastic tray. 'Look at this. Macaroni and cheese. Bread and butter. Creamed corn. Cake and ice cream. Now that's a real balanced meal. Starch, starch, and more starch.'

Rebecca frowned defensively, and Florence protested, 'The cake is homemade, though. Roslyn does try.'

'Alex was upset tonight because of all the starches. I guess he's made kind of a study of nutrition because it's so important when he can't move his body.' Abby paused. 'Alex is real interesting to talk to, you know?'

Rebecca nodded eagerly. 'A lot of these people are.' She and Abby exchanged a smile, and Rebecca would have liked to say more. She'd have liked to talk about the profound satisfaction she got from working here, the excitement that sometimes bordered on giddiness from coming into contact with all these personalities confined in such a small, rarefied space, the sense she sometimes had that she could pick and choose from them to cobble together something for herself. But that seemed silly and melodramatic, not to mention unprofessional, so she contented herself with adding, 'It's an honor to work here, isn't it?' which was risky enough.

'Yeah, sure,' scoffed Maxine. '*You* try wiping ass eight hours a day for minimum wage and see how much of an honor you think it is then.'

'I know,' Rebecca agreed carefully. 'You guys are the ones we couldn't do without.'

'You can tell,' Maxine pretended to confide to Abby, 'because we're the best-paid and most respected workers in long-term care.' Abby smiled uncertainly. Rebecca ran a hand across her tired eyes, wondering wearily whether she could talk Dan into an across-the-board raise for the nurses' aides, knowing that would mean a raise for everybody else, too, which would have enormous budgetary impact while leaving the system as a whole essentially unchanged.

After an awkward pause, the various conversations around the table resumed, and Abby said quietly to Rebecca, 'It must be hard having your dad here.'

Rebecca thought it ought to be harder than it was, but she didn't say that. 'Sometimes,' she admitted. 'But it's also nice having him nearby.'

'Your mom is such a sweet lady,' Abby said.

People often said things like that about Billie Emig, but Rebecca still didn't readily associate such observations with the woman she knew. Kurt said he liked her, although he didn't go out of his way to spend much time in her company; her father made him uncomfortable, and he wouldn't come to the nursing home at all.

It was not that she disliked her mother; even at the worst of her adolescent rebellion, which actually had been rather mild now that she looked back on it, the strongest reaction she'd had against her was irritation. But 'sweet' was not an adjective she'd have used. 'Polite,' maybe. 'Guarded.' She just smiled, which was what her mother would have done under these circumstances.

'And your dad's so cute. Easy to take care of. He's never mean like some of the others.'

Trying for neutrality, Rebecca nodded. 'I'm glad to hear that.'

'It must be hard, though,' Abby said again with an awkward persistence. 'I mean, seeing him like this.'

'Yes,' Rebecca answered minimally, hoping to end this line of conversation. Abby's clumsy though kind commiserations were forcing her to think again about the peculiar experience of her father's senility as an invitation. Abby seemed about to say something else about him, and to forestall her Rebecca inquired, 'How are your girls? I haven't seen them lately.'

Abby sighed. 'They've all had the flu. I just hope I don't get it.'

Abby had just left her husband again. Now she was supporting three little girls on minimum wage. Sometimes she was late for work because she missed the bus or one of the kids was sick or the toilet backed up and flooded the apartment or she had another migraine. Sometimes she missed work altogether. There was no sick leave, so every time she missed work she missed wages, which meant there were more bills she couldn't pay – plumber, doctor, daycare – and then her migraines and her missed days became more frequent.

Rebecca liked knowing about the lives of the staff, too. Craved knowing about them; hungered for detail. Their lives all seemed so much more complex than hers, richer.

When any of them asked about her life – which wasn't often – she had not much to tell them. She lived with Kurt. She was an only child. She had a master's degree in social work and a nursing-home administrator's license. She'd worked in long-term care for several years, but this was her first facility as administrator. They knew her parents; her father had probable early-stage Alzheimer's, and everybody liked her mother.

She took a forkful of the fluorescent orange macaroni and cheese as Abby sighed again and rubbed her temples. 'Boy, am I tired.'

'Not much sleep, huh?'

'No, and we've been so busy today. Everybody's always *wanting* something.'

'What you've got to do,' Florence instructed, 'is train them right from the beginning. Otherwise you won't last the shift.'

'Train them?' Abby's tone echoed Rebecca's own alarm.

'You do things when you're ready, not when they're ready. Otherwise you'll spend all your time running around answering lights, and you'll never get anything done.'

'It's your job to answer lights,' Rebecca objected, not as diplomatically as she probably should have. Florence shrugged and fell silent.

'Alex can't turn on his light.' Something in Abby's tone made Rebecca glance at her. Her long brown hair, parted in the middle and hanging straight, always looked lank and a little sticky; it didn't invite touch, but it did hide most of her face when she bent her head in this characteristic way.

Maxine snorted. 'Don't waste your time feeling sorry for ol' Alex. He knows exactly what he wants – *and* he gets it.'

The Director of Nursing appeared in the doorway. 'Rebecca, I need to talk to you.'

There was anger in the older woman's face and in the way she held herself, and Rebecca heard Maxine say under her breath, 'Uh-oh, you're in trouble.'

Rebecca laid her fork down with a dull click. 'Sure, Diane. Let's go into my office.'

'I think the kids should hear this, too.'

Involuntarily Rebecca glanced at Florence, who was sixty-three and had been at The Tides for nineteen years.

'Are you aware of what's been going on around here?'

Trick question, Rebecca thought, and made herself grin. 'I hope so.'

'Are you aware of what's been going on between Beatrice Quinn and Dexter McCord?'

'What specifically do you mean? I know they're close friends.' Maxine and Larry hooted.

'Are you aware that they have been regularly engaging in sexual activity?'

'How do you know that?'

'We see them. My kids see them.'

'We see them,' Shirley echoed. 'All the time.'

'Do you mean to say that they're engaging in this – sexual activity – in public areas?'

'No. In their rooms. You walk in and there they are. It's embarrassing.'

'I think,' Diane declared, 'something should be done about it. And now is an opportune time, since she is in the hospital. I think we ought not to readmit her.'

Shirley exclaimed, 'Oh, come on!' and Rebecca, taken aback, stared wordlessly at the nurse.

'If it were *my* grandmother in a place where they were supposed to be taking care of her,' Diane went on grimly,

'*I* certainly would not want her taken advantage of like that.'

'What makes you think Beatrice is being taken advantage of?' Rebecca managed.

Colleen spoke up indignantly. 'What makes you think it's any of our business? We shouldn't even be talking about it.'

'Beatrice Quinn is not rational. She's not capable of making decisions in her own best interest. She's not what I would call a consenting adult.'

'How confused do you have to be,' Rebecca demanded, trying unsuccessfully to keep her voice calm, 'before you don't know what feels good? She can say no. Dexter doesn't strike me as a rapist.' Larry and Maxine guffawed.

'So you're not going to do anything to stop it.'

'No. If anything, maybe we need to step up our in-services on respecting people's privacy before Beatrice comes back.'

'Well.' Diane drew herself up to her full height to deliver her final shot. 'How do we even know his hands are clean?' She turned and left the room.

'That's it!' Maxine was on her feet amid the general laughter, shaking her finger at the group. 'I'm going to get another cup of coffee, and when I get back I don't want to hear another word about work. You hear me? I'm sick of it.' She leaned across the table and pointed into Rebecca's face, smiling to pretend she was kidding but raising her voice to show she was not. 'That includes you, too, boss lady. You hear me? I got more in my life than this place, and if you don't you ought to.'

When Abby got back to the floor, lights were on all up and down the hall, bells going off in various beeps and dings, all of them purposely annoying so you'd answer them in a hurry. By 6:30 almost everybody wanted to go to bed. Abby sent the aide who had been watching the floor on to supper and stood by the nurses' station for a minute, fighting back the nervousness that was a constant part of this job because there was always too much to do, trying to decide where to start. It was hard to think, and her body felt strange – heavy, crowded. Maybe she was getting sick. She thought she saw movement in the long hall, about halfway between the nurses' station and the exit, outside Marshall's room, a darkening and then lightening of the fluorescent ripples off the waxed floor, as if someone had passed through. But the hallway was empty.

Abby rubbed her eyes, pressed her knuckles against the buzz of tension in her chest. She was antsy, didn't want to be here. But she couldn't think of anywhere else she wanted to be, either.

The most natural thing for her to do, the thing that she had to think about least, was to answer Alex's light. She went into his room. 'Yes, Alex, what is it?'

'You look tired,' he said at once, scanning her face. His eyes were green and restless, eerie in the stillness of the rest of his body.

'I am tired.' She reached across him to flip the switch that would turn off the light outside his door and silence the dinging. 'We're short tonight. Again.'

'You work too hard,' he admonished gently.

'Tell me about it.'

'I'm sorry to bother you.'

'That's my job, to be bothered.' A thought occurred to her. 'Who turned on your light for you?'

'My roommate. Before he left for supper.' He smiled apologetically, his green eyes darting back and forth across her face as if he were playing a video game.

'Oh, Alex, that was half an hour ago! I'm sorry.' There were tears in his eyes. The nurses had explained that emotional lability was often a side effect of brain damage and you shouldn't take it personally, but Abby was still bothered by his easy tears. 'What do you need?'

'Well, I wanted to use the urinal.'

She was one of the few aides he would allow to do this for him, and, because she didn't know why, his confidence made her nervous. She brought the urinal, folded back the sheets and blanket, unzipped his pants, gently positioned his penis. It embarrassed her, but Alex, a quad for thirty years and, she supposed, used to this, stared quietly at the ceiling while his urine clattered into the pan.

'My wife was in today,' he remarked.

'I heard.'

'I just don't understand her, Abby. She's not reasonable.'

'What did she say?'

'Oh, she said all kinds of things. She was here for over an hour, shouting the whole time. The kids were running loose in the halls.'

'We can't have that, Alex.'

'I know, I know, I told her.'

'They could knock somebody down, running like that.'

'That's what upsets me, Abby. What she's doing to my kids.' His soft voice broke and tears ran down his cheeks. Abby straightened the urinal under him, not knowing what else she could do. 'She's just not a fit mother. She won't even cook for them. She never wants to cook for me when I'm home, either, but I just insist. I can't even go home anymore. She's got the furniture arranged so I can't get my chair through. It's my house. I pay the mortgage payments. She won't get a job.'

His pee had stopped. Abby took the full urinal into the bathroom and emptied it into the toilet, only then remembering that his output was supposed to be measured so the nurse could record it in the chart. Her spaciness annoyed her. She was annoyed with Alex. She had heard all this before.

'Now she's accusing me of having illicit affairs.'

'You're kidding.' Catching herself appraising his body where it lay helpless under her hands, she blushed.

'Don't act so surprised,' he said with a grin. 'It's not impossible, you know.' She busied herself around him and said nothing, but waited to hear what more he would say about that. 'She's accusing me of having an affair with someone here. Someone who takes care of me.'

'Well, you're not. Are you?' She laughed self-consciously.

'Abby, she's talking about you.'

'Me? Why?'

'I guess,' he said, his fly still open, his restless eyes still traveling across her face so that she could almost feel the soft little trails they left, 'I happened to mention what a nice girl you are, what good care you take of me.'

'It's my job. Does she want my job? Obviously not.'

'She used to be a lot like you. I fell in love with her when she was an aide taking care of me, after my first wife put me in a nursing home. She used to say it wasn't a burden taking care of me, it was a privilege.' He smiled wistfully, his eyes on her face, and her heart went out to him.

Scrambling to protect herself, Abby commented, more sarcastically than she'd intended, 'You sure have a way with the ladies, don't you?'

'Who, me? My wife says I'm nothing but a paralyzed old man.'

'You're not old.'

'Before we decided to get married we spent a weekend in the mountains together. She didn't seem to mind my body then. I don't usually approve of such things, but I wanted her to know what she was getting.'

Her face hot, Abby zipped up his pants and covered him, then stood well away with her hand on the doorknob. 'Is there anything else you need right now?'

'I'd very much like to get up.' There was an urgency in his voice. 'If it's not too much trouble.'

'You'll have to wait, Alex. I've already got you up and put you to bed twice this shift. It takes a really long time. I have other patients to take care of, too, you know.'

'My muscles are cramping a lot today. I don't like to be a bother.' He smiled ingratiatingly at her from the bed, his eyes full of tears again and his hands motionless at his sides.

'I don't have time right now. I just don't.'

'Abby,' he began, but she shut the door on his quiet voice and went to answer somebody else's light at the far end of the hall. Out of the corner of her averted eyes she thought she glimpsed somebody flitting past and hovering around Alex's door, and she thought maybe his wife had come back. Unwillingly, she turned around to look. To her relief, nobody was there, and Alex wasn't calling for her anymore.

When she'd finished putting everybody down on the south end of the wing – alone; it was too much for anybody to do alone, but what choice did she have? – she went to help Shirley on the north end. Myra had wet her bed again, so what else was new, and Abby was on her way to the linen closet, hoping there'd be enough clean sheets for a change, when she glanced into Marshall's room and saw him on the floor. Yelling for help, she ran in. At first she thought he was dead. But as she and Maxine got him up and into the bed, he opened his eyes and rasped, 'Faye!'

Maxine jumped, dropped her side of him so that he flopped sideways on top of the blanket. 'Shit. What's he saying?'

'Faye!'

'I don't know,' Abby said, staring at him for a minute. 'Is he calling somebody?'

'You better get Rebecca. Get the nurse and get Rebecca.'

'Faye!'

Although it was cold and they'd been told to come in, Petra and Bob were still out on the front porch. It wasn't in the interests of good patient care for them to be out there, both because of the evening chill and the fact that they weren't wearing coats and because they were doubtless engaging or about to engage in inappropriate activity; Diane, finally on her way home, stopped to give the charge nurse instructions. 'Insist that they come in. You can probably trick them; if you tell Petra her husband's on the phone she'll come in, and then Bob will follow her eventually. Or send Larry and Maxine out to get them.'

Ever since they'd come out here after supper, Bob had been telling Petra a story. A piece here, a space there – it was a mosaic, and whether she received the same picture he sent was debatable, but he kept talking and she kept listening, both erratically, neither looking at or touching the other although that would come.

He'd gone downtown to Woolworth's. He'd bought a hamburger. Today or ten years ago, he went downtown. He sat at the snack bar at Woolworth's. He'd bought a hamburger and fries.

Everybody was looking at him. He didn't care. Fuck 'em all. He sat at the counter like everybody else and ate his hamburger. They were staring at him, they were laughing at him. Fuck you. Take a picture. Then his hamburger floated up in the air. Nobody else acted like anything was going on, so he didn't either. He just waited and it floated back down and he ate it. When the hamburger floated up in the air nobody noticed but when he sat there and ate it like everybody else they laughed. Fuck 'em.

Petra interrupted her own underbreath red-ants monologue to tell him out loud, roughly, 'Shit, I know what causes that.'

He kicked at the wall. He swung his forearm into the wrought-iron post. When she didn't tell him, he snarled, 'So what, bitch? Think you're so smart. Think you're such a smart-ass. I'll show you who's smart. *What?*'

She sidled over to him. The top of her head reached the middle buttonhole of his shirt; that button among others was missing. Not looking up at his face, poking her sharp fingers through the holes in his shirt, she croaked, 'Why, honey, it's *the tides*. You know. It's the power of the tides.'

With that, everything slid into focus for Bob. 'Oh,' he said to her, brimming with gratitude and something like love. 'Oh, yeah. That makes sense. The tides.' He knew that. He wasn't as dumb as he looked.

He stooped and picked her up. She screeched and giggled. He carried her off the porch.

Chapter 5

Five forty-five in the morning and already behind schedule, rushed, because the first feeding had to be done by seven so the second shift could get in and out by seven-thirty in order for baths to get done in time for morning meds. There were morning activities, too, today a book club at nine o'clock and men's group after that, but it wouldn't be the end of the world if people missed that stuff.

Some residents wanted to linger over coffee. Some lingered, not especially wanting to, because their hands were uncertain getting food and drink to their mouths or because they had to swallow three or four times for each bite or because they kept sliding to the verge of forgetting what a fork or a piece of toast was for. Lingerers intentional or otherwise would soon be rousted from the dining room whether they were ready to leave or not, in the constant and constantly frustrated attempt to maintain some sort of schedule.

In the kitchen, Roslyn Curry made as much noise as she could. The radio on top of the freezer was turned to elevator music which she liked, goddammit, no matter what anybody said. Getting to pick the music on the kitchen radio was one of the few perks of being Food

Services Director, and Ros took what she could get.

There was some sort of interference this morning, though, a ghost in the signal so that it sounded almost like somebody singing along, way in the background, to an instrumental version of 'Qué Sera Sera.' This was especially aggravating because it made you want to *listen* to the damn thing instead of just letting it drizzle along the way it was supposed to. Ros frowned, but it was too much trouble to fuss with the dial and try to clear it up, so she'd just put up with it.

She liked this job. She liked these people. She wanted to do right by them. It wasn't easy.

Adele couldn't stand old people or sick people or anybody who wasn't normal, which was sort of funny, considering. Nursing homes made her physically ill. She couldn't fathom why Ros worked there, and she *really* didn't want to hear about it. It was one of the things between them. There were a lot of things. Married to a man all those years who had never taken much of an interest in her, Ros had thought things would just naturally be better with a woman, and it threw her to discover the same old crap.

Stainless steel pots and pans clanged against stainless steel sinks. The louder the clanging the more Roslyn felt both harried and efficient. That was ridiculous, not that she cared.

Bob Morley was hanging around in the doorway. 'Go sit *down*!' she told him. His perpetual scowl deepened but he slunk away. Not very far, she knew. He was like a stray dog, putting up with kicks and curses on the off-chance that you'd drop something edible—not give it to him; she doubted anybody had given him anything in a long time, except maybe Petra. He'd as soon bite you as look at you.

He'd already been sitting in the dining room when she'd come to work at four-thirty – well, she'd been a little late. Four-thirty in the morning was just too early to expect anybody to be at work, if you had any kind of social life. Which at the moment Ros had a lot of, if social was what you could call it.

Fifty-eight years old and as mixed up as a teenager. Trying to figure out who she was, which had been pretty well decided until the afternoon she'd met Adele at the nursery buying tulip bulbs – and they'd spent the day together gardening and having lunch and then the night. Thinking about that night and every other night since, thinking ahead to tonight with Adele, Ros felt sinful and joyful at the same time, both feelings stronger than anything she'd experienced in years, maybe in all her life.

Half-asleep and obsessing over Adele, she'd cut some-body off on the highway and missed the Elm Street turnoff, for Chrissake, which made her even later than she already was. She had trouble with the key in the back door and then stumbled over a bucket the supper crew had left in the way. Just before she'd flipped on the light switch, she'd thought she glimpsed somebody else in the empty, dim, echoing dining room, flitting from table to table, wearing purple. Ros didn't know who it was and couldn't take time to look. By the time she got herself situated, coffee started (stronger than recommended; no self-respecting coffee drinker could stomach the dishwater the budget called for), and went out to do a quick check of the dining room, she hadn't seen anybody but Morley.

She kept looking over her shoulder, though, and squinting into the shadows behind the cooler, behind the doors. She couldn't shake the feeling that somebody else was there, just outside her field of vision, making a disturbance not quite loud enough for her to hear. Amazing what lack of sleep and a sex drive newly awakened and impossible to satisfy could do to you. She'd been better off married and celibate.

Bob Morley gave her the creeps. For one thing, he was tall and big-jointed, kind of like Abe Lincoln. And he looked right at you. Not many people around here did that. His blue eyes were like windows on a war, whole regiments in there, whole armies, most of the bloodshed from friendly fire. You always had the feeling you were walking into an ambush. Ros didn't much like being alone with him early in the morning. On top of everything else, he had a rancid body odor that could curl your hair.

For all that, Ros got a kick out of the fact that Bob Morley and Petra Carrasco were getting it on, not least because it scandalized practically everybody else around here. The two of them couldn't keep their hands off each other. There was a time when Ros wouldn't have understood that. Now, her palms itched to be following the sweet swell of Adele's breast, her own nipples hardened before she was even consciously aware of thinking about Adele, and she felt an unwelcome comradeship with Bob Morley, of all people.

There wasn't enough pancake batter for the second shift. Gordon Marek alone could eat a dozen pancakes, and Ros didn't see why he shouldn't. Annoyed with herself for the oversight and with Adele for distracting her, she hefted the big box of pancake mix and decided there was enough left for another breakfast after this one. She detested using mixes and prepackaged crap, but there wasn't time or money to make things from scratch. For a minute she indulged herself in a fantasy about bran and banana pancakes. Bran would help these people's bathroom problems – they all had bathroom problems of one kind or another – and bananas were good for their electrolytes, which could make old people dizzy and confused if they weren't balanced. Ros knew a helluva lot more about nutrition than anybody gave her credit for.

She poured mix into the huge stainless steel bowl and added water without bothering to measure any of it. She wedged in the big beaters and lowered them into the bowl. The mixer shrieked when she turned it on. Holding the bowl precariously with one hand, daring it to spill or break, she leaned over to check how much fruit she had. Four gallon cans. Sweetened fruit. There was no earthly reason she couldn't serve these people fresh fruit in season. She resolved to talk to Rebecca about that, for all the good it would do. Ros did not like working for a woman, especially one young enough to be her daughter.

The bowl was slowly rotating now; she let the rim slide through her fingers, imagining Adele's earlobe. Jesus. When she straightened up, she saw powdery pancake mix on the floor in the outline of her shoe. She swore. Well, one of the girls could clean it up when they got in at six-thirty. That was another perk of being Director, come to think of it: you could tell somebody else to sweep the floor. They better be on time, too.

Adele had held her face in her hands to kiss her goodbye from the bed, which was now their bed. Adele had whispered, 'I'll be here when you get back, hon,' and Ros, thrilled, was also repulsed. How could she go home to a woman in her bed? How could she stay away, even for an eight-hour shift?

When the pancake batter had been beaten enough that it goddamn ought to be smooth, whether it actually was or not, Roslyn turned off the mixer. The radio was playing a schmaltzy version of 'I Wanna Hold Your Hand,' smoothed out, lots of strings. Ros started to sing along, with feeling. When it dawned on her that she was thinking of – Jesus, *fantasizing* about, getting off on – Adele, she shut up and turned the radio down. Then off.

A whispering rose like crickets, except that there were words in it. Ros stood still and listened. Tender stroking riffled her hair, the sprayed curls at the crown of her head and up under the hair cut close and tapered at the nape of her neck, raising goosebumps and an urgent desire for sex. Soft insistent hands held her face, and soft lips pressed against hers. For a split-second, her vision blurred lavender, and an idea came into her head, fuzzy, hinting at something terrible, suggesting something unbelievably exciting, something she would never have considered herself capable of thinking about, let alone doing. But she didn't know herself anymore.

'Shit.' This was getting ridiculous. It was hard enough to be like a kid in love when you were a kid and it was the opposite sex you were head over heels for. Pushing sixty and in love with another woman was too much. It wasn't that she thought it was wrong. She didn't think she'd ever thought it was wrong, really. But it was such a shock. She didn't have the faintest idea what the rules were. Everything she did these days surprised her. She could not believe she was in this particular fix. This was not what she'd expected to have to worry about at this time in her life.

Out of Roslyn's field of vision, on the other side of the kitchen wall with the steam tables and serving counter, the gauzy presence hovered in the half-lit dining room. When it settled, briefly, over tables and chairs, it altered their contours and outlines for as long as it stayed there.

When it bounced up to suspend itself, fleetingly, from the ceiling, it was like a giant cobweb, a spreading place where the paint was melting, where the very concrete was dissolving. When it raced toward the hall, where fluorescent lights were on all night, it blurred both light and harsh shadow, sound and silence. There was an aura of playfulness about its antics, overlaying menace.

Even when the dining room was full, four people to a table, it didn't sound like a room full of people eating breakfast anywhere but in a nursing home. Plasticware against plastic trays didn't ring or really even clatter, but made scraping and sliding sounds as muted as the colors, grayed pink, brownish yellow. There wasn't the hum of restaurant diners or the separated-out conversations, friendly or hostile, of a family at table. It was a noise all its own. Roslyn thought that when she was a hundred years old and senile – not that she'd have to live that long to get senile – she'd still recognize the sound of a meal in a nursing home. Maybe not, though. Maybe she wouldn't remember any of this. Like a year-old kid, maybe she wouldn't remember anything that was happening to her right now, no matter how real and interesting, even amazing, it was while it was happening.

Ros shook her head at herself. Even her thoughts weren't her own.

The aides were wheeling people in. In a hurry, Florence brought two wheelchairs in at once, pushing Paul because it took him too long to walk and pulling Myra Larsen backwards. Myra hollered, pointlessly.

People did talk – often to themselves or in parallel like toddlers at play, sometimes in brief exchanges, once in a while in extended conversation randomly interrupted when the time allotted for the meal was over. Marshall

Emig was actually quite talkative this morning, and Billie didn't know whether to be pleased or saddened by how chipper he was. Throughout their marriage, he'd set the tone. When he was happy – whistling, playing silly little practical jokes – she and Rebecca had been happy. When he was in one of his moods, everybody'd walked on eggshells. Now, though, she never knew how to take him. His states of mind these days bore the same resemblance to what she was used to as a raisin did to a grape – you knew they came from the same source, were versions of the same thing, but your intuition insisted that couldn't be, they must be completely different.

Marshall was talking about the universe. He'd always liked to talk about such things, and Billie's job had been to nod her head and once in a while say something to pretend she was interested. If he'd ever realized she wasn't the least bit interested, he'd have stopped talking about it, stopped thinking about it, and that would have been too bad. What he was saying now made no less sense to her than what he'd said a hundred times before, but she couldn't trust anymore that he knew what he was talking about, either. Something about black holes which were really made of light, and the universe being infinite but curved at the edges, which Billie thought had to be contradictory. But what did she know?

Marshall said something about the war. What he said was just a part of a sentence, and it didn't make any sense, but Billie tensed. Terrible things must have happened to him in the war. He'd never talked to her about it. It would be awful if being senile made him tell her terrible things he'd never told her before.

She ate her pancakes. Ros Curry always made sure she

got a tray whenever she was here at mealtime, which was more and more often.

Partly, that was because Billie always hoped for a few minutes with her daughter. Rebecca had even less time to visit now than before she took this job, but at least they were in the same building and ran into each other once in a while. She seemed – not happy, exactly, but animated, at least; not so lost. Still, Billie worried about her. Running a place like this was an awful lot of responsibility for a twenty-eight-year-old girl, and Rebecca looked tired all the time. She always had been a loner, never more than one or two friends at a time and those came and went. This Kurt was her first real boyfriend, not counting a couple in high school, and somehow Billie didn't think they were really serious, even though they were living together and almost certainly sleeping together. As far as her mother could tell, the only thing that Rebecca really paid attention to was her work. That wasn't good for anybody, especially not a woman. But she guessed it was better than all those years when Rebecca hadn't seemed to pay attention to anything.

Still, Billie liked spending so much time where her daughter worked, liked having an excuse to watch Rebecca be efficient and compassionate and so grown up. They weren't very close. Billie didn't dare let herself be too close to this daughter. But it was good to be around her while they both, in their own ways, worked at taking care of Marshall, who was the main thing they'd ever had in common.

Billie didn't like the type of people they had here, alcoholics and crazy people like that Petra woman and crippled young people and senile old people all under the same roof. Rebecca said real human communities were like that, all different kinds living together. Billie didn't think that was so in the first place, and anyway this wasn't a 'community,' this was a nursing home. She sipped her watered-down orange juice.

Marshall announced, 'Faye's home.' His face was alight, his gaze fixed on the middle distance of his fractured but expansive interior landscape. Billie wasn't sure what he'd said. A lot of the time she wasn't sure what he'd said, and it bothered her, but if she asked him to say it again he got agitated.

Then, abruptly, he cringed and tried to curl himself up in his chair. The vest restraint prevented him from doing more than bringing his knees up, his head down, his wrists in to cross over his torso, which he'd made concave by bending forward his shoulders and pelvis as though to protect his internal organs.

Across the table from him, not too close but close enough to be identified as his wife, still part of a couple, Billie sopped up the last of the syrup on her plate with the last bite of pancake. The pancakes hadn't been hot when Roslyn had slapped them onto the tray and by now they were positively cold, coated with cold syrup, and they'd come out of a box to begin with. But they weren't bad.

Every meal she ate here, which was almost every supper and sometimes lunch and once in a while breakfast, Billie was offended by all the shortcuts they took in the kitchen, to save money and work. She'd never say anything to Rebecca or Ros, but she didn't think food was where you ought to cut corners, not when food was just about all some of these poor people had left. She and Marshall had always been on a budget, too, especially in the early years. She'd been busy, too. But she'd never in her life served pancakes from a mix.

TIDES

On Marshall's behalf she took offense, even though he didn't seem to notice any difference between this food and what she'd cooked for him all their lives together. He'd always been so persnickety about food, and he wouldn't have eaten instant pancakes if he'd been starving to death. Here he ate a tall stack, and would want more. Billie couldn't understand where he put all that food; he was so thin. Frail. Frail was a disconcerting thing to think about your husband. Senile was, too.

Marshall always said the food was good, affectionately told *her* it was good, as if she'd cooked it for him. He was always so pleased. His pleasure made Billie feel good as if she really had cooked it with him in mind. It also made her terribly sad.

The funny thing was, Billie herself didn't mind the nursing-home food as much as she thought she ought to. Even the cold pancakes out of a box tasted pretty good, and she'd actually liked the chicken last night. Roslyn did the best she could. Billie decided she'd ask for the recipe; she'd never go to the trouble of fixing it just for herself, but still.

They made her feel so welcome here. At home. Marshall didn't always exactly know her, and that broke her heart, but she was known and welcomed in this place. Dexter and Gordon always spoke to her by name, and both of them flirted, Dexter declaring at the top of his lungs, the way he declared everything, that her husband was a mighty lucky fellow, a *mighty* lucky fellow, and Gordon presenting her with flowers he'd pilfered from neighbors' yards. Gordon called Rebecca 'Princess,' which Billie thought was cute, but she didn't know about this dog of his; who ever heard of animals in a nursing home? Mrs Quinn would come and have a cup of coffee with her in the evenings, sometimes just the two of them left in the dining room. Fervently, Billie hoped Mrs Quinn would be all right. What an awful thing. It wasn't Rebecca's fault, you couldn't be everywhere at once, but those nurses ought to have been watching better.

Billie liked the old people, when she didn't dwell on the fact that they were her own age, many of them even younger. Gordon was sort of endearing, although she didn't think this was the best place for him; didn't they have places for old drinkers? She didn't mind Paul, really, and she felt so *sorry* for him, but his drooling and lurching made her nervous. Alexander Booth could be charming and he had some interesting things to say, so she guessed he was all right.

But the insane ones bothered her. Like that man standing over there against the wall watching her – he always seemed to be watching her; he always seemed to be watching everybody – and that woman of his and the old lady who screamed she was Cleopatra and Jesus Christ. Billie shuddered. People like that didn't belong here, and more of them were being admitted. What was Rebecca thinking of? Her own father.

Instinctively Billie moved to block Bob Morley's view of her husband. She'd have been able to ignore what he'd said just now if he hadn't unfolded himself and said it again, pitifully, as if he hardly could believe it himself. It was almost a question. 'Faye's home?' Then he looked right at her, and his eyes cleared, and he said brightly, 'Faye. You're home. Welcome home.'

Stunned, Billie protested, 'Marshall Emig! I'm not Faye! For goodness' sake, Marshall, I'm Billie! I'm your wife!'

Marshall exclaimed again, pleased as a little boy, 'Faye!'

And strained across the sticky table to hold out both old hands to her.

Billie didn't take his hands. In fact, she leaned back out of his reach. Her fingers had turned numb with the shock of what he was saying, but she knew it wouldn't really sink in until later, until she got away from him. He thought she was Faye. He thought Faye had come home. And he was glad.

Marshall relaxed then, while maintaining that awkward position; though she was terribly hurt, Billie fretted that the restraint must surely be cutting into his ribs. His face slowly went blank. Billie watched as energy drained, muscles slackened, eyes clouded over. His head drooped toward his outstretched arms, as if to rest there, but the Poscy – an awfully cute name for such a contraption – held his torso upright. He was asleep.

Billie wanted more than anything to get out of here. Why should she care about Marshall if he was going to think she was Faye? She'd thought they were rid of the woman years ago – and yet, she found she wasn't completely surprised that Faye had reappeared now in Marshall's scrambled mind. Tears filmed her eyes but she refused to let them fall. Lots of people around here shed lots of tears, but she was not going to be one of them. She'd cry at home, alone.

But she couldn't leave him just sitting here asleep, not with that madman staring at him, not when he was seeing Faye. And she couldn't manage him by herself when he was all sprawled out across the table like that. She looked around for somebody to help her. All the girls were busy hurrying people out of the dining room whether they'd finished their breakfast or not.

Billie got to her feet and stood by the table, hoping

she'd be able to catch somebody's attention, hoping Marshall wouldn't wake up. Faye, of all things. To have to think about Faye again at her age. She waved to Shirley, but couldn't catch her eye. Shirley was arguing with Dexter McCord, who didn't want to leave the dining room yet, didn't want to take a bath. He was holding onto the edge of the table and bellowing. Shirley was prying his fingers loose. One of them was going to get hurt.

Billie looked away from the unpleasant scene, wished she could close her ears. Except for Shirley and Dexter, herself and Marshall, and that man hunkering by the back door, the dining room had been emptied. Billie had the feeling somebody else was there, but she scanned the room more than once and saw no one. The radio was on in the kitchen, but it was always on and she couldn't tell whether Roslyn was back there or not.

Her legs went wobbly on her and she groped for the back of the chair, sank into it. If she weren't so heavy she'd be better off, but she couldn't see herself losing weight now. She rested her elbows on the table and her head on her hands, defeated, bent over like Marshall but a little less so. This was beyond her. All she could think to do was wait for somebody to notice that Marshall wasn't in his room and come looking for him. It shamed her that she couldn't handle her own husband. That's why he was in a nursing home, because she couldn't do right by him.

Roslyn came out from the kitchen, as she did most mornings, to have coffee with some of the residents who lingered. She wasn't supposed to do that; she was supposed to be cleaning up after breakfast and starting prep for lunch. Let the girls do that; if they didn't know what to do by now they were all in trouble. She had enough on her mind, like Adele. The salesman from ARA would be here this morning and she didn't have her order ready. Screw it. What was the point of this job if she couldn't take a few minutes to talk to the people she was cooking for?

Not that she liked all of them. She kept trying to explain it to Adele. Just because they lived in a nursing home didn't mean they were all interesting or decent human beings or even – Roslyn's bare minimum – not irritating. Bob Morley, for instance, was practically nothing *but* irritating. There he was now, hulking just outside the back door. Smoking, probably, or feeling up Petra, or jerking off. Ros wondered if he'd eaten breakfast. A lot of the time he wouldn't eat with the others. Ros suspected he couldn't stand their company, and she could relate to that, so more often than not she'd fix him a tray later, by himself. She wasn't supposed to do that, either. Screw it.

Beatrice Quinn was one of her favorites, but the old broad was still in the hospital. The last time Roslyn had visited, Beatrice had patted her hand and said not to worry, she'd be back in a few days, but who knew? Roslyn missed her. Shame, what had happened. Ros wondered whose fault it was. The driver's? The nurses' and aides', for not watching her better? Beatrice Quinn's? If she didn't knock it off, Bea was going to wake up in one of those locked wards someday. But if Ros herself was ever in a nursing home, she'd be doing her damnedest to escape all the time, too. They'd have to tie her down. Maybe that's what they ought to do with Beatrice.

Juggling her enormous coffee mug and the morning paper, she pushed aside the dishes and crumbs on one of the vacated tables the girls hadn't got to yet, brushed off some sort of cobweb on the back and seat of the chair, and sat herself down. Sooner or later somebody would join her. By now it wouldn't surprise her if Rebecca showed up, never mind that the administrator had no business here this early in the morning. Rebecca was naive and in over her head, and according to Diane the only reason she had got this job so young was because she slept with Dan Murphy. To hear Diane tell it, everybody from the new little housekeeper to the Health Department nursing surveyor was sleeping or had slept with Dan Murphy, which, looking at him, was hard to believe, and as if Diane would know anyway. But you couldn't accuse Rebecca of not working hard.

Having in this way started thinking about sex and trade-offs for sex, Ros was well into thinking about Adele some more – picturing herself in Adele's arms, fantasizing about Adele's tongue and her own – when Bob slammed open the back door and strode toward her. 'Hungry,' he grunted.

Over the top of the paper Ros fixed him with a baleful stare. 'Should've eaten your breakfast, shouldn't you? It's a long time till lunch.' She knew and he knew she'd get him a tray, but she wasn't going to make it too easy. One of Rebecca's more ridiculous ideas was that residents ought to be able to get snacks whenever they felt like it, just as if this really were their home. Roslyn openly scoffed at that one.

'Fuck you,' Bob said clearly.

With difficulty Ros stopped herself from decking him; the muscles in her arm actually clenched. She didn't even raise the verbal obscenity stakes, though a dozen more imaginative rejoinders sped through her mind. 'And the horse you rode in on,' was what she said back, which was probably over his head. With a furious rustle and snap she raised the paper in front of her face again and simply pulled rank, an option always available to her and any other staff person no matter what Rebecca said about equality and shared power. 'Get out of here,' she ordered. 'Breakfast's over.'

'You'll be sorry,' he snarled, then stormed out the back door, slamming it. She was surprised that he'd left without a struggle or at least an argument. If he got hit by a car it would be her fault for not giving him breakfast whenever the hell he wanted it, no matter how obnoxious he was. Ros scowled.

There was nothing worth reading on the front page. She tried to fold the paper to page 2, but it buckled and the inside sections slid out onto the floor. Bending to pick them up, she grunted and cursed.

The intercom crackled: 'Roslyn Curry, call on line 1. Ros, line 1, please.' So Rebecca was here already; who did she think she was? The page broke into the relative quiet of the early morning, started the yap that would go on all day. Even at night there were phone calls to announce and nursing staff to summon from one wing of the facility to the other, and occasionally, when things were slow, the night shift would play on the intercom, sing or tell jokes or call mischievously to each other, just to break the monotony and keep themselves awake. Not everyone who lived there was awakened by this. Some were deaf. Some were so inured to the erratic stimulation of their environment that even the electronically enhanced shouting, laughter, crackling, and whistling didn't really bother them. Those who were disturbed often didn't sleep again that night unless they were sedated, for which all of them had standing doctor's orders in their charts; the insomnia and the medication were, most of the time, duly charted and reported as a problem in patient-care conferences, but regarded as routine.

Ros sat there, not wanting to answer the phone. She spent half her goddamn life on the phone. It was just the ARA guy, confirming their appointment, which was his sneaky way of making sure she was ready for him, which she never was. She successfully ignored the page until Rebecca repeated it, then slapped the paper down on the still-uncleaned table, said, 'Okay, okay, keep your pants on,' and stalked into the kitchen to pick up the phone.

'Roslyn?' came Adele's voice, and she sounded funny. Adrenaline surged through Ros, making her queasy.

'What's the matter?' Silence, and Ros had to ask again, 'Adele, what's wrong?'

Adele took an audible breath and said in a rush, 'There's somebody else.'

For long moments Ros didn't consciously know what Adele was talking about, although the sudden gauziness of her senses, followed by abrupt, terrible clarity – the cracks in the ceiling three-dimensional, the odors of pancakes and syrup and coffee acrid – probably signalled comprehension at some visceral level. Everything that came into her head to say seemed both ridiculous and dangerous, life-threatening. She heard the back door open and didn't hear it shut. The son-of-a-bitch never did shut the door.

Adele said, 'I'm in love with somebody else,' and now there was no question what she meant.

Ros said, stupidly, 'Who is he?' and Adele gave a shriek of outraged laughter. The salesman from ARA knocked on the doorframe, stuck his head in, gave a jaunty wave, and settled himself and his order forms at the nearest table, still in full view and earshot. Ros said, 'Shit. Okay, who is she?'

Predictably, Adele said, 'It doesn't matter who she is, Ros. Things just aren't going to work out between us.'

Roslyn was having trouble breathing; her throat was clogged and scratchy, as though a fine net scarf had been shoved into her esophagus. She turned her back on both Bob Morley and the salesman and managed to ask through the obstruction, 'Why not?' She didn't know what the rules were here. Did a lesbian lover – that was the first time she'd allowed herself even to think the word 'lesbian' – break up with you the same way and for the same reasons a man would?

Apparently so, because Adele said, 'Oh, Ros, we just aren't right for each other. We haven't been right from the beginning, but I kept hoping things would get better,' and Roslyn had the same Alice-in-Wonderland headrush she'd had when her husband had left her, telling her things she should have known all along and had never even guessed.

She found that she had been staring at the flickering ceiling fixture; her vision was starred now with bursts of multicolored light and their auras. Her head buzzed, less like a swarm of mosquitos than like the electric zapper that incinerated them.

'I won't be here when you get home,' Adele finished, and broke the connection. Ros did not hang up right away.

Since Billie Emig had heard her daughter's voice on the PA, sounding awfully bossy coming out of the speakers all over the building like that, she'd been waiting for Rebecca to come into the dining room, see her father, and help her mother get him to his room. No such thing happened. Billie sat there. In a fierce undertone, she said to Marshall, 'You notice who's here taking care of you now that you're senile, don't you? Not Faye,' but of course he didn't have anything to say to that.

A man she'd never seen before, in a suit and tie and carrying a briefcase, walked past their table, whistling. He smiled down at her and patted her shoulder. 'Good morning, dear.' Rebecca hated it when people talked to Billie like that; she said it was patronizing, but to Billie he was just being nice. The man peeked into the kitchen, waved to Roslyn, and, still whistling, sat down at a table near the door, where he opened his briefcase and spread out papers.

Rebecca didn't come, and neither did anybody else. Billie resolved to ask Roslyn for help; she hated to do that, since it wasn't really Ros's job and the man in the suit was obviously here to see her. Billie hesitated, increasingly angry and afraid.

With a cry, Marshall woke up and jerked himself back so hard that the chair moved. His eyes bulged, and there were bubbles in the corners of his mouth. Billie got to her feet and went to him. He tried to get away from her. 'Leave me alone!' he was hollering, all the more awful because his voice was raspy and hollow, stuck in his throat. He struck out at her, batting her hands away. He'd never hit her before.

'Ma'am? Need some help?' The salesman pushed back his chair and came across the room. Before she'd told him what she needed, he'd caught Marshall's flailing hands. 'Now, you don't want to do that, sir.' The 'ma'am' and the 'sir' emphasized, somehow, that he was in charge of the situation, which Billie found immensely reassuring.

'He thinks I'm somebody else,' she confided to the man. 'Sometimes he gets a little, you know, confused.'

'Oh, that's okay, I get a little confused now and then myself,' the man said heartily. He had dropped one of Marshall's hands now and was pumping the other one gently, pretending to be shaking hands. Billie thought that was nice. 'Sir,' he went on, bending close as if Marshall couldn't see very well and raising his voice as though he couldn't hear, 'my name's Stanley Bartlett. I'm the guy that supplies your food here.'

Saying by rote, 'Glad to make your acquaintance,' Marshall heard his own voice and suddenly snapped into an understanding of where and who he was, what was happening, what was expected of him and what he could expect. The residual effect of the earlier state of mind – a sense of having been terrified and with good reason – threatened to leave him tremulous, but he managed to steady both his voice and his grip as he, in fact, shook hands with Stanley Bartlett, repeated gravely, 'I'm glad to meet you,' and even added, comprehending almost completely what this interaction concerned, 'We appreciate all that you do.' He still saw Faye superimposed on his beloved Billie, but now he knew she wasn't real. It wasn't the first time he'd dreamed about her, or imagined he glimpsed her in a crowd (or felt her hands on him the way they would be when she was loving him, or felt his hands on her).

'Would you mind helping me walk him back to his room?' Billie appealed to Mr Bartlett, although she wasn't sure she'd need his help now that Marshall was almost himself again, as much himself as he ever was anymore. She spread her hands apologetically. 'I don't know where the girls are. They must be short-handed today.'

'Sure,' Bartlett agreed, but she could tell he didn't want to and she was embarrassed that she'd asked. He glanced toward the kitchen and at his watch. 'Looks like Ros isn't ready for me anyway.'

Marshall stood up on his own. Bartlett reached

helpfully for his elbow, which threw Marshall off-balance; he tipped sideways but righted himself by pushing off against Billie's shoulder, eluding her grasp. Then at a respectable pace he got himself out of the dining room and down the hall to the right, which was the direction of his room. Billie and the salesman followed to make sure he got where he was going. Faye followed, too, a short distance, before spinning back to meet Ros as she slammed out through the swinging kitchen door.

Distraught as she was, Roslyn Curry would be easy to enter. Faye slid right in, just as Bob Morley stepped in front of her demanding his breakfast. 'Sure! No problem!' Ros hissed, bringing her face close to Bob's and locking gazes with him. 'Sit down right there, sir, make yourself comfortable, and I'll be just pleased as punch to serve you.'

Bob didn't know what to do. He was slow; he didn't always get things. He sat down. He was hungry.

But she didn't come back out of the kitchen. She didn't bring him his breakfast. He got hungrier and hungrier and madder and madder. He could hear funny noises from back there, like a woman crying. It pissed him off when a woman cried. He got up. He knocked over the chair. 'Hey! I'm hungry!' Nobody did anything.

Fists clenched, mind completely focused on food, Bob kicked at the metal swinging door into the kitchen and it opened. He hadn't exactly known it would open, but when it did he barged in. Somebody was over by the big refrigerators. She was shaking, and all kinds of colors fizzed out from her. Bob stayed away. He looked for food. The stove that didn't look much like a stove didn't have any food on it. There was a garbage can in the corner with its lid off, and he peered down into it and saw pancakes.

He pulled them out. They were specked with coffee grounds but he didn't care. Now he needed syrup. 'Syrup!' he grunted.

Somebody told him, silkily, 'Under the counter. Right in front of you. In the big plastic bottle. You can have as much as you like.' Bob *liked* syrup.

Clutching the gritty pancakes in one hand, he squatted to look under the counter. There was the big plastic bottle the voice had been talking about. He tugged at it but it was heavier than he'd expected. He needed both hands, so he laid his pancakes down on the floor and managed to get the jug out. Somebody was coming, he heard footsteps and voices outside the kitchen. He had to hurry. He jerked the cap off and poured lots of thick syrup onto the pancakes right there between his feet and grabbed the sticky mass and shoved it into his mouth.

It smelled funny. It tasted funny. It burned his throat going down. His belly *hurt*.

Chapter 6

From the supine position in which he'd had Abby place him on the bed, Alexander Booth could see only the ceiling and a few inches of the walls on three sides, with attendant variations in color and texture. This ceiling was institutionally typical, in need of scrubbing and painting; most people, he thought wryly, didn't observe ceilings as extensively and intensively as he did, even those whose responsibilities would seem to demand it.

Little besides the neglected ceiling was in his field of vision, but he had other ways of determining who was in his presence. His method was not infallible, but over the years he had come to trust his own perceptions, and the greater his confidence the greater their efficacy. Perhaps it was a form of intuition risen out of his need, far greater than normal, for self-protection and vigilance about the environment, or perhaps it was simply that his senses had developed in compensation for other lost or diminished functions. He was even willing to entertain the possibility of extrasensory perception given room to manifest by the weeding out and paring down of ordinary physical perception.

Whatever the mechanism and its purpose, Alex knew Abby was there. She was standing in the doorway in what he guessed she imagined to be silence; she would be unaware of the minuscule rustlings and tappings a normal human body made in the space it occupied; at her age, before his accident had, in a split second, rendered his body absolutely motionless and still, he had been unaware of them himself.

She was watching him, taking his measure, attempting to understand him and, he hoped, her feelings for him, assuming he didn't know she had finally come in answer to his summons. His lips actually ached from whistling so long and hard. He was on the verge of saying something to her, though he hadn't decided whether it would be greeting or reprimand, plea or complaint – most effective if he could pull it off would be a mixture of all of the above – when he perceived another presence as well, and he decided to wait until he had an idea of who else was there.

But now there seemed to be no one other than Abby, and she made herself known to him in the conventional manner, speaking aloud to him, moving to where he could see her, touching his shoulder where he would feel her although the sensation was much muted compared to what it once would have been. Although he had all but given up the dream of finding a woman with whom he could fully communicate, in all the ways available to them both, Alex was nonetheless struck by this further evidence of Abby's conventionality; for one so young, she was shockingly unimaginative. On the other hand, she was easy to read because of it, easy to predict, which would be an advantage to him. And there was something quite appealing about her innocence and simplicity.

'Yes, Alex. What can I do for you?'

Alex felt his eyes fill with tears. He had no control over the emotional lability that commonly resulted from a high spinal-cord injury such as his; indeed, the external manifestations – tears, flushed and contorted face, penile erection, unsteady voice – were no longer directly expressive of contemporaneous emotions. But he could control the use to which he put such symptoms, and in the decades since the accident he'd learned, albeit unwillingly at first, that opportunism could be quite as effective as forethought. 'I'm so sorry to be a nuisance,' he began now.

There was a pause. A more analytical person would have been deciding how to respond. He doubted, though, that Abby consciously considered her interactions with him or anyone else; he hoped his assessment was accurate in this regard. 'I'm sorry to take so long to answer,' she said.

'I know you're busy.'

'Actually, it's not so bad tonight. Everybody on the schedule showed up for a change.' Alex said nothing, but he made his silence heavily expressive, and she said, almost at once, defensively, 'But we were tied up with another – patient.'

He heard her voice quaver slightly, saw embarrassment redden the curve of her cheek, and was gratified to realize their relationship had progressed to the point where referring to him as a patient caused her discomfort. This was a good sign. He was gaining influence over her more rapidly and more deeply than he had over his current wife and the girls before her. Experience and wisdom acquired with age assuredly had their advantages.

Fondness for Abby welled, gratitude toward her along with an appreciation of his own power that never failed to move him, and he was weeping again. Alex regularly visualized himself crying, as well as laughing, making love, excreting, eating, sleeping, performing any physical function he could think of, in order to accustom himself to the image, to divest it of its horror and render it familiar, acceptable – even, eventually, welcome. It was a technique he had discovered a long time ago, some years after the accident, taught to him by no counselor, modeled by no other quad, and so he suspected he might well be the only one who knew it, a patentable method for turning misfortune into advantage. Lemons into lemonade, if you will; dross into gold. Alchemy. Off and on he considered launching a career as an inspirational speaker and writer, but was reluctant to share what he knew with the public at large, out of apprehension that the efficacy of the insight would be diluted if he broadcast it.

Again, now, he put the visualization technique to use, not so much to view himself as Abby might be seeing him – Alex didn't take much interest in other people's opinions – but in order to reinforce the way in which he perceived himself:

Fifty years old. Giving the impression of being at once older and younger than that, because of the long-term flaccidity of his muscles, his skin well-tended – smooth, no breaks or tears, virtually no wrinkles – over underlying sagging flesh. Many were put off by this age-indefinite appearance, regarding it as 'unnatural'; it was, of course, fundamentally natural for him.

Light brown hair, graying now and thinning. Green eyes, not the green more properly termed hazel which changed hue according to surroundings or mood, but brilliant, clear, consistent emerald. Tanned skin. He had his aides place him for a few carefully monitored minutes in the sunshine every morning and every afternoon, and was pleased to be living in a climate which afforded him three hundred days of sunshine in a typical year. The pallor of the invalid which pearled under his tan was inescapable and, therefore, a factor he incorporated into his self-image. He had come rather to like the way it looked.

Abby didn't respond immediately to his tears; Alex didn't begrudge her her hesitation, but he noted it. When finally he did feel the drying of his cheeks by a tissue in her hand, she was saying gently, but with a quasi-professional detachment that did not bode well, 'I'm sorry, Alex. It must be hard to have to wait for somebody all the time.'

Alex pressed the slight advantage he felt he had. 'You said you weren't especially busy.' Deliberately he stopped short of direct accusation.

'We were having a problem with another – a patient.' She squirmed again, which was precisely what he'd hoped for.

Delicately he inquired, 'Oh?'

She shouldn't tell him, but she did. 'Myra Larsen went off on us again.'

'Who did she think she was this time?' Alex found Myra Larsen vexing, pitiable, occasionally amusing, sometimes – although less and less so as time went on – interesting in a clinical sort of way. Depending on whom he was talking to, he emphasized one or another of these reactions, all of which had equal claim to honesty. With Abby, he had guessed, correctly, that sympathy would be the most appropriate; she would not be the sort to find humor or intellectual diversion in what she would consider another's misfortune. 'Poor lady,' he murmured, for good measure.

'I'm not sure. Shirley thought she was saying "Faye," but it could have been "Hey" or any other word like that. She seriously tried to hurt Shirley.'

'Are you all right?' His concern for her was genuine, the alarm with which he expressed it perhaps a trifle exaggerated since he could tell she was, in fact, unhurt.

Directly in his line of vision now, she smiled. Satisfaction warmed Alex's heart and belly, in the part of his body – by far the majority – in which he could feel nothing external. She had a lovely, winsome smile. 'I'm fine. She just pulled my hair a little.'

He took a breath and made certain the exhalation was a bit tremulous. 'I wish you didn't have to endure such abuse.'

'It's not a big deal, Alex.' But he could tell she was shaken, and pleased by his concern.

So he expressed it again. 'You deserve better than this.'

'I like my job,' she said, a little sternly, and he thought perhaps he had gone too far, but then she reached toward him, and he felt her gentle fingertips on his brow. He allowed this gesture to play itself out, enjoying both the physical sensations and their mental and emotional ramifications. She really was a very sweet girl. 'Everybody's having trouble keeping their mind on their work. After what happened.'

Alex knew she was referring to the patient who had died as a result of eating oven cleaner instead of pancake syrup. He had heard about the incident from various angles, first the alteration of the ambient noise of the facility indicating something out of the ordinary, then the rush and clamor of emergency vehicles, the distinctive clatter of the gurney wheels rapidly down the hall, the Carrasco woman's red-ants-in-the-rectum monologue perhaps slightly more urgent than usual. Staff had openly discussed the matter in his presence, as they often did. He had made a few discreet inquiries.

He considered concealing his rather extensive knowledge and asking Abby to tell him what had happened, but that strategy seemed unnecessarily cumbersome, so he said quietly, 'I heard about Bob. What a terrible way to die.'

'Nobody knows what will happen to Ros.'

She should be in jail sprang to his lips, but he decided such a comment was too risky at this point, since he hadn't yet gauged Abby's position regarding the cook.

Abby went on. 'She didn't do it on purpose. He got the wrong bottle himself. Patients aren't allowed in the kitchen. He knew that.'

Alex hazarded, 'Still, it was at the very least gross negligence.'

'I guess. And it wasn't like Ros. She's always so careful. And she takes a special interest, you know? She always made sure Bob got fed, even when he wouldn't eat at the right time.' Alex held his peace until Abby sighed, shook her head, and asked, 'What did you need?'

What he had needed, still needed and was not getting, was *her*, her responsiveness, her attention, her company. What he had devised to say was not different from that, but slightly reconfigured. 'I am terribly lonely tonight for some reason, Abby. Do you think you might be able to stay with me a while? Perhaps read to me?'

She stared at him as though he'd requested something perverse instead of only very much out of the ordinary. 'Read to you? While I'm on duty?'

Alex turned his head so he wasn't looking at her except out of the corner of one eye. 'I suppose you're right,' he said softly, without a trace of irony. 'Actually spending time with your patients isn't in your job description, is it?'

It was a calculated risk. A more experienced aide would have laughed at him or responded in kind to the underlying sarcasm, and he'd have paid for his temerity with slowed response time to his whistle and surly if not downright careless handling. But Abby, as he'd surmised, was susceptible to the view – in her case, largely unarticulated – that having to ask for such a thing in the first place was a human tragedy. Flustered, she scrambled guiltily for some way she could do what he wanted. 'I – could stay a little while after my shift. Not very long. My neighbor lady's watching the girls and I can't—'

Alex was shaking his head back and forth on the thin pillow. 'That's eleven o'clock at night, Abby. I can't be awake that late. I'm sorry. This just isn't going to work.' The balance between them had shifted nicely, so that now it was as though *he* were regretfully denying *her* a request.

'No, wait, I'll come in on my break.' He saw her blush a little. 'But I'm not exactly a good reader.'

Alex had strong opinions about the state of the American educational system, but he chose to put them aside for the moment. 'When will you eat?'

'I'll eat with you.'

'Are you sure?'

'Sure. You're better company than most of them anyway.' He didn't know how seriously to take that last comment, whether she was patronizing him or not.

Judging, though, by the haste with which she asked if he needed anything else, the relief with which she accepted his assurance that he did not although it would actually have been nice to be up in the chair for a while now, and the clumsiness of her movements as she hurried out of his room, Alex surmised that she did, in fact, prefer his company to that of the other staff, and he was quite pleased.

Before Abby could get back to him, though, someone else came in. Alex's first thought was that she'd managed to get away early for him, and he was touched and triumphant. But it wasn't Abby. It wasn't his current roommate, either, a burly and lame old man whose gait – whose entire presence – was much heavier than this light, gauzy disturbance of the air. Perhaps there was a new nurse. Alex did not want to deal with a new nurse tonight, but he would, of course, if the situation warranted. He could see nothing of this person – the word *intruder* came to him, which rather surprised him, since he had honed a detachment from the spaces which he inhabited that generally did not allow for the concept of personal boundaries capable of being intruded upon. He didn't hear anything definitive, voice, tread, breath rhythm. With a calm that had little to do with patience, he waited to receive more information.

Now there was a peculiar tapping on the inside of his skull, like nothing so much as someone requesting – *demanding* – entrance into a locked room. Training his considerable powers of concentration full on the sensation, Alex was nonetheless able to smile in bemusement at the image; his mind was indeed locked, barricaded, although the effectiveness of this security depended to a great extent on presenting the illusion that it didn't exist.

Therefore he had, as it were, constructed apertures that would look like windows, through which other people were convinced they could see in, but which were actually one-way mirrors.

The staccato sound and jarring were insistent. Alex was reminded of a hand with long nails, tapping, rather than cruder knuckles knocking. He was briefly tempted to open his mind to it out of simple curiosity, but the foolhardy impulse had not even enough time to be rejected before the tapping had stopped and he was alone again with his thoughts, excellent company that they were, roiled now by this odd experience.

Alex shifted. Not physically, since he could move nothing below the neck, but quite literally. Perfectly, intimately aware, of course, that there would be no corporeal response to the orders issued by his brain to his shoulders to move an inch to the right, to his hips to slide slightly downward, he nevertheless issued those orders, and the sensation of having moved was as palpable and released as much tension as though he'd physically shifted.

He must not allow stray outside forces of any kind to influence his mental processes. There had been distractions before; whatever this newest one was – and he suspected it was in some way connected to the development of his relationship with the sweet Abby – he was more than a match for it.

Across the hall, Myra Larsen was singing. Her bony hands waved in the air, knobby fingers twirling as though they were graceful, wrists like coat hangers on which might have been draped soft variegated scarves.

Hearing her from the other end of the building, Rebecca looked up with a start, sat back in her chair, laid down her pen and turned off the calculator to hear her better. There was something eerily familiar about the song the crazed old woman was singing, though its melody was so fractured and its lyrics so nearly incomprehensible that it could hardly be called a song. Rebecca listened, didn't want to be listening but was mesmerized. Gooseflesh rose on her arms and legs. A hot sensation like panic geysered into her chest, from where she could not imagine, unless it rose out of the roiling sadness and guilt she felt about Bob Morley and Roslyn Curry.

After a few minutes she roused herself, came out from behind the desk, and shut the door. She could still hear Myra. Frustrated far beyond what the situation called for, she gave the dial of the radio on the shelf above her desk an angry twist, and mellow, undemanding jazz trickled out into the room as she tried again to work.

Marshall had been sitting in his room staring at the wall, staring at his interlocking and disentangling fingers, peacefully, waiting for Billie, waiting for Rebecca, waiting, not waiting for anything. When Myra had been singing for a while, he was singing along. He knew this song. It made him happy. It frightened him. It took him back, and forward.

Dan Murphy stuck his head into Rebecca's office. He wasn't the only one who disobeyed the bright red *Do Not Disturb* sign Gordon Marek had made for her in craft class and hung with a flourish on her doorknob. Gordon himself loved the sight of it hanging there but paid scant attention to its purported message. Other people usually acknowledged it with an apology or a joke; Dan just ignored it, though it flapped against his hand. 'Hi, babe. Busy?'

Rebecca looked up frowning from the spreadsheet of accounts payable, which had just begun making sense. Then she sighed, smiled, and rested her chin in her hand. 'Never too busy for the boss. Come on in.'

He was already in, flyaway red hair looking badly cut although it undoubtedly was not, expensive sports jacket rumpled. He was followed by the woman whom Rebecca recognized – still incredulously – as his wife Naomi: small, thin, colorlessness so thorough it had to be purposeful, very quiet. Dan settled himself into one of the new captain's chairs he had insisted Rebecca buy for the office and lifted his feet onto her desk, his boots smudging the three-page staffing report she was almost a week late completing in triplicate for the Health Department, which required the same information as the weekly reports for the management company but in different combinations. His wife stood by the door.

'You'll be getting a refund check from Vic Andres,' Dan said. 'Deposit it.'

'Vic Andres? The guy from Surgical Supply? What's he refunding? We got the order.'

'Don't worry about it, babe. Just stick it in the bank. Vic and I go back a long way. So what's this I hear about a patient dying under suspicious circumstances?'

Rebecca shuddered, and the nausea that threatened every time she thought about the oven-cleaner incident – and there were few moments when she did not think about it – rose again. She passed a hand over her eyes. 'Nothing suspicious about it. We know what happened.'

Dan guffawed harshly. 'Jesus, what was she, drunk on her ass? Oven cleaner instead of pancake syrup? I mean, wouldn't you think she'd have smelled it or something?'

Rebecca could only shake her head. 'She wasn't drunk or stoned. She said she was tired. She said she was distracted by personal problems.'

'Shit, that's some fucking distraction, not to even notice a patient pouring oven cleaner on his goddamn pancakes. On the kitchen floor, no less.'

Not sure she ought to be telling him this, Rebecca went on. 'She was absolutely hysterical. She kept saying she tried to get to him before he put it in his mouth but she couldn't move. As if it were happening to somebody else.'

'Great. Just what The Tides needs. A psychotic cook.'

'Or as if somebody held her back. She said she actually thought she felt hands on her arms, fingernails digging in.'

'Even better. A possessed cook.' Dan was up and pacing. 'You'd think the guy who died would have noticed. You'd think he'd have smelled it, or it would have burned his tongue. How could he eat enough of it to kill him? Christ, that's what institutionalization will do for you.'

'He was a burned-out schizophrenic, controlled for years by massive doses of Thorazine. Thorazine suppresses olfactory sensations, among other things. I doubt he noticed much of anything.'

'Family?'

She shook her head. 'None.' She thought of Petra Carrasco, who had shown no reaction at all to Bob's death, but couldn't bring herself to tell Dan about her.

'Jesus.' He sat for a moment, not still but, for him, subdued. Then he said several of the things Rebecca was thinking, though she wished she weren't. 'Jesus, what a way to live and what a way to die. But at least there's no family to raise hell.' Rebecca nodded unhappily. 'Health Department been here yet?'

'No. We notified them, of course. I expect them any minute.'

'They'll be all over this place.'

'Well, they should be. I'd worry if they didn't look into something like this.'

He narrowed his eyes. 'It won't be fun, babe. Trust me. They'll have a field day. At the very least, you'll get written up. I'll do what I can to keep it out of the papers, but I can't guarantee anything. This is not the kind of attention I need right now. So what does this do to your census?'

She hesitated. When Sandy had come running to tell her what had happened to Bob, census hadn't been the foremost of her reactions, she was glad to note, but it had been among the first. 'A hundred and thirty-five.'

'Damn.'

'Referrals are down. I suspect we were already being blackballed because of this "patient mix" business. And Bob's death won't do much for our reputation, either.'

'Patient mix,' he repeated scornfully. 'Shit. I've been in this business a long time, and they've never complained about having different kinds of patients in the same facility before. Hell, everybody does it.'

'We sent them our policies so they can see that we know what we're doing. And I have to admit we're being more selective about admissions than we were.'

'Can't afford to be too selective,' he reminded her, almost breezily, springing to his feet. 'Gotta pay the bills. Listen, babe. Naomi and I have a favor to ask you. Naomi needs a job. Anything. I was thinking maybe she could help Lisa with the social work stuff. Something to take her mind off herself. We all get a little crazy when we don't get enough outside stimulation.' He touched his wife's cheek anxiously, tenderly. She kept her gaze out the window and finally Dan turned away from her, his face rigid. 'I don't know,' he said quietly. 'Maybe it won't work out. But talk about it, will you? I gotta be someplace.' He shut the door behind him, then opened it again as Rebecca's phone began to ring. 'By the way, babe, the place stinks. You better get your housekeepers on the ball.' He shut the door again and was gone.

Rebecca wrote 'odor' on a piece of paper taped to the top of her desk and answered the phone. It was an anxious supplier calling about an overdue account. She promised to pay him in full in thirty days. She did not add: *If the Medicaid check comes through on time. If census holds. If the roof lasts another few months.* He harangued her about the problems of small businesses and the size of his payroll; she commiserated, actively listened, and allowed her voice to tremble. Finally he said he'd call again in a month if he didn't have a check, and would she be free for lunch sometime? She hedged. When they hung up she crossed the name of his company off one of her lists.

With an effort, then, she turned her attention to Naomi Murphy. 'What kind of work do you think you'd be interested in?'

It seemed to take a beat or two before it registered with Naomi that she was being directly addressed. 'I don't know. I really don't know much about nursing homes.'

Naomi Murphy's father was Ira Goldberg, principal partner in Western Health Care Associates, the corporation that owned The Tides and one of the largest nursing-home chains in the state. Besides that, she was married to

Dan. How could she not know much about nursing homes? Rebecca regarded her curiously. 'Actually I don't have any openings right now. My staff is pretty well stabilized and the budget won't allow me to add any more people, much as I'd like to.'

Naomi nodded and rose. 'Thank you for your time.'

'Wait.' Rebecca was suddenly reluctant to let her just vanish again. 'What about volunteer work?'

Naomi shrugged. Her hand was on the doorknob and her back half-turned to Rebecca, but it seemed she was listening.

'We always need good volunteers. One-to-one visiting, writing letters, family contacts, accompanying people to appointments outside the facility.'

Naomi took the few steps required to get her across the room to the chair her husband had vacated, sat down, crossed her legs at the ankles, folded her hands in her lap. Then she said quietly, her eyes averted, 'This is my husband's idea. He thinks I spend too much time in the house. I like my house.'

Somewhat vaguely, Rebecca nodded. There was a silence. Rebecca started worrying about her paperwork again. Thoughts of Bob Morley's gagging and Roslyn's hoarse screams burst like fireworks in her memory. Not quite consciously, she saw again the odd sheen that had stained the kitchen floor around them; she'd assumed it was vomit or some other bodily fluid, but it hadn't been there when she'd looked again, so it must have been some peculiar trick of the fluorescent lights and the sunrise through the window above the counter.

She tapped her pen on the desk and said briskly, 'Well, at least let me show you around. Give you some idea what our people are like.'

Naomi made no objection. As they left the office the phone rang again. Rebecca hesitated, then shook her head irritably and shut the door firmly behind them. Whatever it was could wait. Sandy could take a message.

Chapter 7

Billie didn't know why in the world she bothered to talk to Marshall as if he was in his right mind, but for almost thirty years she'd been talking to him and old habits died hard. 'Why would she come back now? Becky's grown.'

'She wants her,' Marshall moaned, as if that explained everything.

'Anyway,' Billie said, shaking her finger at him, 'you told me she was dead.'

'I think she is dead.'

'Well, then, she can't be here, now can she?' But Billie drew her sweater more snugly around her in the close cramped room. Here was another way she'd been betrayed: Marshall had promised that Faye's name would never pass between them again, because she was dead and couldn't hurt anybody anymore. Until now he'd kept his promise, too; maybe he'd thought about Faye – Lord knew Billie had, and Marshall had even more reason – but neither of them had mentioned her in decades.

It appalled her to be talking about Faye. The woman had been in her mind for as long as her husband and daughter had, which seemed like her whole life even though she knew better. But she'd kept her in the airless and lightless dusty dungeon in the back of her mind, where she belonged. Now, because Marshall was losing himself right before her eyes, Billie was being forced to think about Faye and talk about Faye, and she didn't like it one bit.

The danger was that she'd say something she shouldn't. One good thing about senility was that more than likely Marshall would forget whatever either one of them said, but he might not, and she definitely wouldn't. The danger was that she'd tell the one thing she knew about Faye that Marshall didn't. In fact, right this very minute she could hardly resist the temptation.

And why should she? You didn't see Marshall holding anything back these days. She could always deny it later, to Marshall and to anybody he might tell and even to herself; Marshall had Alzheimer's, after all, so you couldn't believe anything he said.

Apparently Marshall had forgotten she was there. He might have forgotten all about Faye again, too, since he didn't look scared anymore. His expression was almost happy. There was a little smile on his lips, as if he was thinking about something funny that he wasn't going to tell her. His hands were relaxed in his lap, and the Posey restraint could have been a nice vest on him, grayed from washing but with a lot of wear and even a little elegance left in it, instead of what it really was, something to tie him down. His eyes were focused somewhere past her. If he'd known she was there he wouldn't have known who she was.

That was what did it, the fact that her husband had had the nerve to forget who she was. Billie set her jaw, leaned forward, and reached toward him, thought better of it just before her fingertips would have come into contact with his knee and drew back, didn't touch him after all. She didn't say his name, either, though it was all but filling her mouth. She just started talking, telling the story she'd never told anybody that had sometimes seemed to be what her life was all about.

A few doors down on the other side of the hall, Jenny Booth had just showed up for a surprise visit with her husband. Alex knew the instant she appeared in his doorway that she was under the influence of alcohol. He had no reason to suspect, though, that she was not alone, that her presence – needy, increasingly hollowed by the drink that pretended to fill it in – would have been greeted as an invitation, and that she was under another influence as well.

With an effort certainly substantial though perhaps not quite as enormous as he hoped to make it seem, he turned his head away. 'You're drunk,' he stated.

Jenny trapped his head between her hands to kiss him lingeringly on the mouth. 'Hi, honey,' she crooned, her breath rank. 'I'm glad to see you, too.'

In order to lean over him, she was bracing herself on the rails of his bed, an outrageous violation of his personal space. She must be shaking, for the rails rattled. The smell of her nauseated him and he couldn't turn his head far enough away. So he narrowed his eyes and levelled his gaze, which he knew to be formidable, directly into her face.

'Look, I brought you a present. Sweets for my sweetie.' She set a box of chocolates onto the unresisting mound of his stomach.

'You know I don't eat chocolate. You know I must be very careful about my diet.'

The box slid down between his legs and she retrieved it, never acknowledging that she had rubbed against his genitals, a contact of which he himself was aware only in theory since he could neither see nor feel it. Reaching across him to set the candy on his very orderly bedside stand, and thereby disturbing the order, she kissed his mouth again in passing as though she had a right to do so. 'There. That's for my favorite boy.' Noting that the plastic wrap around the box had been removed, he wondered icily who had given her this candy.

Rolling his head back and forth on the pillow to generate momentum, he braced himself – thought as if he were bracing himself, although of course his body made no such motion – gathered his meager breath under him, and shouted, 'You are drunk!' It came out a whisper, rasping in his throat.

Jenny brought her face very close to his, and Alex thought she had the aspect nearly of a stranger. Even though the pupils of her eyes were dilated and the muscles around her mouth slackened by drink, there was a purposeful meanness about her that he had never seen before. This was somewhat alarming, but more than anything else, it interested him. It had been quite some time since he'd actually been interested by Jenny, and he did not welcome this complication, for if it persisted it would require a change in the strategy he'd already devised. If he could have drawn back he would have, simply to give himself a little time.

Jenny closed her eyes and brought her mouth down on his again. Pressing hard, she opened her lips, which opened his; Alex was attentive to the fact that, although he didn't actively resist, he also had not initiated this erotic and aggressive act, and that was a most unusual dynamic between them. He felt her teeth against his, then her tongue in the cavity of his mouth, and, for just a moment, he thought he would choke. He managed to spit out, 'Jenny, no,' but she acted as if he hadn't addressed her, and that was unlike her, too. The kiss, the assault, went on and on, and Alex found himself fantasizing that this was some other woman kissing him, a stranger, some other woman fondling him and whispering his name.

'It was while Faye and I were still friends,' Billie was saying, looking past Marshall in much the same way he was looking past her. 'Or I was still under her spell, not that I was ever really Faye's friend. Not that anybody was. It was before it ever entered my mind that there'd be anything between you and me.' She smiled and shifted her gaze to him to say, fondly, 'Imagine that,' but he didn't acknowledge that there was anything between them now. Hurt, Billie looked away from him again and went on with her story.

'I had no idea she was pregnant. Nobody did. Well, maybe you did, but nobody else. She didn't show. She kept herself belted and corseted or she wore those loose flowing filmy things she always wore, and you couldn't tell. And you'd certainly never think of Faye with a baby. You'd never think of her as a mother.' Billie gave a short, harsh laugh to show how ludicrous the idea was even now.

'I hadn't heard from her for a while. That wasn't unusual. The other person always had to take the initiative with Faye, always had to be the one to extend themselves, unless she wanted something. I missed her. I wanted to see her. Don't ask me why. When I went for so long without seeing her, I missed her. Like she was some kind of a drug, not that I know anything about drugs. But I knew about Faye. So I went over to her house.' Billie glanced sideways at her husband. 'Your house.' Marshall was quiet, but his eyes were open. She'd have kept on talking even if he'd fallen asleep. If truth be told, she wished he had, so she wouldn't even have to pretend she was talking to him.

'When I knocked on the door she didn't answer, but it wasn't locked and it swung open, almost like she'd left it open for me. Faye did that to everybody, remember? She made you think you were special to her and she was thinking about you when she wasn't, not for a second. Anyway, I called her name and then I let myself in. Don't ask me why. I always thought maybe I shouldn't have done that, maybe it was rude, but at the time I really thought she wanted me to. I could hear her in the kitchen – remember how the kitchen was a straight shot from the front door, through the dining room? She was singing, like she did.'

Marshall, who'd been aware of his wife's waxing and waning voice like waves on the other side of the belljar that enclosed him, suddenly broke free into singing. He heard Faye's singing both in his memory and now, and he closed his eyes and held his breath and let it wash deliciously over him, knowing he would drown.

Jenny Booth walked around to the head of the bed where Alex couldn't see her. Because he'd taught her not to do that, Alex understood that either she fully intended it to be disrespectful or she was simply being flagrantly, disrespectfully careless. 'I had a few drinks after work, if that's what you mean. Hell, a few beers.'

'You gave me your word you'd stay dry. That's the only reason I took you back. I should have known.'

'Well, Jesus Christ, I have reason to drink, don't I? What else have I got in my life?'

'Your children, for one thing,' he said severely. 'Our children, Jenny.'

'Oh, please. Don't throw the kids up to me. What do you do for them? You don't even pay child support.'

'I've explained to you that as long as you're drinking, their money goes into a trust account for them. I will not support your filthy habit, and if you have enough money to drink you obviously don't need me to help you support the children.'

Jenny snorted. 'You pitiful little bastard. You think you know everything, and you don't know shit, you know that?'

Her grammar and sentence structure were ludicrous enough almost to make him laugh, but he focused on indignation. 'Get out of here. I will not tolerate a drunk in my presence. I must be very careful—'

'Flat on your back, helpless, can't do a goddamn thing for yourself, can't even take a piss by yourself, and you're telling me to get out? You're a vegetable, Alex, look at yourself!'

No one had ever said such things to him before, least of all his own wife, though of course people thought them routinely. Alex was hurt and offended, but only mildly; predominantly, he was on the alert. Jenny was different. Jenny, whose salient characteristic he knew to be predictability. Jenny, whom he could count on never to have an original thought in her head. Jenny, utterly malleable and flat.

She was not herself. It was not just the alcohol, either; sadly, he'd seen her drunk more than a few times before. A peculiar animation had hold of her, a brittle and dangerous playfulness, a self-confidence that alarmed him.

She was smiling. Her eyes sparkled. She leaned over him in a proprietary way. 'Come on, baby,' she cooed.

Baby? 'Let's you and me stop fighting and have ourselves a little fun. Know what I mean?' Her hand dropped full on his penis; amazed, he watched it land, then flex and stretch, like a five-legged insect. Even more astonishing was the fact that, although of course he didn't feel its tickling and massaging, its sheer unexpectedness stirred in him what he'd come to identify as sexual arousal, a most unwelcome response under the present circumstances.

Alex was silent for a few moments, working to regain his equilibrium and wondering that he had ever lost it. His mind seemed oddly fuzzy, and meticulously he reviewed what he had eaten and drunk in the past twenty-four hours, what medications he had taken. There was the matter of the constipation, a chronic problem more serious this time than usual, perhaps well on its way to an impaction, and the strong dose of castor oil he had taken this morning that ought to have had an effect by now.

But that hardly seemed sufficient to account for his disturbing mental condition, which he would describe as a mixture of susceptibility and malaise, shot through with erotic desire such as he had not experienced in years. Whatever the cause, he could not allow himself – which was to say, his mind, what he sometimes thought of as his soul – to be compromised.

At last he said, very calmly, 'Please leave, Jenny. You are not welcome here.'

But she had collapsed against him and didn't reply. He rasped a few variations of the ineffectual command and then, for the time being, surrendered to circumstances beyond his control, a strategy which he had learned to regard as another way of regaining control.

Billie said, 'I walked up beside her, and I said, "Hi, Faye, I hope you don't mind, I was in the neighborhood," or something silly like that, and she said, "Hi, Billie," just like she'd been expecting me although I'm sure no thought of me ever entered her pretty little head, and I saw she was giving a baby a bath in a basin on a red oilcloth. I can still remember how the sun came through the window on that bright red oilcloth.

'I looked at her and I looked at the baby. I remember thinking what pretty hands she had, covered with water and soapsuds like that. The soapsuds looked like those scarves she always used to like, remember? Pink and lavender and sort of bubbly. The baby was just a tiny little thing – I didn't know a thing about babies but I thought it was probably ju a few days old.'

Billie paused and took a deep breath. 'Then I realized something awful was going on. She was trying to—'

Marshall erupted, 'Shut up! You just shut up! I don't have to listen to your nonsense! I don't even know you! Who do you think you are? You just shut up!' and when she stubbornly tried to finish the story she'd been waiting so long to tell he just talked right over her.

'My eyebrows itch,' Alex said suddenly, then said it again. *My eyebrows itch.* It was not a ploy, but it might well have been.

Jenny stirred. 'What?'

'Oh, my eyebrows itch!'

'Your eyebrows itch?'

Alex nodded frantically and twitched the muscles under his brows as hard as he could, which had no effect on the ferocious itching. He did not believe he had ever before experienced any visceral sensation like this. It was quite as though someone were drawing the tips of long fingernails back and forth across one eyebrow and then the other, skimming the surface of the flesh and the hair follicles, leaving trails of itching he could not reach.

Without moving her face from his neck, Jenny rummaged in the drawer of the bedside stand and finally found the tube of cream. She squirted some into her palm and spread it across Alex's eyebrows; not watching what she was doing, she came perilously close to the corner of his left eye. As she massaged the cream into the thin dry skin, he relaxed unwillingly but undeniably in her arms. 'Thank you,' he whispered. Jenny brushed the sandy hair out of his eyes. It occurred to him that she might have tickled his eyebrows herself, purposely, to humiliate him, to demonstrate the extent of his dependence on her. But such a theory made little sense; surely he would have noticed. In his situation, it was crucial to resist the temptations of paranoia, which were sometimes considerable.

She lay on top of him, her breath hot against his neck. He couldn't precisely smell the alcohol from this angle, but he could feel it, adhering to his skin and to the cilia of his lungs where he was forced to breathe it in. She turned her face into his pillow and he realized with horror that she meant to fall asleep in his bed.

He wanted her to leave. Failing that, he wanted her to make love with him. Recognizing the jeopardy he was in, Alex seemed unable and – far more dismaying – unwilling to extricate himself from it.

Billie said – directly to her husband this time, bringing her face close to his, 'I never told you. I never told anybody. After a while I didn't know what I saw. But I know now. She was *playing* with that baby, some awful game, dunking her under that soapy water and then pulling her out and then dunking her under again. I saw her do it twice with my own eyes. At first I figured she was just, you know, toying with her, the way Faye toyed with all of us, being mean, showing she could do anything she wanted to. But now I think she was going to drown her.'

Marshall's eyes bugged out and his hands reached for her, to hold her or to hurt her or both. But he was tied in his chair and he couldn't reach her unless she made a move to close the distance between them, and she didn't.

'By the time I gathered my wits about me – but honestly, Marshall, I don't know to this day what I would have done, because this was *Faye*, you know, and Faye could convince anybody of anything, she could sell ice to the Eskimos, she could make a person believe the sky was yellow when you could see with your own eyes it was blue – she'd picked that baby up out of the sink and handed her to me, naked and crying and wet and covered with all those pretty soap bubbles, and she just walked out of the house. Remember? You came home and found me with Rebecca, me who knew nothing about babies, who'd hardly ever even held one before, and that was the last time we saw Faye. Remember?'

Marshall bolted out of his chair. Billie shrieked. The strings of the Posey he'd somehow managed to untie floated raggedly behind him like strips of toilet paper stuck to somebody's shoes.

Jenny's breaths had become shallow, roughened by snores at beginning and end. Her flesh exuded the stench and slime of fermented grain. Alex forced himself to inhale as deep a breath as possible, and wet and pursed his lips to whistle for Abby. As he did so, he caught the sudden strong odor and taste of roses, and a firm pressure came over his mouth, like a hand being laid there to silence him.

Then, though he did not will it, his body – an ally after all these years of learning to live within the casing of it that others regarded as unresponsive and all but dead – came through with a daring rescue as if of its own volition. Warmth and wetness formed under his hips and between the fronts of Jenny's thighs, and the room reeked with another sharper odor. Knowing at once what it was, and incredulous, Alex nearly laughed.

Blearily Jenny struggled off the bed and stood away, staring, as a semi-liquid stream of feces cascaded between Alex's legs and feet. The bodily event created no sound, only the yellow-brown stream across bedclothes and flesh and the yellow-brown pool forming on the white floor. 'The castor oil,' Alex breathed. 'It's finally working.'

The torrent went on for several minutes; there was no way to stop it. It seemed impossible that anyone could hold so much. Alex lay with his eyes closed and his hands limp at his sides, legs spread where Jenny had shoved them in her haste to get away from him and the assault of his excrement. He simply waited on the overflowing bed. When he could, he began to whistle.

Rebecca and Naomi Murphy were making their way down the long main hallway. Rebecca was thinking unhappily that the spray of gladioli at the central nurses' station gave the place a somber, funereal air – probably had, in fact, been recycled from a funeral, whether or not of a person known to anyone at The Tides – when she heard Alex's whistle and, simultaneously, saw her father coming. Carrying his walker with all four legs well off the floor, leaning forward at an alarming angle and trailing the ties of the restraint, he was virtually running.

Rebecca started toward him, thinking to catch him when he fell, as he surely would. But he raised his walker like a chair against an attacking beast, and she saw how wild his eyes were, how red and hollow his gaping mouth.

'Get out of my way! Get the hell out of my way!' he wheezed. 'I have to find my daughter!'

'Dad,' she started to say, 'Dad, I'm your daughter, I'm Rebecca,' but her assurances of alleged facts obviously contradicted by his own senses only made him more frantic.

Afraid to frighten him more than he already was – curiously reluctant to intrude into an experience so private; he was her *father*, after all, and entitled to his own private madness, as she was entitled not to be presented with it – Rebecca looked around for help. Someone was behind him; her first reaction was relief that she wouldn't have to handle this. She received a few quick impressions – a small figure, female, wearing something pale purple and dark gray, moving somehow both rapidly and languidly; someone she knew – but then she looked past him again and saw that no one was there.

'Excuse me,' she said to Naomi, who had paused in front of the grinning and glassy-eyed Paul, whether out of discomfort or interest Rebecca hadn't yet discerned.

She had taken her eyes away from her father only for an instant. When she turned back to him now, there seemed to be a pastel aura behind him, lavender and pink and buttercup yellow. Even with the shadows that shot through it, the lowering slant as if of light from a deep hole, it would not have been sinister except that it was clearly in pursuit of her father, who was clearly fleeing.

Rebecca was well aware of the visual distortions that the shiny waxed white floors, white walls, and fluorescent lights could generate. But this was more organized than that, more definite, and gave the impression of having intent, mischievous if not malevolent. It didn't fade as she stared at it, squinted, shielded her eyes, but swirled and seemed on the brink of coalescing into a recognizable form, which Rebecca, suddenly, did not want to recognize.

She whirled, which put her between her father and the shimmering apparition, and saw with relief that her mother was there, sturdy and of considerable bulk, hands on the bars of the walker next to his hands, holding it down on the floor the way it was supposed to be. 'For goodness' sake, Marshall, get ahold of yourself. This is ridiculous,' Billie Emig declared, and Rebecca felt herself relax at her mother's familiar no-nonsense tone. She started to turn back to Naomi Murphy, who had moved close to the wall and placed a hand on the handrail, not exactly huddling but obviously intending to stay out of everyone's way, a strategy at which she was accomplished.

Then Rebecca's father stiffened and screamed. His voice was hoarse and not very loud, but the sound he made was definitely a scream, and the smallness of it sent shivers through Rebecca. She did not want discourse with her father's demons. Marshall let go of his walker and gave a clumsy little sideways leap, then collapsed.

Larry came out of a nearby room, and Rebecca put one hand under her father's forearm and the other arm around his waist. Together, she and Larry managed to get him into the wheelchair Shirley brought, and as soon as she could Rebecca stepped back from the slumped, frail, semi-conscious old man. 'Thanks, guys,' she panted.

'Is he all right?' asked Shirley.

'I'll get him to his room and we'll check him out,' Larry said briskly.

Rebecca watched. There was no cloud. Larry's strong, squat figure shimmered a little at the edges as he passed from one fluorescent pool to the next, especially at the intersection with another hall where light came from the sides as well as from above and, blurrily reflected, from below. That must be what she'd seen; no wonder her father, already confused, had been so badly disoriented. Maybe grants were available to experiment with the architecture of nursing homes, or maybe a design firm could be interested in using The Tides as a demonstration project.

It was far more gratifying to think about grants and research projects and publishable papers than about Bob Morley dying from oven cleaner on his pancakes or about her father's hallucinations. Or, for that matter, about Naomi Murphy's alleged need for a job. Rebecca forced herself to go to her mother. 'He's not the only one to get confused by light and shadow and reflection,' she began, meaning to comfort and explain.

But her mother would have none of it. Grim-faced, arms folded protectively across her ample middle, she turned on Rebecca a look of such piteous terror that Rebecca stepped back. 'What am I going to do, Becky? What am I going to do?'

Rebecca steeled herself and put her arms around her mother. She did not remember the last time she'd done that; it might, in fact, have been when she was a small child. The older, larger woman was rigid, and the embrace didn't last long, but Rebecca did say, 'You're not alone, Mom. We're in this together.' When her mother didn't say anything, Rebecca dropped her arms, eased away, and asked, 'Did you – see anything?'

'What are you talking about?' Billie snapped, swiping at her cheeks although there were no tears.

'I thought I saw – something in the air around him.'

'I didn't see anything except my senile husband,' her mother fairly spat.

'I'll get Dave to check out the furnace, and call Public Service to make sure we don't have any toxic chemicals in the air.' That's all I need, she thought ignobly, but it did make her feel better to list things she could do to address a problem, even if it wasn't the real problem. Her mother gestured vaguely, turned, and walked away, leaving the facility by the side door that visitors weren't supposed to use.

Rebecca let her breath out and reached past Naomi to inspect the loose handrail she'd thought Dave had fixed last week. Naomi was quite still. When Rebecca glanced up at her, her face, in place of its customary careful neutrality, had acquired a peculiar brittle animation that seemed to bespeak anger, then horror, then inspiration. Her body, too, assumed one stance, one attitude rapidly after another, its characteristic unprepossessing contours and bearing now sharp and tense, now bowed as in a free-form dance. All this took only a second or two, and then Naomi shivered, looked down again, folded her hands in front of her again, and was again still.

Chapter 8

Usually Larry didn't mind working graveyard. In fact, he preferred it, which wasn't the same as saying he liked it. He didn't *like* this line of work. Who would? But he didn't have any better ideas at the moment, and working eleven to seven helped. For one thing, you almost never actually had to deal with the patients.

Other than bedcheck, which nobody knew whether you did or not, there wasn't a lot to do. You could sleep. This new administrator acted all high and mighty when she caught them napping, but every place Larry had ever worked, which was a lot of nursing homes, that was one of the perks of working nights that nobody talked about but practically everybody did, so he didn't know what her problem was. She wouldn't last long anyhow. They never did, and she was young and a woman.

Sometimes there'd only be him and the nurse for an eight-hour shift, at least till the housekeepers and the kitchen crew came on. You could do just about anything you felt like. He'd done just about everything. He'd had girls meet him at the back door; there were plenty of empty beds. He'd taken stuff out of patients' rooms, only the ones who were bedfast and out of it, stuff they'd never miss and their families just brought it to make themselves feel better about dumping them in a place like this. A couple of times he'd even seen his chance when the nurse left the med cart unlocked and he'd scored some Percodan, which gave a nice little buzz. Larry wasn't exactly proud of all the shit he'd pulled, but it was probably what kept him from quitting, and he was a good orderly so bottom line was he was helping out everybody.

You could study. Every time Larry was in college, he'd studied on his shift, not that it had done him any good, he never had managed to finish an entire semester. He wasn't cut out for college. He wasn't cut out to be an orderly, either. He didn't know what he was cut out for.

Lately he'd been reading the Scriptures at night. Sometimes he read them out loud. Nobody else wanted to listen. Just a few months ago Larry wouldn't have wanted to listen to the Bible, either, but now he couldn't understand why not, and he felt even more alienated from the rest of the world than usual but in a better way, for once in his life like he was right and they were wrong instead of the other way around.

Sometimes if a patient was awake he'd read the Scriptures to them. You weren't supposed to do that, but he couldn't see why not. Guy like this Paul, for instance; what else did he have in his life? If anything ever happened to Larry like had happened to Paul, he'd take whatever he could get that would show him how to go on living. Paul, actually, didn't seem especially bummed out, but Larry knew that couldn't be real. *Larry* was bummed about his own life, and he wasn't brain-damaged or senile or anything.

At the ajar door of Paul's room, Larry paused to peer up and down both halls. It was worth waking him up to read from the Word of God, but the others wouldn't like having a patient awake on their shift. He didn't see anybody. He hadn't expected to. It was three-thirty in the morning, and unless the administrator showed up for one of her bogus 'staff meetings,' there wasn't likely to be much stirring until they started getting them up at five.

Paul was already awake. The minute Larry stepped into the room he could hear him moving around in bed and grunting. What was even more surprising was that he had a visitor. Larry himself had checked the doors at eight, when they were locked for the night, and nobody could have gotten in unless somebody'd let them in. At first he thought it was that Abby; she didn't usually work nights and he didn't know her very well, and it did look like a young woman with long hair like hers. But the hair was fluffy, not straight, and this woman had really long painted fingernails; he could see them glistening in the shaft of bright light from the hall when she lifted her hand over Paul's face.

Larry found that he'd raised the Bible in front of him, and it seemed like not a bad idea so he kept it there as he made himself step toward Paul's bed. 'Hey,' he said, keeping his voice down. 'Hey, what are you doing in here?'

'Waiting for you, honey,' the woman said, and came into him.

Abby was trying to stay away from Alex tonight. She hadn't wanted him to know she was on, but somebody'd told him or he'd heard her or sensed her or something, because every time she turned around he was whistling for her and nobody else would do.

She hated working nights. The girls were with the neighbor again. She could hardly keep her eyes open, and napping in the hard chairs in the lounge only made her more exhausted, and she couldn't bring herself to actually sleep on one of the empty beds the way some people did. But the money was worth it. She needed the money. And she'd imagined she could at least avoid Alexander Booth.

She didn't know how to think about Alex. She didn't want to be thinking about him at all, except as one more patient she had to take care of for eight or sixteen hours at a time, but he didn't exactly seem like a patient. It was true that he had no control over his body from the shoulders down and you had to do everything for him, but he gave her the impression of power and even motion. 'The power of positive thinking,' was what he called it. 'Getting things done. Taking charge of your life. Being a hammer rather than a nail. Knowing who you are.'

He'd catch her staring and sometimes he would wink: 'It isn't every day a pretty girl looks at me that way.' Or he would frown and turn his head away as far as he could: 'Cut it out, Abby. You make me feel like a sideshow freak.' Whatever his reaction, flattery or offense, she could never think of anything to say, and she'd feel found out. She would just finish whatever she was doing for him and leave the room. But then he'd call her back. Didn't he ever sleep?

She thought about him more and more. Playing with her kids, sitting in a meeting, taking care of the routine intimate needs of some other patient, she would find her mind wandering to Alex. In bed waiting for sleep, which sometimes took a long time to come especially if she was really exhausted, she would try to make her body limp and numb like his, to imagine being paralyzed and making love, or making love with a paralyzed man.

She shouldn't be having thoughts like that. Maybe she'd have to go find another job. It wasn't hard to find work as a nurse's aide in a nursing home – there was such a high turnover – but the prospect made Abby tired and scared and, for some reason, sad.

He was whistling for her now, very softly. Sometimes she thought only she could hear it. She went the other way, hoping, for once, that there'd be lots of lights on. But everybody on her wing was asleep, or they didn't want anything, or they'd given up asking for what they wanted. She'd just finished bedcheck, and all her wheelchairs were washed.

Alex was whistling, like a voice that didn't need words inside her own head. Maybe he was having diarrhea again. She ought to go take care of him if he was having diarrhea, make up for the other day.

Her nose wrinkled. She didn't smell anything worse than the usual nursing-home smells. The other day she'd known it was diarrhea by the smell. She'd have thought she was used to it by now, between her kids and the patients, but her stomach turned. She'd told herself it couldn't be much fun for Alex, either, and that had helped some. She'd detoured to the clean-linen closet, hoping she'd remember to tell somebody that they were running low on clean sheets, but probably she'd be the one who didn't have any when she needed them.

His wife was standing with her back against the wall, fists pressed over her mouth. 'You did this on purpose!' she was choking.

Alex was covered from the waist down in b.m. His bed was soaked, and Abby had stepped in a puddle of it before she realized it had spread. 'Oh Alex,' she groaned, and hoped he'd read that as sympathy instead of scolding. But the expression on his face confused and angered her. He didn't look embarrassed or upset. He looked pleased with himself.

'I'm sorry, Abby,' he said, but he didn't sound sorry.

'I can't stand this anymore!' His wife had edged toward the door but wasn't showing any real signs of leaving. Abby couldn't do what she needed to do for him with his wife looking on.

'Jenny, please,' Alex began in his reasonable, insinuating way, so much quieter than the women's voices and the background noise in the hall that everybody worked hard to listen to him.

Now Jenny Booth was addressing Abby. Abby didn't want to talk to her. She just wanted to get Alex cleaned up. She didn't think she could stand the smell much longer. 'Ten years ago I was just like you. I was an aide in a nursing home, we took good care of our patients, too, and he was married to another woman at the time, and he used to tell me awful things about his wife just like he's telling you about me. What are you telling her about me, Alex?'

'Jenny,' Alex said.

'Did you tell her you had the power turned off? My four-year-old had a terrible cold, it could have been pneumonia for all he knew, and her daddy turns the heat and the lights off on her for three days and nights in the middle of February. How could you *do* that, Alex?'

'I had to do something to get things off dead center between us. I do not intend to spend the rest of my life in a nursing home, not when I have a home of my own to go to and I'm paying the bills. Even though they do take better care of me here than you ever did.'

'I need to get you cleaned up—' Abby started.

Sobbing, Jenny pushed past Abby and out of the room. Her loose sandals made an awkward sound as she rushed down the hall. Then the door at the end of the hall swung open and shut, its heavy spring slowing and muting the slam. Abby stood there breathless, clean linen in her arms, tasting the fecal odor now on the roof of her mouth.

Alex sighed. 'You see? You see what I have to put up with?' Abby didn't know what to say. She hated nasty talk and yelling. 'I think she's gone crazy,' Alex said under her hands. 'I think she's actually had a psychotic break.' There was a pause. Abby worked. Alex said in a different tone, 'Maybe I can make use of that.'

Abby was going to be sick. She dropped his cold leg onto the bed and backed out of the room. Behind her the whistling started up again.

Somebody came into the bathroom with her. Abby was too sick to care. She made it to the toilet and threw up, rested her forehead on the edge of the toilet – which wasn't very clean – and then threw up again.

When her daughters threw up, she held their heads and wiped their lips with a damp washcloth. Somebody was doing that for her now. In between heaves, she tried to see who it was. As far as she could tell, nobody was there. She must really be getting sick. Who would take care of her kids if she got sick? She kept retching even after there wasn't anything left in her stomach, and her throat filled with hot bile. Ordinary throwing up was bad enough, but at least you knew your body was getting rid of something it couldn't use; dry heaves made her imagine parts of her body itself coming up, stomach lining and lungs and other things she didn't know about but that her body needed even if it didn't know it did.

She stayed in the bathroom for a while after she'd stopped throwing up, just to make sure, and because her knees were too shaky to support her, and because she couldn't face cleaning up Alex's mess or listening to him bad-mouth his wife while he pretended that wasn't what he was doing.

Somebody suggested that she could just sleep in here and nobody would be the wiser, a soothing and alluring voice hinting at a lullaby, and Abby did fall half-asleep on the floor, which wasn't entirely clean and wasn't cool anymore but was smooth. Her head was filled with pink and blue perfumed gauze that floated like a soft scarf in a soft breeze, very pretty, hard to hold onto but worth the try.

She made herself get up. She wasn't being paid to sleep. She wasn't being paid to be sick. Her patients needed her. Alex needed her. She washed her face at the sink and dried it with the last paper towel, telling herself not to forget to tell Dave that the dispenser was empty. Her mouth tasted terrible and, naturally, she didn't have a toothbrush or even a mint. She sucked water from cupped palms and swished it around in her mouth, spat it into the sink and made sure to rinse the sink out. Her head was clear now, and she felt better. Who could that have been, talking to her?

Florence and Shirley were just coming out of Alex's room with giant white plastic bags full of dirty laundry. 'We got it,' Shirley said cheerfully to Abby. 'He wanted you, but we told him he had to put up with us, so he did.'

'Sorry. I didn't mean to leave it for you.'

'He's on my assignment sheet tonight, not yours,' Florence pointed out.

'But I'm the one who found the mess. I should have cleaned it up. I meant to.'

'You okay, hon?' Shirley asked on her way past. 'You look a little peaked.'

'He just really got to me,' Abby started to say, but

Shirley and Florence, lugging the bulky bags, hadn't stopped on their way to the laundry chute.

Abby's memory of the incident was unpleasant, but it also didn't seem very real. Clearest was her feeling of having failed, which she felt a lot anyway, and the impression of the pretty colors, pretty fragrance, cool hands, soft voice she'd had to resist of whoever had been in the bathroom with her while she was being sick. She didn't think there really had been anybody. Could a person just imagine something like that?

She became aware that a buzzer somewhere on Wing 2 had been going off for a long time. Where was that guy Larry? Hiding somewhere reading his Bible, probably. She'd been warned about him, but so far he hadn't tried to convert her. From the nurses' station she could see that Paul Brautigan's light was on, and she went to answer it, chased by Alex's whistle whether he was actually still whistling for her or not.

Paul was standing at his open window. Before she'd even taken in the whole scene, Abby was remonstrating, 'Paul, what in the world are you doing? It's four o'clock in the morning! You can't have your window open, you'll catch cold!'

It took Paul a long time and a lot of effort to move, and he didn't even try to turn around by himself. But at the sound of her he started yelling, like a toddler unable to form words but full of emphasis and intent. His arms flailed. His pajamas, mismatched and too big for him, had slid off his hips and shoulders, and his heels were on the bottoms of them so that he'd surely trip and fall any second. Abby rushed toward him, and was horrified to see him lean out the screenless window, bend almost double over the sill. She grabbed his skinny hips and tugged him backward, but she always forgot how strong he was and he barely budged. His yelling sent vibrations through his body and into hers.

This was stupid. She knew how to handle Paul. She didn't let go of him, but she moved her hands on his back and sides, massaging a little, soothing. She stepped up beside him. 'What's wrong, Paul?' she asked, hoping her voice was more or less calm.

Still yelling and waving his arms, he let her bring the top half of his body back some, not completely inside the room but a little better balanced. Hanging onto him, she looked out the window, saw nothing out of the ordinary, then lifted her gaze to the expanse of the empty lake behind The Tides, which seemed to go on forever in the night. She could have sworn it had water in it, and that the water was rising, and that sent a buzz of unaccountable fear through her even before she saw the bodies on the bank.

Two of them, she thought at first, but then she saw that it was just one, Larry, sprawled over the rim of the lake-bed with his head at a wrong angle to his body and something dark and glimmering oozing out of a hole in his throat.

Chapter 9

Many of the residents, routinely sedated and in any case acclimated to commotion at all hours and little explanation afterward, slept through the night as well as they ever did. Others, though, were to a greater or lesser extent disturbed by the phones ringing, by the rushing footsteps and echoing voices in the halls, and by the lights and sirens outside, including out where the lake had been in the field behind The Tides.

In her new baby-doll pajamas, Petra was down there with the police, declaring in her furious undertone that it was the Mafia that did it, she had proof. She was so small and her speech so soft that one officer after another bent low to hear her, whereupon she'd grab his front uniform pocket and stand on tiptoe to murmur a proposition: a look at the red ants nesting in her rectum in exchange for three cigarettes. Okay, okay, two.

Gordon Marek hovered around his cache of wine bottles under the scraggly back hedge, some empty and one or two with a little left in them, hoping he wasn't being too obvious. Feeling bad for his Princess that she had to come out in the middle of the night for something bad like this, some guy stabbed in the throat, but wishing she'd get here and take care of things so the fuzz would leave.

The nurse tried to get Paul to go back to bed, but he was too agitated to stay put even after she called the doctor and got orders for an extra shot. He kept talking, his speech even less intelligible than usual. He kept crawling over the bedrails and he was going to fall and hurt himself, so finally they gave up and got him dressed and let him sit in a chair by the nurses' station. Every time a uniformed police officer or ambulance attendant went past, Paul's eyes lit up, his loopy voice rose, and his hands shot out more or less in the direction of the person he wanted to stop.

Rebecca, hurrying with a detective into Paul's room again, was struck in passing by the sound he kept making, a sibilant F followed by a long bray: 'Fff-aaaaaaay.' More than a few times lately, she'd heard her father make that sound.

But this odd coincidence was obscured almost at once by the questions the detective was asking, most of which she couldn't answer: Had Larry seemed depressed? Had there been anything unusual in his behavior lately? Was there anything in his employment history that would indicate mental instability?

'I don't know,' she kept saying. 'I don't know. I hardly ever saw him. I hardly knew him,' and was vaguely ashamed to admit it, although not knowing a night orderly would not have shamed her if he hadn't killed himself.

Suicide, almost certainly; they'd found a note under Paul's window – unsigned, but presumably in Larry's handwriting – saying he'd done things he couldn't live with, and the bloody knife had still been in his hand.

It was well after six when Abby finally got to Alex to get him up. He smiled when he saw her and said a pleasant, 'Good morning, Abby,' with a personal, affectionate spin on it, making it clear he was glad to see *her*, not just anybody. She couldn't believe he didn't know what had happened. Alex knew everything. But he didn't say anything about it, and so, stubbornly, neither did she.

Alex's morning routine was long and complex, like all his activities of daily living. Abby knew perfectly well what to do, and she should have been in a real rush because they were so far behind, but she found herself perversely waiting for him to tell her each step. She could feel his displeasure in the stiffening of his body, which was making it harder for her to do what she had to do for him. Handling him almost carelessly, she was very aware of his helplessness and of the power she had over him. She'd never thought of that before and didn't like to be thinking it now, but she couldn't seem to help it. She was tired. She was badly shaken by the events of the night. Her thoughts didn't seem to belong to her.

She stripped and bathed him. First the water in the basin was too hot and then it was too cold, though she noted nastily that he did not flinch, because he couldn't. She soaped and rinsed his body, running the washcloth between his fingers and toes and quickly between his thighs. His toenails needed trimming and his penis was soft. Some of them got woodies when you took care of them, which could be enough to scare off a new aide. Abby took a sort of nervous pride in his skin, which was intact without even any reddened areas. Buzzers were going off all up and down the hall and she thought she heard someone calling her name, but she ignored it, taking care of Alex, doing it right.

It wasn't working, though. Concentrating on Alex wasn't making her stop thinking about Larry. She kept seeing his body the way it had looked from Paul's window, draped over the edge of the lake-bed, throat turned up and cut open as if to let something out, the way you'd lance a boil. She kept seeing his blood. She'd never seen anybody stabbed before, but on this job she'd seen blood and all kinds of other bodily fluids and she'd never seen anything that looked like that. Gushing out. All different colors, though now she couldn't understand how she could have seen colors when the only illumination had been from the city streetlights around the edge of the field, none of them close, and the security light mounted on the back of The Tides.

And she kept wondering what Paul was trying to say. 'Fff-aaaaay,' he whined and whispered and hollered. 'Fff-aaaaay.' Ever since she'd known him, Paul had said things you couldn't understand; the older aides said they didn't mean anything, they were just noises, but this time especially, Abby wasn't so sure.

'Now the lotion,' Alex prompted as she towelled him dry. 'Don't forget the lotion.'

'When do I ever forget the lotion?'

'You're awfully rough this morning, Abby. Usually you have such gentle hands.'

'Beggars can't be choosers,' she snapped, astonishing herself. She was sure she'd never used that saying before, couldn't think of anybody she'd heard say it, but his offended gasp gave her an ugly little jolt of satisfaction. 'It's been a long night,' she added, rummaging through his bedside table in search of the tube of lotion, disturbing his things.

'Are you mad at me?'

'Not everything in the world revolves around you, Alex, you know.' Why was she talking to him like this? Worse, why was it fun? She dribbled lotion onto his skin before it had had time to warm up against her own. He didn't move, and she reminded herself resentfully that he couldn't even feel the cold lotion or her hands in the crevices of his body. She didn't know why she should be mad about that, but she was.

'Abby, Abby, you're in such a hurry. You're not taking time with me.'

'I don't have time, Alex. I have a whole floor of people to take care of, and you're not even in my group.' You're in Larry's group, she thought but did not say. He was, after all, a patient.

'Well, you're not doing anything right.'

Before she had time to realize what she was doing, Abby had slapped him hard across the face. The lotion on her hand left sticky white streaks on his cheek. He didn't move. He lay naked in front of her, his green eyes narrowed and his tongue protruding slightly between his teeth. She stared at him in horror as his penis hardened and rose.

At the very stroke of eight, a tall balding man in a gray suit and gray tie found Rebecca serving trays in the dining room and introduced himself as Ernest Lindgren, Administrative Specialist, State Department of Health, flashing his state ID. Rebecca finished her last table and led him to her office, trying to decide when and whether to tell him about Larry. Unless that was why he was there – but it didn't seem likely that things would have moved that fast.

'We've been expecting you,' she said, because that was what she'd rehearsed to use when the Health Department showed up, wondering too late whether it was a politic thing to say. 'Here's all the documentation about the oven-cleaner incident.' To her own ears, the term 'incident' sounded euphemistic, even cavalier.

Lindgren did not accept the folder, and Rebecca felt something akin to socially awkward as she laid it back down on her desk. He consulted his notes, although she had the impression he would not have needed to. 'I'll get to that. But I am primarily here to investigate a series of other complaints.'

'Complaints?' Rebecca echoed. Her knees weakened and she held onto the edge of the desk as she sank into her chair.

'On September fifteen two residents reportedly had some sort of altercation in the dining room.'

'Oh yes.' Gordon Marek and Cardenio Martinez, but she didn't tell the man from the Health Department their names. Doubtless he already knew. There was an argument over who would sit where. Not an uncommon conflict when people don't have much that belongs to them anymore.

'Later that same month, on the twentieth, a resident allegedly threw a cup of hot coffee at a staff member.'

'That was me.' Rebecca couldn't help chuckling, had to consciously stop the laughter before it veered into nervous giggles. 'We have a lady here who believes she owns the place. That's who she is, The Owner. When I tried to get her into her room for a fire drill, she threw her coffee at me. She missed, by the way.'

'That kind of behavior is unacceptable in a setting like this.'

'What would you recommend?'

'Discharge her.'

'She's been here over ten years. This is her home.'

'Allegedly there have also been several incidents of residents using foul language against staff.'

She blinked. 'Occasionally people become angry, yes.

Even at staff. Maybe it's a way of retaining some sense of self, of resisting the effects of institutionalization.'

'You are taking a risk whenever you encourage the expression of strong emotion.'

'Yes,' said Rebecca, giving up, 'we are taking a risk.'

'The complaint alleges that you have alcoholic patients who actively drink despite doctors' orders to the contrary.'

'None of them has ever been declared legally incompetent, so we have no right to control what they do with their money. To my knowledge they've never been really abusive, except that now and then Gordon Marek likes to play the piano at three in the morning.' She smiled, recognized her need to relocate the little markers of normal life at The Tides.

Florence burst into the office without knocking and stopped short at the sight of the investigator. Breathless, her usually ruddy face florid, the aide announced, 'Sorry, Rebecca, but Mickey just went through the window!'

To her chagrin, Rebecca's first reaction was to glance at Lindgren, who had turned sharply in his chair to look up at the flustered aide. 'A new resident,' Rebecca explained hurriedly to him.

'Schipp,' he said, without consulting his notes. 'Admitted directly from the State Hospital.'

Rebecca ushered Florence out of the office, firmly shutting the door behind her. Unsure whether there could be conversations about nursing-home business kept private from a Health Department official, she half-expected Lindgren to come out and join them, but he didn't. 'What happened?' she asked Florence.

'Nobody knows. He was on his bed asleep last time I checked. Next thing we knew he'd gone out the window.'

'Is he hurt?'

'Not a scratch. We've got him restrained in bed now and he's putting up quite a fuss. Diane's afraid he's fixing to have a seizure. He's seeing things, too. Says some woman's trying to get inside him. Says this place is possessed.'

'Ask Diane to request that the doctor review his meds, would you? He's probably been on the same ones for years.' Florence nodded, glanced at the closed office door, and went off down the hall.

Reluctantly, fighting her impulse to rush to the scene of any crisis anywhere in the facility, even though she knew she was often only in the way, Rebecca went back into her office. Lindgren wasn't there. Stretching across the desk as she rounded it to sit down, not needing to look up the number or to see the phone while she punched it in, she dialled the Mental Health Center and was put on hold before she could cut in. A page came for her to take another line. She was afraid to lose her connection to Mental Health; sometimes you could get a busy signal for an hour. But she was still on hold when Sandy repeated the page, so she switched to line 2.

A creditor. Finding the file for his company in the correct spot in her file cabinet, correctly labeled and arranged in approximate chronological order, afforded her considerably greater satisfaction than it warranted, until she saw the light for line 1 go out.

Meanwhile, Mickey Schipp bellowed and did his best to fight off the voice, the tongue, the teeth and painted nails. Tied down, there wasn't much he could do; there really never had been. But the creature that had been trying to choke him this time, in this place, by filling him with itself so there was no room left for him, had eased up, and abruptly Mickey slept.

In the room where Viviana Pierce lay dying, her son and

grandson, keeping vigil, both thought they saw something drift around her. The grandson wondered with a chill whether he was seeing his grandmother's soul leave her body. But the phenomenon was so subtle neither spoke of it to the other.

Viviana stirred, gave a soft moan. Her grandson brought ice chips in a thin cloth to her lips again, all he knew to do; her lips parted. Her son murmured, 'Ma?' His mother didn't answer, nor had he expected her to.

Viviana was aware of certain sensations: cool dampness between her lips, murmuring, the fragrance of roses, sunlight glimmer, music from the bedside radio and noise from the hall, hunger and thirst and loneliness and an utter lack of desire to satisfy any of them, all in the middle distance and receding. More immediately, she was aware of the presence insinuating itself into the spaces that emerged in her as she approached death. It seemed no more strange than dying itself, or than still being alive. It nudged to get in. It made promises and threats.

The longer she'd lived, the surer Viviana had been of who she was. She knew now, too: a woman dying. Almost, she absorbed the thing that was trying to absorb her, almost she took it with her, but it pulled free.

The Administrative Specialist came back into Rebecca's office, red-faced and gesticulating. Still on the phone, Rebecca had just talked at some length about Mickey Schipp to somebody at Mental Health, and she held up a restraining hand in Lindgren's direction as someone else came on the line. He scowled and took his seat again. She hoped she hadn't seemed insolent. More than that, she wished he wouldn't sit there listening. But a harried voice was at last saying, 'Intake,' and she couldn't miss this chance. Rebecca identified herself again and again outlined the situation. 'I'll need to have that intake worker call you back.'

Rebecca rested her forehead in her hand. 'Aren't you intake?'

'I deal only with the first half of the alphabet.'

'This is an emergency,' Rebecca pointed out helplessly, gave her name and number and hung up.

'It really is not acceptable to have a public restroom in that condition,' Lindgren said to her at once.

Thinking Gordon might have sprayed the wall again or the housekeepers might not have cleaned the toilet well enough, Rebecca felt herself redden. She half-rose. 'I'll get somebody on it—'

'First I'll need your policies and procedures book, and a place where I can work in some peace and quiet.'

She didn't say how unlikely that was around here. She showed him to the staff lounge, closed the door behind him, and went in search of a mop and cleaner to clean the worst of the offending restroom herself.

Her dad, weeping, was just then faltering in the front door, his walker like the cage a tomato plant might lean on, but tipped and wobbling. Hands full of cleaning supplies, bucket clumsy over her arm, Rebecca backed out of the utility closet and called to him. 'Dad? What's wrong? How was your trip?'

'I got lost,' he told her plaintively. His voice and body quavered. His spine scarcely supported him. He still didn't know where he was. But now he was with his daughter and so he must be all right (once their being together had signalled that everything was all right for *her*). He didn't know who this young woman was, but she was someone familiar, someone important to him, so that was all right (he wanted it to be all right, but he was cognizant of the fact that perceptions could be altered by innumerable internal and external factors and that his might well be being altered at this moment without his knowledge or permission, most likely by Faye). People pushed to get past him. He stood his ground. This girl was a stranger, wanting something from him he didn't dare give, and he recoiled. Rebecca was right beside him, but she was his daughter and he shouldn't be depending on her. Marshall pitied the man who'd been lost and who was still so scared of being lost. 'I didn't know where I was.'

Alarmed, thinking he must have wandered away from the group, Rebecca looked at Colleen, who shook her head. 'He was right with us the whole time,' she said brightly. 'He was just fine.'

'You weren't lost, Dad,' Rebecca assured him. 'We all knew where you were.'

'I'm sorry. I'm sorry, Becky. I got lost.'

'You weren't lost, Dad,' she repeated. Marshall knew full well he deserved the rebuke. 'You were on an outing with other people from this facility, this nursing home, where you live. You went for a bus ride to the mountains. Everybody knew where you were. You weren't lost.'

'*I* didn't know where I was, young lady. Why wasn't I told?'

Rebecca set the disinfectant and cloths on the nurses'-station counter and reached to button up his shirt, wondering how long it had been open like that, wondering if it ought to matter to her since it obviously didn't matter to him. The fact that he'd always taken pains with his appearance was often given both as rationale for paying attention to it now in his stead and as tragic evidence of how he was no longer himself. But he *was* himself, here and now: a man who didn't care whether his shirt was buttoned right or not.

He flinched and drew back, then saw what she was doing and allowed it, even smiled. 'Mom's coming for lunch today,' she told him cheerily. 'It's eleven o'clock now, so she'll be here in an hour or so.'

'Who? Mom? My mother?' Eagerly he glanced from one side to the other in an arc constrained as much by limited imagination as by muscle constriction or vertigo.

'*My* mother. Billie.' It was hard to call her parents by their names. When he still looked blank, she tried, 'Your wife.'

His face stiffened and his knuckles whitened on the bars of the walker. 'Here? Where? My wife, you say? Where is she? What is her business here?'

'She'll be here in about an hour to have lunch with you, Dad.' Rebecca was ashamed of her own impatience, but Sandy had paged her for another call, hopefully Mental Health intake, who wouldn't wait long. 'Go with Colleen down to your room now so Mom will know where to find you.' She patted his arm and turned away, ashamed, then, of the patronizing tone used to mask and make up for the fact that she didn't want to talk to her father anymore.

She went around the counter to pick up the phone and was relieved to hear someone with whom she'd had at least cursory contact before. Rummaging for Mickey's chart – out of place because it had been in such recent and hurried use – she described the situation again, listening to Mickey's renewed shouts now every minute or so. 'I'd like you to look at his meds.'

'I'm sure he's organic. Not amenable to treatment.'

Rebecca closed her eyes. She'd heard this with every referral she'd made to the Mental Health Center. Again she said, 'I'd like you to review his meds. Just in case he's over-medicated or is experiencing side effects from long-term use of anti-psychotics.'

'We can look at the patient and determine whether a medication review is indicated,' the intake worker said. 'You do have an SI194?'

Rebecca flipped through the chart and found no such form. She gritted her teeth. 'No.'

'Well,' said the intake worker, 'we can't do anything without an SI194.'

'How do I get one of those?'

'It should have come with him from the State Hospital.'

'It didn't.'

'That's because you didn't go through us on this admission. Every psychiatric admission to every nursing home in this county is to come through us.'

'I had no idea.'

'We can initiate the paper trail here.'

'Good,' Rebecca said warily, waiting for the catch.

'That's another department, so it will have to wait until Monday.'

'We can't keep him over the holiday weekend like this.'

'That's the best I can do.'

Angrily Rebecca summarized the conversation in the progress notes and slid the chart back into its slot on the rack. The top hinge loosened, riffling the contents onto the floor. She bent under the desk to retrieve the papers, then sat crosslegged on the floor arranging the flimsy, multicolored sheets behind their proper tabs.

'Call the doctor,' she told Diane, too frustrated to make the instruction sound like a suggestion. 'Tell him what the bozo from Mental Health said. Tell him we need to get Mickey admitted to a hospital.' She expected an argument and was ready, even eager, but the Director of Nursing picked up the phone without a word.

By the time Rebecca had reassembled the chart, Diane had reached the doctor's office. 'She won't put me through to him,' she told Rebecca, not covering the receiver with her hand. 'She says he's already spent all the time he's going to on this patient.'

'God*dammi*t.' Rebecca took the phone. 'This is Rebecca Emig, administrator of The Tides. You tell Dr Pratt it's essential I talk to him.'

Obviously reluctant, the woman muffled the receiver and said something in the background. Before long the doctor came on the line, sounding bored. 'Pratt here.'

'Dr Pratt, we have a real emergency here with one of your patients.'

'Which one is it anyway?'

'Mickey Schipp.' Rebecca spelled it. 'He transferred from the State Hospital yesterday afternoon—'

'Look, it's your nursing home – do what you want.'

'What I want is to have him hospitalized so his meds can be evaluated and he can have a complete physical. We can't do that without a doctor's order.'

'Well, I won't give you an order. How's that?'

Various obscenities sprang to her lips, but she only asked, more or less evenly, 'Why not?'

'Tell me, young lady, are you a physician?'

When she didn't answer, he repeated the question. 'No.'

'Then kindly allow me to practice my profession. This is nothing more than a chronic psychiatric patient. Just restrain him and sedate him and he'll be fine.'

'I don't like—'

'If you can't handle patients like this, don't take them in the first place. Now, it's Thanksgiving weekend and I'm

going home. I suggest you do the same. Good day, Miss—'
He hung up before he had thought of her name.

'He can't hospitalize him,' Diane told her, a bit smugly.
'Pratt lost all hospital privileges years ago.'

'Then why does he still have patients here?' Diane
shrugged.

Rebecca hurried away to call Kurt and tell him she'd be
late again. He wasn't home, and she was just as glad. She
hated hearing the message she'd recorded on the machine;
it sounded just enough like the voice she heard when she
spoke to be eerie. Holding the receiver away from her ear
until the beep, she left a message, hoping it was sufficiently
contrite without encouraging him to call back. She really
didn't like it when Kurt called her at work. He was going
to his brother's tomorrow for Thanksgiving and she would
have dinner here with her parents, so they'd planned,
somewhat vaguely, to mark the holiday together tonight.
Now, she wasn't sure she'd get home in time.

Not for the first time, it occurred to her how much
more real work was to her than home. While she was at
work, she found it hard to imagine home – the house, the
neighborhood, even Kurt. During the increasingly brief
and infrequent periods when she was at home, work was
almost always on her mind. Often there were phone calls
from The Tides. If not, she called in every hour or so.
Often she'd intend to be concentrating on something else
– television news, conversation or lovemaking with Kurt –
when an idea about some work problem would percolate
to the forefront of her consciousness, far more vivid than
whatever activity she might currently be engaged in and
demanding immediate action.

In theory, this was distressing; probably she ought to
have a more balanced life. But The Tides was endlessly

fascinating, endlessly frustrating and gratifying, and because of it she felt better – more directed, more sure of herself, more *together* – than she ever had. She could not imagine herself anywhere else.

She supposed Kurt must be unhappy. He complained that she was never home, objected when the phone rang during a rare dinner together or in the middle of the night, once had gone so far as to take it off the hook while they had sex and lashed back at her when she protested. She supposed she wasn't being fair to him. But Kurt's displeasure – Kurt himself – was easy enough not to think about. It was The Tides that claimed her attention, refused to be set aside.

Retrieving the cleaning supplies, she went into the bathroom Ernest Lindgren had used. It didn't stink, which was a pleasant surprise. She set the mop down and turned on the light.

At first she thought, foolishly, that someone had papered over the dingy off-white paint without telling her; at first, naively, she rather liked the colors. Great loops and, she saw as she inspected more closely, tiny slashes and dots adorned all four walls and the ceiling, using the entire red end of the spectrum – hot pink, scarlet, peach, tangerine. Lipstick, she realized, and the scrawls were not random, but were full-fledged graffiti spelling out words. Spelling out her name again and again, Rebecca and Becky and Rebecca again, and the repeated phrase like an invective: 'You're mine!'

Gordon, she thought, incensed. This was the sort of thing Gordon might do, to prove his 'love' for her. But she dismissed the idea almost as soon as she'd thought it; she really couldn't envision him putting this much energy into anything.

Could her father have done this? The prospect chilled her; could he be this far gone already? Unpleasant as it was to contemplate, it was not inconceivable that he might be mentally capable of something so bizarre, but surely he didn't have the physical stamina or steadiness – or reach; there were squiggles and swaths of the garish color in the highest corners.

Hastily Rebecca filled the bucket with water from the sink, sloshed in more than an average amount of the potent cleaner, and saturated the mop. As she wrung it damp and brought it up firmly against the opposite wall, she found herself casting about for anyone else she might be said to belong to with such a vengeance: 'You are mine!' Certainly not Kurt. Her mother, maybe; her mother had such a claim on her. But Billie Emig would never make a public spectacle like this. Oddly, Rebecca almost wished she would.

The disinfectant fumes in the tiny enclosed space made her eyes water and her head pound, but the waxy graffiti were impervious. To be sure, she scrubbed a few times at the wall, moved the mop to the wall behind her, beside the sink. And saw on the mirror, scrawled in iridescent black lipstick, the name: 'FAYE.'

That, she was abruptly certain, was the name her father had been saying, and Paul – and, now that she thought about it, other residents. She'd heard Gordon singing a song about Faye, and last night, in between tales of the Mafia and aliens from outer space, Petra had mumbled at least once that Faye had killed Larry.

Faye. Rebecca didn't think she'd ever known anybody named Faye. Was the FAYE slashed across the mirror the signature of the perpetrator, or another name, like hers, scrawled in a bathroom like a dirty word, and on a day when a Health Inspector was in the facility? Anger shook her, then fear.

She plunged the mophead back into the bucket and leaned the handle against the wall. It slid down, bringing the dripping head up, and water splattered. Rebecca swore and left the room, shutting the door behind her. She swung by Sandy's office to tell her to post an *Out of Order* sign on the bathroom door and to find Tillie right away to figure out whether the lipstick could be cleaned off. Sandy, wide-eyed, wanted to talk about it. Rebecca kept her instructions terse and did not stay.

Still seething, she determined to finish the damn October month-end books today no matter what else happened. On her way back to her office, she glanced into Myra Larsen's room to see Naomi Murphy feeding her. Thoroughly absorbed in each other, neither woman acknowledged her presence, and Rebecca lingered before she turned the corner to inspect the room Dave had painted that morning.

Myra, of course, was talking, trying on life-stories, spinning identities, and she was swallowing one spoonful after another without interruption in her monologue. Naomi was rapt.

Rebecca just stood and took them in. This, she thought with a catch in her throat, was the pay-off; this was the reason she did this work. Fleeting and based on the only approximate intersection of disparate realities, this contact between Myra Larsen and Naomi Murphy lit up the place.

'My name is Myra Larsen and I don't belong here. Everything I've ever done I've done on my own, without a speck of help from anybody, and you can bet your life nobody's going to help me now. Sit down, girlie, listen and you might learn something.

'My name is Myra Larsen and I taught school for forty years, over forty years, and I was a good teacher, too, my students learned. But I had enough of the classroom, and I retired early and I took a cruise around the world. By myself. It was lovely.

'Oh, I've had some experiences, girlie, some experiences worth listening to. You just sit there and listen for a while, you might learn something. If you're going to keep me in this hellhole you might as well know something about me.

'Ohh! Ohh! They're killing me! They're killing me! Ohh!'

Suddenly and for no apparent reason, Myra's head rolled on her shoulders and her eyes bulged. Naomi waited patiently for her to be finished. The first time this had happened she had been badly shaken, but it hadn't taken long for her to become accustomed.

'I spent everything on myself, everything, and I made a pretty penny in my lifetime, too, for a woman. Why should I save it? Hah! Let my daughter do for herself like I had to do, the greedy little bitch!

'Don't leave me, girlie, stay with me just a few minutes and you might learn something.'

Myra's sharp hands closed around Naomi's wrist, spilling the applesauce on its way to her mouth, and the hollow eyes stared right at her. Naomi separated the clutching fingers and studied the dry cracking flesh between them, riveted by the undeniable physical reality of the hand in hers and the stale breath in her face, listening to Myra's shape-shifting story and trying, in fact, to learn something.

'My Papa was a well-respected man, and his death was

the tragedy of my life, the touchstone of my life. Mama couldn't cope. Mama was frail. I detest frailty in a woman. I've never been frail in my life. My sister took me in, fed me and clothed me till I was eighteen and married, but it was out of Christian duty, never out of love for me. Nobody's ever done a thing for me out of love. Understand that, girlie, and you might learn something.'

Again Naomi nudged the laden spoon against the pale lips, and finally, as if against Myra's will or beneath her interest, they parted and accepted the food. Naomi was pleased, as if she'd accomplished something. There wasn't much time before they would come to take the tray away, whether Myra had eaten or not.

'Hey, babe,' Dan Murphy hailed Rebecca. With him was Ira Goldberg, Naomi's father and one of the owners of The Tides. 'What's happening? Ira's here to take Naomi to lunch.'

'The state's here,' she told him, sorry to sum up everything that was happening in such a reductionist way, but aware that that was what he'd want to know.

His small eyes narrowed. 'About that oven-cleaner shit? Don't tell me they're already moving on that orderly's suicide last night.'

'Primarily to investigate a complaint about patient mix.'

'Patient mix.' His lip curled. 'You know something? I'm getting fucking sick of hearing about patient mix. Who's here?'

'Ernest Lindgren.'

'That figures. Ernie loves crap like patient mix. Where is he? I'll just go say howdy. Pay my respects. Ask about his daughter. She just got herself knocked up by some sleazebag and flunked out of Harvard.' He strode off down the hall, raising a hand to Diane as he passed the nurses' station, clapping Dexter McCord on the shoulder.

Myra was allowing Naomi to feed her another bite, this time not from a spoon but a bit of bread and butter directly from her fingers. Still watching them but unable now to lose herself in the beauty of the tableau, Rebecca said to Ira, 'She's so good with her.'

Scowling, Ira relit his pipe. 'Better she should work with young people. Children. Where there's hope. Where there's life. Where the present and the future are not already decided. Look at that. She wastes her time.'

Wanting to protect the delicacy of the interaction between Naomi and Myra from his cynicism, Rebecca made herself a decoy. Regretfully she moved away, and Ira did come with her.

As usual, Trudy Belker drooped sideways in her chair, the restraint dragging on the floor. Rebecca spoke to her, touched her shoulder, then stood behind her and lifted her upright. The old woman was hardly any weight at all in her arms, and she smiled gratefully, but Rebecca flinched, afraid she would leave bruises. 'I'm sure,' she heard herself challenging Ira, 'you've seen worse.'

'Of course I have seen worse. My wife and me, we were in the camps. I've seen things you don't believe. True horrors. This – this is nothing.' He waved his hand contemptuously, then brought his bearded, pipe-smelling face close to hers. 'I tell you. The human beings died and the animals lived. That's all.'

'Come, Myra,' Naomi was saying, so quietly that she spoke more to herself than to Myra. 'Let me wash your face.' She touched the warm cloth to Myra's cheek and the old woman howled.

'I am Pocahontas and they're selling me to the white

man! I am Pocahontas and they're selling me to the white man! Ohh!

'I am going to the gas chamber! I am going to the gas chamber! Take me to the gas chamber! Ohh!'

Naomi listened to Myra Larsen with the same mixture of awe and deep shame she had always felt toward her parents. Naomi herself had never suffered; her parents had seen to that. Suffering was mythical, untransferrable, ennobling, degrading. Only the chosen suffered; without suffering, one could not know who one was. Myra Larsen was the closest Naomi had ever come to genuine, present suffering, and she couldn't get enough of her.

Suddenly hands were pulling Naomi's hair, forcing her head down. The hands were strong, nails sharp. Naomi held her breath and made herself very still. Myra leaned as far over as the Posey would allow, put her mouth close to Naomi's ear, and shrieked, 'Listen to me, girlie! Be still and listen to me and you might learn something! Ohh!'

Painfully on her knees now, Naomi had a sudden image of herself lying unconscious at Myra's pale feet. Myra screamed and thrashed, twisting Naomi's hair.

Naomi held her breath, waiting, thereby intensifying her lightheadedness. The pain was considerable, and there was humiliation in it. Was this suffering?

Now hands whirled to cover Myra's mouth. Naomi's hands, though she first didn't know it and then willed them desperately to stop. The side of her left hand worked itself between the hard gums, a gag, while her right thumb and forefinger pinched shut the wide flanged nose.

Suffocating, Myra still did not shut up. She kept right on inventing herself, stringing tales about herself haphazardly together, stealing other people's stories for her own. 'Ohh! Ohh! I am Faye! I abandoned my husband

and my child, and I never once looked back! Why should I? The greedy little bitch! Listen to me, girlie, and you might learn something! Ohh!'

Naomi tried to pry her hands loose from Myra's straining face, but the fingers were frozen, and a terrible pressure was being exerted on them, pressing them in, manipulating the stringy flesh like old clay. She would fill the old woman. She would swallow her up. Her thumbs would punch through the papery skin. Her nails would scratch the harridan voice into silence, leaving the stories free-floating as birds needing a place to land. Rage made her press harder, reach more deeply. Rage, and raging need.

Naomi struggled to throw herself onto the floor, thinking in that way she could break her own hold. But she was held upright on her aching knees, until the screeching subsided into a whisper – 'I am Faye. I am going to the gas chamber. I am Faye. Ohh' – and the tangled grip on her hair loosened and Myra Larsen slumped against the restraint, eyes and mouth wide open, all the suffering she could access finally used up.

Chapter 10

Without warning or even prelude, Rebecca's mother told her, 'Your father was married before, you know.'

Rebecca stared, a gesture wholly expressive rather than communicative since her mother's broad back was stalwartly turned to her. She did not want to have the conversation that loomed here; she did not want to be in possession of the information her mother was threatening to impart; she did not want to receive any secrets about her parents, especially not painful secrets. Especially not now.

Busy at the sink and counter – Rebecca's sink and counter, doing Rebecca's dishes although Rebecca had specifically asked her not to – Billie said, 'She was a mean, selfish woman. Dangerous. Evil. She can't have him back. She can't have my husband or my—'

'Evil?'

'Yes, evil. She fed off other people. Used them for her own purposes and then just threw them away.'

'Evil's a strong word.' Rebecca was bemused by her mother's vehemence, imagining youthful jealousies – made to seem quaint by the passage of time and by the angle of her own perspective. She even rather liked the image of two girls setting their caps for the young man who would be her father.

'Now sometimes he thinks I'm her. All these years and now he's going to die thinking I'm her.'

Rebecca asked cautiously, 'How long were they married?'

'I don't know how long they were *married*,' her mother said disdainfully. She was scrubbing at a spot on the counter, and Rebecca was trying to pretend that this industriousness wasn't a comment on her housekeeping. 'I don't really know if they ever were legally married. Your father has never produced the marriage license or the divorce decree. For all I know, they're still married. For all I know, he's a bigamist.'

'Oh Mom, come on. That doesn't seem very likely, does it?' Rebecca laughed. Her mother did not. 'What happened to her?'

'She left.'

'He just never heard from her again?'

'I didn't say that.'

Rebecca waited. Either the spot finally yielded or her mother gave up.

'Oh, he's heard from her all right.'

When nothing else was forthcoming Rebecca ventured, 'Why did she leave him?'

'Couldn't stand the responsibility, I suppose. It tied her down.' Rebecca's mother was folding the cloth she'd used to clean the counter, although it was wet and dirty now. She put two corners together, smoothed it out. But the cloth wasn't square, and it didn't fold right. Frowning in frustration, she tucked the uneven edges in, making a deceptively neat little package, which she placed on the back of the sink. 'Or she used him up. Got all she could from him. She was a user.'

'What was her name?'

Her mother spat, '*Faye*.'

Rebecca's breath caught, and blood rushed to her head, blackening her vision for a long moment and making her ears ring. Tillie had not been able to get the red and pink and orange lipstick off the bathroom walls or the bold black FAYE off the mirror; they'd had to repaint the walls and ceiling and replace the glass.

What did it mean that her father had once been married to a woman named Faye, whose name she now seemed to be encountering on all sides?

'Becky, where are your paper towels?' her mother was demanding, as though she'd asked the question before.

'I – I don't use paper towels,' Rebecca said. 'It's bad for the environment.' As her shock subsided, she was distantly amused and annoyed by her own defensiveness. 'There's a rag bag under the sink.'

'I don't see how you can keep house without paper towels.' Rebecca got up to get the rag bag. It contained only one piece of corduroy, too small, too linty, and not nearly absorbent enough to make a decent rag. She handed it to her mother anyway, who didn't disguise her contempt for it or the burdensome necessity of making the best of this bad situation.

'Just being married was too much responsibility for her?' She didn't want to say the name, but she had to. 'For Faye?' It was obvious she was pushing the limits of tolerable dialogue between her mother and herself, but Rebecca hoped to find out a few more tidbits of information before she was shut off completely. 'This Faye person – ' she said the name again, and shivered ' – must have been a real free spirit.'

Her mother snorted. 'That's not what I would call her. A woman who deserts her husband and her—' Without much finesse she interrupted herself and demanded, 'Where do you keep your broom and dustpan? I'll just sweep up the cat fur on this floor.'

Rebecca stopped herself from explaining that the cats were Kurt's, and crossed to the basement door. 'Her what?' She pulled out the broom, saw the dustpan lying in the gloom at the bottom of the stairs and went down to retrieve it. Emerging, she pressed, 'Abandoned her husband and what?'

But her mother had had enough. 'Look at this broom!' She was holding it aloft and overhand as if about to use it to squash vermin. 'There are hardly any bristles left on it! This wouldn't sweep up a thing!'

It was the broom from the garage. The house broom, in somewhat better shape, was supposed to be hanging on one of the hooks in the stairway but was nowhere to be found. More embarrassed than she ought to be, Rebecca didn't want to explain. 'Don't worry about the floor, Mom. It'll just get dirty again.' She wished she hadn't said that. 'Tell me what you started to say about Faye.' The naming again; again, the shiver, unpleasant but leaving her craving more.

Hands on hips, balefully regarding the floor, her mother shook her head. 'I shouldn't have told you about her.'

'Why not? Why didn't you guys tell me before?'

'Your father made me promise not to.'

'Why?'

'He didn't want you to know.'

'Why?'

But her mother said again, distractedly, 'I'll just sweep this floor,' and started in. The broom left bits of itself on the linoleum.

After a pause, which Rebecca could have ended by saying any of a number of things that crossed her mind, she stood up. 'I'm going into work.'

'It's after six o'clock at night,' her mother admonished. 'You work too hard.' It was as much an accusation as an expression of concern.

'I have a lot to do.' And I want to talk to Dad, she very nearly said. About Faye.

'Won't Kurt wonder where you are?'

'He's not going to be home until late, either.' She couldn't remember where he'd said he'd be, or whether he'd said.

Her mother looked at her and looked away without comment. Although it was never likely that they'd talk about anything more personal than housekeeping, she was actually a little disappointed to escape a maternal observation about her relationship, such as it was, with Kurt. She'd been ready. *Independence*, she'd have said. *Our own lives. I'm still trying to find myself.*

For the first time, she was saddened by how separate she and Kurt were from each other. For the first time, she envied the bond between her parents, which persisted, apparently, no matter who either of them became.

She hugged her mother goodbye, keeping her distance, feeling her mother keeping hers. This was their way with each other, as though it would jeopardize both of them to come too close. 'I guess I'll go on home,' the other woman said, and abruptly Rebecca understood how much her mother missed her father. She didn't want to know that, and her mother wouldn't want her to know.

Driving to The Tides, against the flow of rush hour but still in traffic, she tried to think about this Faye. But that was an unsettling line of thought, and anyway, she'd already decided what to do about it. As soon as she could, when her father's mind was reasonably clear, she'd ask him some questions, take advantage of the weakening of his intellectual defenses. Such opportunism made her feel a little guilty, but not much.

So her thoughts sailed automatically, happily, toward work. Certainly there was plenty there to occupy them. Such as whether she'd done the right thing about Mickey Schipp.

Last Saturday morning, she and Lisa had loaded Mickey, wooden-faced and croaking rhythmically ('Faye'? Had Mickey been saying 'Faye,' too?) but without much remaining energy, into the back of her station wagon, and had taken him to the emergency room of the public hospital, which was mandated to treat everyone. Diane had refused to have anything to do with the plan, because there was no doctor's order.

The sights and sounds of the E.R. had agitated Mickey, and his bellows had risen again, louder and much more frequent until he seemed to be not even pausing for air. Lisa and Rebecca had sat with him until an orderly came to wheel him away, then stood together and watched him disappear through the metal swinging doors. 'I'm afraid we'll lose him,' Lisa had sniffed. 'I'm afraid the system will just swallow him up, and we'll never see him again or even know what happened to him.' And, indeed, when Rebecca had called the hospital today to find out how he was doing, no one would talk to her because she had no legal relationship to the patient.

Census, for another thing. With Mickey's discharge and Myra's death, they were down to 131. Anxiety tightened her throat.

She thought, too, about the memorial service they'd

held for Myra. The dying of people in The Tides without anything to mark their passage had come to seem wrong to her, never mind Diane's testy remark that they couldn't take time from the nursing schedule every time somebody died, considering that death was a not infrequent occurrence in a long-term care facility. Lisa and Colleen had helped organize it, and people did come, residents and staff, no family. Sandy wept a little, said at least Myra'd gone peacefully, just stopped breathing, saying she felt sorrier for Naomi, your first time losing a resident you were close to wasn't easy, and to be *right there*. Naomi was no more or less withdrawn than usual.

Rebecca had come away from the service feeling worse than before, for she'd had no clear image of a person to mourn and she didn't think anybody else did, either. Pocahontas, Joan of Arc, Cleopatra, Myra Larsen. All constructs. All tall tales.

Then, altogether unwillingly, she was thinking about Faye – a woman she'd never heard of until half an hour ago but about whom, now, she seemed to have always known. Dread rippled through her, and a profound longing.

Suddenly she was remembering something, just a flash:

Being left. Not alone, for someone else warm and solid was there, but something was gone from her, a fragrance, a soft pink and lavender touch. Lost.

'Jesus,' she said aloud, shaking her head to clear it. Her suggestibility was unnerving; nothing more than hearing about Dad being abandoned by a first wife she hadn't even known existed could cause her, just like that, to feel abandoned, too. She was relieved to turn onto Elm Street, nearing her facility.

But some impulse drew her past the parking lot and

around the long block behind The Tides, so that she came up on it this time from the rear. In the snowless winter evening, the bowl of the vanished lake in the unlit field caught stray light and shimmered. The building itself, long and low and harshly lit, looked alien.

Rebecca parked along the road and got out, vaguely wondering what she was doing but seeing no harm in it. The cold instantly set her shivering and she hugged herself, tucked her hands under her arms. But there was also the peculiar sensation of proffered warmth, an invitation and a tease, tingling and sparkling just beyond her like moonlight on water, like poison gas.

Dead frozen weeds pricked through her stockings and deposited small, annoying debris in her shoes as she cut across the field. Now and then the slipping of her heels on the hard ground was abruptly interrupted when they sank in and then came away with clots of mud that altered her pace and gait. Forced to unfold her arms and extend them to the sides to keep her balance, she was cold and keenly aware of being alone out here, though a building full of people she was responsible for lay not far behind her and, indeed, the city surrounded this place like an incandescent fairy ring, not really as far away as it looked.

Something wet was rising over her shoes. She looked down. Her feet were almost entirely obscured by cold grass and shadow, but she caught a glimmer across her left ankle, a fluid streak up her right shin. She must have stepped into a boggy section of ground she hadn't realized was there; she'd been under the impression that the water table here was low, seepage minimal – in fact, they'd had trouble keeping the lake full, and lack of drainage had made it stagnant, more swamp much of the time than lake.

She veered to one side, searching for a more solid

route. With some irritation she told herself that she ought to just give up and go inside, but instead, she went farther out toward where the lake had been. Now the sensation of lapping water was at her groin and waist, but her clothes were not wet.

Her feet found the slope of the lake-bed before her eyes did, and though her hands flailed, there was nothing to grip that could stop her brief, jarring descent. There were veritable currents of trash, papers and cans, a single shoe and, she swore, parts of human bodies and faces – a watery crooked bony hand like Myra Larsen's, Larry's grin above the mirroring gash in his throat, the glowering blue eye of Bob Morley.

She hit bottom. It wasn't very far down, and the depression showed itself now to have nothing in it but dead field grass and ordinary litter. But, in what must be a last remnant of this hallucination – stress-induced, it had to be – Rebecca was surprised not to splash, for all around her rippled a substance that she expected either to soak or to sear, while at the same time she knew it was not real.

It did neither, precisely, but somehow it was getting through her clothes, through her skin, into her flesh and bone, into her heart and the cavity that housed her heart. This, she realized, was the false fulfillment of the earlier promise of warmth, but it was not warm.

A cheat, a trick. A trick of the light and atmosphere, certainly, that had caused her to feel tides where there were none, see debris far different from the paper sacks and soft-drink cans and occasional used condoms that Gordon and Dave cleaned up out here every once in a while. A trick of her own mind, frayed by overwork and worry, obsession and prolonged insufficient sleep. But a trick, also, perpetrated on her from some source just outside herself.

She could not stay out here anymore. She could not think about this anymore. She scrambled out of the depression and hurried across the field. The back door of The Tides would be locked now, unless Gordon had propped it open again, and she went around one end of the building toward the front.

Through her physical and emotional discomfort, intense by this time, her attention was caught by a mark on the wall that she was sure had not been there before. Maybe eighteen inches higher than the foundation, it created a demarcation below which the brick was noticeably darker than above.

Out of professional obligation, she stopped in what had become nearly a headlong rush and crouched to run her fingers over the darker brick. It was wet. She straightened, forced herself to walk more slowly around the corner of the building. The moisture mark wasn't consistent, faded altogether in some places and fairly dripping in others. She could detect no obvious source for it, nor any actual damage. She'd have Dave check it out in the morning, if he showed up for work. She'd check it out herself.

Petra was in her usual sentry position just inside the front door. No more or less crazed than before Bob had died, she caught Rebecca's sleeve and murmured confidentially, 'You know what? I have a nest of red ants in my rectum.'

Rebecca patted her hand, which caused Petra to flinch away. 'You know what? There are times when I feel that way myself.' She went on past. Petra, of course, was one of the people the Health Department surveyors had most in mind when they objected to inappropriate patient mix, which was why she'd lived in ten or twelve facilities over the past fifteen years. Rebecca was, in fact, more than a little embarrassed to think of her accosting the next person through the front door with her tale of insectoid colonic invasion, but it didn't seem grounds for exile.

She waved to Beatrice Quinn, back yesterday from the hospital. Beatrice had a yellowing bruise on her hip and her characteristic leftward list was more pronounced than before her encounter with the Volkswagen, but otherwise she seemed all right. She waved back, a little acknowledgment that might have been nothing more than a social grace but that pleased Rebecca inordinately and made her very glad to be back inside The Tides, where she belonged.

It was not because of her father that Rebecca felt at home there, and her father, in the same building, felt no connection to her, either, as she was now; he didn't even know her as she was now, and certainly had no intuition that she was only a few hundred feet away. His attachment was to his child, as he remembered her, as he had imagined her in the first place, a person not unreal but forever incompletely formed.

Marshall had been taken to his room after supper and put down for the night. His roommate – who could put himself to bed and often did not until well after the night shift came on at eleven, much to their consternation since it was in their job description to wake people, not to put them to bed – was watching television in the lounge, and so Marshall was supposedly alone. He wasn't alone, though (he was in the company of others, who were so close to him that they invaded him, inhabited him not unlike Petra's red ants, of which he had not heard). He was cradling the infant Rebecca. He was talking to his mother. He was pleading with Faye. He was hoping his mother, who had died when he was seven, could protect him and Rebecca from Faye (who might be dead, too; he never knew).

Not nearly asleep but not precisely awake, either (he'd lately discovered plenty of states of mind imprecisely identified by pairs of supposed opposites like asleep and awake, confused and alert, oriented and disoriented; more and more he was drawn into those states, and not always was it a terrifying experience; not always did he resist), Marshall asked of Faye, 'What do you want?'

But it was his daughter Rebecca who answered. He knew it was Rebecca when she sat down beside him and took his hand, but he forgot he knew that and something about her was just like Faye. 'I wanted to talk to you, Dad. Are you up for company?'

Marshall understood that she was evaluating his degree of orientation and the state of his sensorium and otherwise taking his measure. As well she should. He turned his thin, cool hand over in her warm one, his still so much bigger than hers, and meant to smile at her, though he couldn't be sure either that he'd smiled or that the smile, if there was one, had reached her. Faye might have stolen it. Faye had always had a passion for pretty baubles that she had no use for; she'd swiped his mother's wedding ring and then pouted and begged until he'd allowed her to wear it, and she'd left with it still on her finger. Or in her pocket. Or between her teeth. At that Marshall found himself tempted to laugh. He should have said something to Becky, who probably had asked him a question, but the opportunity for meaningful discourse, brief as it always was, seemed once again to have passed.

'Mom told me something today,' she said.

Mom was Billie. Marshall knew that.

'But she wouldn't tell me very much, and I was hoping you would. It's about Faye.'

Shock blew through Marshall's mind like a cold black wind with no color in it, a frigid white wind using up all colors, and he pulled himself upright by wrenching his daughter's hand and digging his fingers in. She winced but didn't let go. 'We had a pact. We were never to mention that name. You were never to know about Faye.' Such blatant vocalization of the name made his teeth chatter, his lips itch as though a scarf had been trailed across them, his tongue curl.

'Why not, Dad? Why keep it a secret from me?'

Marshall was trembling now, and his mind shook. He heard Faye laughing, that peal and howl he'd so loved and grown to loathe. He felt her reach inside him, and reach out through him to grasp his daughter, and he could not let that happen. He flung out his hands.

Rebecca caught them like tossed discs. 'Dad?' she urged. 'Dad?' But Marshall's mouth was full of Faye as he struggled to swallow her back down, and he couldn't say any more.

That was about the time Abby saw the three people come in. She was busy, and at first she didn't think much about it. But when, out of the corner of her eye as she was pushing a wheelchair into the hall for the night shift to wash, she saw one of them unlock the medical records office, she went to get Rebecca.

Rebecca was leaning over her dad, who was curled up in his bed crying like a baby. Abby felt so sorry for him, and for Rebecca, who, once she'd heard about the visitors, glanced over her shoulder to ask, 'Can you stay with him while I go find out what's going on?'

Abby hesitated. She had a lot to do. 'Sure,' she agreed,

coming forward. 'What's the matter?'

'I don't know. He thought he saw something. Somebody. He thought somebody was trying to hurt me.' She passed his hand from between hers to between Abby's. Her father didn't seem to notice the transfer. Rebecca paused another minute or so, then shook her head, muttered, 'I'll be back when I can,' and hurried out of the room.

'Danny sent us.'

'At eight o'clock at night?' Rebecca kept her hand on the doorknob. The woman was considerably taller than she, and the two men loomed over them both.

'He wants all the records from all the facilities centralized in the main office.'

'It's against regs to take medical records out of this facility.' The three of them advanced on her, and involuntarily she stepped out of their way. But as soon as the woman had the door open, Rebecca was inside first, standing with her back against the file cabinets and her arms folded, feeling a little ridiculous and unsure whether she might be making too big an issue of this. 'Suppose we had a survey tomorrow? I'd be held responsible for those records.'

The woman shrugged, her considerable breasts in motion. Annoyed with herself for noticing, Rebecca deliberately stared. 'Danny's orders,' the woman said, almost languidly.

'I don't give a shit whose orders they are,' Rebecca said evenly. 'I'm in charge here.'

'If you don't box them up for us, we'll do it ourselves.'

'No,' said Rebecca. 'You won't.' She rested her hand on the phone. It was not quite an empty gesture; whether or not the police had jurisdiction, calling them would complicate things for a while.

There was a charged silence. Finally the woman shrugged again. 'Hey, he don't pay me enough for this. You'll be hearing from Danny in the morning. Come on, you guys, we got other places to be.' They left by the side door, and Rebecca pulled it tight behind them, making sure it locked, wondering what the hell had just happened.

'Go get 'em, little lady!' yelled Dexter McCord from his place among the half-dozen old men who sat all day in a row against the wall, not talking much among themselves but observing.

'I don't know what that was all about,' Rebecca said, smoothing her clothes and working to catch her breath as if she had been in a physical scuffle.

'I'm ninety-two years old,' Dexter blustered, 'ninety-two years old, and I never saw anything like that.'

'She's got no call to talk mean to my Princess,' Gordon declared. His round face, dusky from broken capillaries under dark brown skin, was made even more childlike than usual by his scowl and protruding lower lip, and his puppy squirmed and squealed between his fat knees.

Rebecca wished she could feel more respect and less fondness for Gordon; she wished she didn't think of him as cute. Resisting the impulse – which she wished she didn't have in the first place – to pat him on his bald head, she instead rested her hand on his shoulder for a minute. 'Thanks, buddy.' The puppy gave a miniature growl and scrambled up Gordon's chest for Rebecca's hand, managing to sink its needle teeth into the ball of her thumb. 'Hey!' She shook it loose. As it tumbled into Gordon's lap, a thin wet trickle appeared across his shirt and left suspender.

He didn't seem to notice the urine. He scooped up his puppy in both big hands and raised it to eye level, peering at it anxiously. 'Don't hurt my dog!' he meant to shout at her, but his voice cracked. 'Don't you hurt my dog, you hear me?'

Her thumb stung. 'He's not hurt. But he is peeing. Get him outside, Gordon.'

'You scared him.' He hauled himself to his feet and lumbered away with his dog cradled in his hands against his bouncing belly.

Rebecca didn't watch to make sure he headed for a door. As she passed the nurses' station the pool nurse remarked, 'One of these days that dog's going to seriously bite somebody.'

She left urgent messages for Dan Murphy everywhere she could think of, then managed to finish the census report and the Plan of Correction from Lindgren's investigation before, finally, Dan returned her call. 'I suppose you know we had a little visit tonight?'

He was calling from someplace noisy. 'What are you talking about, babe?'

'Dammit, stop calling me that.'

'Hey. Sorry.'

'What's the name of the woman in the management office? Tall, blonde?' Although he'd surely have known immediately whom she meant had she referred to the woman's breasts, she did not.

'Joni. Jesus, haven't you ever been introduced?'

'Joni said that all the records from all the facilities are to be "centralized." By your orders.'

'She did?' He gave his characteristic mirthless chuckle.

'I didn't let her take them, Dan.'

'Is that right? Wish I'd seen that.' His amusement

caused her to question her judgment again.

'Danny—'

'I'll take care of it,' he said. 'Trust me.'

It was after eleven when Rebecca finally got back to her father's room. He was asleep. Abby had finished her shift and gone home, and the night crew knew nothing about the earlier upset. Things happened around here and then vanished as though they'd been washed away, important things, profound things. Rebecca shuddered and, because she had to, left the facility.

The pines around The Tides bent like serene old ladies who knew what their lives had been about; Rebecca wondered whether there was really any person like that. Gordon was out on the porch without a shirt, swigging from a brown paper bag. Chewing on something, his puppy gave a puppy growl; Rebecca didn't look to see what it had. 'You'll freeze,' she told Gordon crossly. 'It's winter.'

'Hey, boss-lady.' He tried to slap her hand in greeting and missed. 'I got my love to keep me warm.'

'Your love, huh? They sell love for a dollar forty-nine a pint these days?' She shook her head at him and went on out to her car, leaving him humming and executing a precarious softshoe shuffle on the porch.

She was tired. More than that, she was overstimulated. Her heart raced. Her head ached. Her thoughts were edging into the surreal, the way they'd been when she'd walked out into the lake. She kept going over the events of the day, mentally completing lists, crossing things off (the census report; the Plan of Correction, though she'd have to go over it again in the morning when, hopefully, her head would be clearer), adding things (the water mark on the wall). Dutifully she tried to guess what Kurt might have done today and what questions she might ask to indicate interest without inviting a whole exhausting conversation.

The house was completely dark when she got there, not even the porch light left on for her. Unaccountably hurt by the darkness, she let herself in with more noise than necessary. One of the cats zigzagged toward her, mewing. She picked it up and cradled it against her chest but, responding to her tension or to some feline disquiet of its own, it twisted in her arms and jumped down.

Rebecca frowned, feeling unwelcome and out of place, things she never felt at work. 'Fine,' she said aloud, though the cat was long gone.

She took the new *Time* – already, she noted irritably, dogeared – into the bathroom, where she drew a hot bath. When she sank into the water, it was not quite hot enough, only tepid around her shoulders, and she shivered. She propped her feet on the edge of the tub and felt, with a grim sense of vindication, the ends of her hair getting wet, which meant she'd have to take time in the morning to curl them.

Abruptly she was remembering being bathed in a dishpan set on a red oilcloth. She remembered streaks of sunlight on the red oilcloth, the particular way it gleamed. She remembered the water getting cold. The water over her face like a rainbow ribbon, then withdrawn. She remembered crying, being comforted.

That must be a very early memory, she thought, shaken, and it didn't seem to be a pleasant one because she felt exposed, vulnerable. Dimly, she wondered why.

Finally, so tired now that her body didn't seem to be performing its automatic functions automatically and she couldn't consciously quite think what to do, she climbed out of the tub, dried and lotioned her skin, put on her nightgown and robe after some struggling with the sleeves. With great effort, feeling self-righteous and put upon, she hung up her towels and cleaned the ring out of the tub. She turned off the lights and stumbled upstairs to bed.

Kurt didn't move or speak to her. She couldn't tell whether he was really asleep, but he might as well be. Relieved, Rebecca slipped in beside him. As usual he was wrapped in the covers like a burrito, leaving none available for her. Enormously annoyed, she tugged at them until they unwound, and by that time she was well into an exaggerated mental harangue about his thoughtlessness. He muttered something, ostensibly in his sleep, and flung an arm over her. She stiffened and thought how more often than not these days she cringed from his touch. But the thought barely registered before it was obscured by impending sleep and the need for sleep.

In the hypnagogic state between wakefulness and sleep – which now seemed to her probably not unlike the state of mind her father was in much of the time – her thoughts did not turn but flowed toward the mysterious Faye. Buoyed and pulled by a fear that felt ancient, for which there weren't words, she made herself small and waited for sleep.

Marshall was buoyed by a dreamy fear, too, and by old love. On his hands and knees between his bed and the wall, he might have been swimming in love and fear, drowning. Faye danced erotically around him, inside him, tenderly, as she had when he'd been able to hope she loved him, and her scarves crossed his face like bands of a rainbow, now swishing, now snapping, hurting his eyes, soothing. 'You can't have her, Faye!' Marshall shouted.

'You left her when she was a baby, and you can't have her now!'

But Marshall may not have said anything out loud, and the nurse and two aides on the night shift were either dozing or playing cards, and nobody heard him, but Petra Carrasco, desperate for Bob or for her husband or for somebody, anybody, who came into Marshall's room, observed him and muttered to herself and went away again.

When Rebecca's phone rang, she squinted at the clock as she always did. 3:12 a.m. 'Yes?'

'Rebecca, this is Linda at the nursing home. Did I wake you up?'

Too sleepy to react to the foolishness of the question, Rebecca managed, 'Yes, Linda, but that's all right. What's up?'

'I'm sorry to disturb you in the middle of the night.'

'What is it?'

'Well, you know that guy? That maintenance man?'

'Dave.'

'Yeah. Dave.'

'What about him?'

'He's here.'

'What do you mean, he's there? What's wrong?' The heat again, or another broken pipe. Maybe that was where the water was coming from. Rebecca groaned and began considering ways to readjust the budget, which wouldn't be easy.

'He's been in the basement for a couple of hours. I don't know what he's doing down there. I keep hearing him talking to somebody, or talking to himself.' Linda paused. 'Is he, you know, all there?'

'Oh, Jesus.' Rebecca sat up. Dave was the third maintenance man she'd had, and all she knew about him, really, was that he could hammer a nail and wield a paint-brush better than she could, which wasn't saying much. From his red-rimmed eyes and constant dry sniffing, she'd surmised a cocaine habit, and his reliability left something to be desired, but he was better than having nobody to make the myriad repairs around The Tides. 'Go get him,' she told Linda. 'Tell him I want to talk to him.'

Linda hesitated. 'Then he'll know I called you.'

'It's your job to let me know about unusual things on your shift.'

'I called Diane. She said it wasn't a nursing problem and I should call you.'

'She's right. Go get Dave.'

'I'm afraid of him. Somebody that weird, you don't know what they'll do.'

'Then call the cops. Or I will.'

'He'd still know it was me. Oh, wait.' From the sound of it, Linda turned from the phone, then back. 'He's gone.'

'Are you sure?' Was she telling the truth?

'I just saw him leave. I can hear his truck now.'

'Okay.' Rebecca let her breath out. 'Make sure the back door's locked. I'll talk to him in the morning.' If he comes in, she thought unhappily, but there was no point in saying that to the nurse.

'There's something else.'

'*Tell me*.'

'Well, I'm the only one here.' Rebecca had a sudden, extravagant fantasy of The Tides completely emptied of all life but this one nurse. 'The only staff,' Linda elaborated helpfully.

Still half-asleep, Rebecca couldn't compute the scheduled staffing pattern. 'Aren't there supposed to be three aides on with you?'

'Two. Since – Larry. Diane hasn't found anybody. But Edie and Nancy were scheduled tonight.'

'Neither one of them showed up?'

'They showed up.' Of course – she'd seen them both. She rubbed her eyes. 'They walked off. Quit.'

'Just like that? Did something happen?'

'They said the place is haunted.'

'Haunted? By somebody besides Dave?'

'Supposedly they saw a ghost.'

'I don't think I've ever heard of a haunted nursing home. Where did they see this ghost?'

'Nancy said she caught her in bed with Paul.'

'This is amazing. Did Paul mind?'

'Edie saw her in your dad's room.'

Rebecca was speechless. Finally, she found her voice to ask, 'Are you okay? Is Dad okay? Should I come in? Not that I can help much with anything medical.'

'Diane said she'd come in if I needed her. But it's only a couple of hours till the day shift come on. Everybody's fine.'

'As long as you don't have an emergency.'

'As long as I only have one emergency at a time.'

Rebecca replaced the receiver and set about the task of retrieving some of the blankets from Kurt, who had not stirred again. She ought to go in. Linda shouldn't be there alone. She ought to see about her father. She fell asleep.

Chapter 11

Naomi awoke trembling, a tide of fire in her throat. She hadn't heard Dan come in, but here he was asleep beside her. What else was in her house that she didn't know about? What else that ought to be here was not? Hands were at her, sharp thumbs in the hollow of her throat, bones pressing hard against her gums. But the pain of them was small and she could still breathe with no trouble, so it was not enough.

Naomi listened. Nothing was amiss in her morning house. She would get up soon and search every room to be sure, as she always did, but she knew everything would be the way she'd left it last night. Everything would be fine. No one taken out while she slept. No graves filled in.

She reminded herself that cancer could be spreading in her body right now without her knowledge. A secret spark could have taken hold in the attic. Just before the Gestapo knocked at the door (why would they *knock*?) her mother might have come awake like this, checking to be sure everything was all right.

But that horror was not hers. Suffering, which made a life authentic by defining it, was not hers. She flattened her face against her pillow, but she could still breathe.

Naomi missed Myra. Myra, with her shrieking and her

opaque, reflecting eyes and her sinewed throat that vibrated like a distant alarm. Naomi missed Myra—

—and was assaulted by a flood of guilt like excrement, like her own feces, cramping, tearing.

The feeling passed, as strong emotion and physical sensation always did. This was no more her guilt than were her memories of killing Myra, of nudging the willing breath out of the wizened mouth, then of lowering her hands, damp from Myra's spittle. Over the years Naomi had come to realize, despite her own vivid perceptions to the contrary, that very little of what she experienced actually belonged to her.

Other people had often understood this before and better than she did. When she and Dan were first married, she had tried to tell him a little about the camps, but he had never known what to say and it had ended up embarrassing them both, because, of course, she wasn't any closer to the concentration-camp experience than he was; it didn't belong to her. She hadn't been there, not even in the womb. For a long time she'd tried to adjust her personal chronology so that that might have been true, so that she might really remember the absurd terror of knowing you'd done something so terrible that it was punishable by being in this place but never knowing what it was you'd done, the oozing of human slime between your palms, the sharp cold in your fingertips and the backs of your knees, the chitter of machine-gun fire, the rancid smoke, the swelling of Wagner to the doomed rhythm of marching feet.

'I am Joan of Arc and they are burning me at the stake—

'I am Pocahontas and they are selling me to the white man—

'I am Faye. I am Faye.

'I am going to the concentration camps. Take me to the concentration camps—'

None of that suffering was hers, even now. None of it had been Myra's, either. Taking great pains not to touch Danny, Naomi crawled out of bed.

When Alex woke it was the middle of the night. He couldn't see the clock; no matter how many times he told them, housekeeping could not seem to understand the importance of placing the clock where he could see it. But he could tell by the quality of the air and by the nature of his own consciousness that it was the middle of the night, and somebody was in his room, and Alex was inexplicably afraid.

He tried to whistle for help but his lips were too dry. 'Abby!' He cried out for her with all his strength, trusting that she would come when he called, despite – because of – the fact that she'd lost control with him and would, by nature, be blaming herself. But he managed only a low groan and there was no answer.

That was inaccurate. There was an answer. Not from Abby, but from the figure dancing around him, leaving trails of multicolored spangles like a vicious pinwheel.

The spangles came closer, surrounded him, and there was a sweet odor that made his head reel. A soft pressure parted his lips, and something flicked into his mouth. Nausea and sexual arousal swelled.

His vision blurred, his throat caught, and his head began to thrash. The motion was out of his control, back and forth on his pillow, and there was an enormous clatter and thump in one ear and then the other, inside his head, faster and faster. Terror and pain rose in his throat, and he was so aroused he could all but feel the throbbing of his penis, the swelling and straining of his scrotum, which he had not felt for most of his life.

Soft strong hands, a woman's hands, on his shoulders, on either side of his head, holding him, saving him from falling off the bed, restraining him from flying out of this body and away. Tears of relief filmed his eyes and he couldn't wipe them. 'Abby.'

It wasn't Abby. It was a woman he didn't know whose pale blonde curls were bright and deceptive as a cloud around her piquant face, whose lips and eyelids were painted bright as a Mardi Gras mask, whose breath reeked of roses. He fought the hands at first, or tried to, but they were too much for him and before long he felt himself subsiding. He coughed and choked; something yellow and gauzy, a soft roughness, was brushed across his face, then fed into the pulpy back of his throat.

He was coughing, choking. Vomiting; he would drown in the tides of his own vomit. The woman had slid down his body and was, he knew, squatting between his legs, where he could neither constrict his muscles to draw her down onto him nor flex them to fling her away. He heard a wet thick sound, the spurt of his own ejaculate, the gluey rivulets of it waxing and waning. He heard her exuberant cry.

He was wailing now, howling, and astonishing himself. Was it an expression of dread or of desire, of surrender or of triumph? It was quite unlike him not to know his own mind and heart.

But he did know. His mind focused. The pumping of his heart steadied. He turned his head to the right as far as it would go, farther, the entire right side of his face buried in the pillow, his neck straining. Then he gathered himself, more determination and will than strength, and flung his head hard and fast to the left, as far as and farther than it would go.

Anyone watching would have seen that Alex's body shifted hardly at all, the mass of it from the neck down too much dead weight for only his head to move. But Alex knew otherwise, and so did Faye, who left with that part of him she'd been able to take in.

Alex waited. Then he moistened his lips and began to whistle. No one heard him, though, and eventually he fell asleep, until someone – not Abby – came to get him up in the morning. He was glad it wasn't Abby, though he missed her. He hadn't decided whether to tell her anything of what had happened to him in the night, because he hadn't decided what to make of it, so he had planned to behave as he would on any other morning. She'd have bathed and dressed him as usual, and the slowing of her hands over the crusted spots on his upper thighs and lower abdomen would have been imperceptible to anyone but Alex, who would have smiled. As it was, the aide who readied him for the day was, though not a stranger, also not someone who tested his abilities to remain charming and distant, and so the interaction was blessedly uncomplicated.

When the two women stopped at the nurses' station and announced they were there to see Beatrice Quinn, the pool nurse scanned the charts, looking for the room number. 'Two two one,' shouted Dexter McCord from his place in the old men's row against the wall. 'Down there on the south end, next to the last room, cattywumpus from that wall they painted. Can't miss it. Oh, hell, follow me, little ladies, and I'll steer you right. Come on, come on.'

The young women exchanged indulgent smiles. The

nurse shrugged. Finally one of them said, loudly and sweetly, 'Why, thank you, sir. That's very nice of you.'

'Ninety-two years old and I'm just a kid.' Wheeling his chair energetically though not very fast, he boomed over his shoulder: 'You believe I'm ninety-two years old, missy?'

One of the women said at once, 'You certainly don't look it.'

'Damn right. Just a kid. What do you want with Mrs Quinn?'

At first they didn't answer, but when he said, 'Eh?' and stopped his wheelchair in the middle of the hall and laboriously turned it to face them, one of them said cheerfully, 'Oh, we're just here to ask her a few questions, that's all.'

'What kind of questions?'

'Just questions.'

'Where you from?'

'I'm from Pennsylvania originally and my friend here is – where are you from, Harriet?'

'No, goddammit,' said Dexter. 'Where do you work?'

A pause. 'We work for the county.'

'Which office?'

They gave up then and told him. 'The Mental Health Center.'

'The funny farm, eh? Thought so. That granddaughter sic you on her, did she? And that nurse, that Diane? I been expecting you. She kept saying that granddaughter wouldn't do a thing like that, but I knew better. Well, let me tell you something, little ladies, save you some time. Mrs Quinn is crazy as a bedbug, that one, but I don't think it's your kind of crazy.'

During this speech he'd maneuvered his chair around

again and continued down the hall. They followed, Harriet thinking how she'd been so fond of old people before she took this job and how nice it was to run into one who, though probably diagnosable, was not overtly hostile.

'This here's her room.' He stopped and motioned them impatiently around him like a traffic cop. A man with a walker edged between them, muttering under his breath. 'Just hold your horses, mister,' Dexter told him. 'You got no place to go that won't wait. We none of us do.'

Petra Carrasco insinuated herself between the two women, put her hard hand on the arm of the one not named Harriet, and leaned close. 'I got a nest of red ants in my rectum, did you know that?'

There was a beat of silence. Then the mental health worker said evenly, 'I'm very sorry to hear that.'

Petra pulled herself up on tiptoe, reached to tweak the woman's cheek, and rasped, 'Hey, no, they're my *friends*, know what I mean? We look out for each other.' Then she let the woman go and moved off, looking for somebody else to tell about the red ants.

'Don't fret your pretty little heads over her,' Dexter advised. 'The time to worry is if she ever shuts up.'

Petra was intercepted by the pool nurse with her med cart. Almost graciously she accepted the cup of orange juice in which her Thorazine was contained, then raised it over her head and threw it. Involuntarily the women from the Mental Health Center stepped back. The sticky liquid splattered across the mural and the white waxed floor. Thin body bent back on itself like a paper clip, Petra jigged in a half-circle around the baffled pool nurse and jabbed one forefinger and then the other in her direction. 'Devil!' Petra screeched at the nurse. 'Murderess! Try to poison me! Try to poison my little friends!'

Quietly Naomi entered her kitchen. Somebody else was there. The light was odd, a soft lavender hue, sinister for all its prettiness, like musical accompaniment to the ovens, like variegated gray smoke from them against blue sky. She stood in the doorway, waiting, but the presence didn't reveal itself; in fact, it vanished.

A piercing need drove her to the door without a coat, though the cold assaulted her. She had to get to The Tides. She had things to do there that could not wait.

These were not her thoughts. This was not her need. But Naomi was used to responding to urges that she didn't own, understandings that she could not claim, and she allowed herself to be rushed.

When the mental health workers knocked on the open door and entered Beatrice's room, she was sitting on the edge of her bed, leaning sharply leftward, ruminating about home. About herself at home and away from home; was it the same self? How would it change her if she gave her things away? How would it change home? 'Mrs Beatrice Quinn?'

In a sense, Beatrice didn't know. But of course, really, she had the answer. 'Yes,' she said pleasantly. She turned around slowly and ran her fingers distractedly over her hair, bringing her thoughts back to this time and place. 'Good day, girls. I am Mrs Beatrice Quinn. May I help you?'

'Yes, Mrs Quinn. My name is Gina and this is my friend, Harriet. We're from the county Mental Health Center. Your granddaughter, Mrs Byrne, and your nurse Diane asked us to come and see you.'

'My granddaughter Mary Alice? That was nice of her. Why did she ask you to do that?'

'Oh, she's a little concerned about you, that's all. We

have a few questions to ask you. Is there someplace we can go that's more private?'

'Mental health?' Beatrice regarded one and then the other, mindful not to stare.

'She says you keep trying to leave the nursing home. Is that right?'

A smile caught at the corner of Beatrice's mouth, though she was also a bit frightened now. 'I see. Well, you girls just make yourselves to home.'

The two women sat down awkwardly on the edge of the bed, their knees humped over the lowered siderails, and put their clipboards in their laps. Because the bed was pushed against the wall on one side, all three of them were now sitting in a row, which made conversation awkward. Beatrice folded her hands in front of her expectantly. One of the workers cleared her throat. 'I wonder if you can tell me, Mrs Quinn, what day it is?'

Beatrice blinked. 'Oh, dear,' she said, 'I've been sick for so long, don't you know. I think it might be Tuesday?' She looked at Harriet questioningly and Harriet nodded encouragement.

'No,' said the other one, making a checkmark on her paper. 'I'm afraid it's Friday, Mrs Quinn. Friday.'

'Oh, me.' Beatrice smiled self-deprecatingly and tugged at her ear.

'And the year, Mrs Quinn? Can you tell us the year?'

She hesitated. 'Oh, my dears, it's been a long time since I thought about days and years. I mean, things like that don't matter much to me anymore.'

'Do you know what year it is, Mrs Quinn? Can you guess?'

'Well, let's see. 1989.'

'Almost.' Another checkmark. 'And do you know, Mrs

Quinn, who the President of the United States is?'

Beatrice, still polite, lost patience. She patted the woman's knee. 'Now, my dear, why in the world would I be interested in a thing like that?' Gina and Harriet took pains not to look at each other, but Beatrice plainly saw them nod in unison and knew that she'd failed.

On her way to The Tides, though she knew there was something important she had to do, Naomi went to see her mother. Maybe her mother would stop her. Maybe her mother would tell her what it was.

Her mother's house was haunted: horror in its bones, evil always caught out of the corner of its eye. 'Mama, please, tell me about the camps.'

Esther Goldberg looked at her daughter across the brown living room, recently turned brown-and-gold from teal-and-white. The décor changed so often that Naomi couldn't remember what it had looked like while she was growing up; she often couldn't remember what it had looked like when last she'd visited, was only aware of being unnerved by its appearance this time. She felt the jolt of her mother's eyes locking on her. 'Why do you ask this now? It was a long time ago.'

'Tell me, Mama. I want to know.'

'It has nothing to do with you. Your papa and me, we make sure it has nothing to do with you.'

Esther's eyes left her again for their customary focal point in the middle distance, and Naomi was on her knees beside her mother's chair. She saw the blue numbers on her mother's wrinkled forearm, close enough to be pressed into her own cheek, though they were not. She imagined the old woman's mittened hands tangled in her hair, pulling her head back until she could hardly breathe and someone had to come and rescue her. She imagined her own hands, as if they were not her own, as if they were guided by someone else, around her mother's throat, forcing out the story that was not hers. Saw herself lying unconscious at her mother's pale feet. But her mother would never touch her like that, had seldom in fact touched her at all for fear one of them would contaminate the other with what she knew of the world, would never allow such intimate contact as for one of them to murder the other.

Esther said nothing, did not look at her daughter, did not move in her chair. Naomi put her arms around her mother's knees and laid her head in her lap. The body under the clothes made her skin crawl, as if she hadn't known there would be flesh and blood.

'Mama,' she wailed, against her mother's skirt, 'tell me why you never visit the nursing home.'

'I do the books,' Esther answered automatically. She kept her arms on the arms of the chair. Naomi opened her eyes and saw again the awful wrinkled numbered flesh of her mother's wrist. It hung from the bone. She closed her eyes against nausea in her throat, then opened them again and saw that the flesh was beautiful. Where her own arm was flattened against her mother's thigh, she saw the beginnings of the same tiny dry wrinkles, the same soft folds. 'I do the books,' her mother repeated. 'That's all.'

There was a long pause. Once, Naomi thought she might actually be falling asleep in her mother's lap. Then the older woman spoke, still not touching her, speaking over her head.

'Everybody looks the same. Everybody smells the same. Everybody sounds the same, and they all have the same eyes and the same voice and the same skin, and they all have the same name. *Musselman*.'

'Oh,' Naomi started to protest, squirming around so that she was looking up at the underside of her mother's pocked chin. 'They're not the same. Not at all, Mama. Myra—'

'The sickest ones. The thinnest ones. The ones with the eyes that see things you can't see, things you don't want to see, things you will see soon enough when it comes your time. The ones who are the next to go, the next to be chosen, for no reason, left or right, every second one, every sixth. You touch them and they cry out, and your hand goes into their flesh. And you find you are crying out in the same voice, and you are all the same. You cannot look at them. You cannot look at yourself.

'You walk among them and you're covered with the stink of their waste. Your own waste. You're assaulted by your own waste, and by the pain that doesn't hurt anymore of your own body rotting away. In that place, you are *Musselman*, daughter. You are next.' The old woman's fingers tangled in Naomi's hair and tightened around her skull.

After a while Naomi whispered, though she didn't want to, 'I have to go. I have to go there, Mama,' and the old woman nodded.

Chapter 12

When Rebecca got to work that morning, two cars with state license plates were parked in the parking lot, and the discoloration on the side of the building was clearly visible from the street, undulations in the stain indicating where the water level had risen and fallen more than a few times. How was it possible that nobody had noticed this before?

Already on edge from interrupted sleep, Rebecca was dizzied and nauseated by the adrenaline that shot through her, but she couldn't allow herself time to calm down. Hastily she gathered her things, got out of the car, slammed the door, then realized she'd forgotten the yellow pad with hand-scrawled drafts of half a dozen letters to be typed and mailed today. She fumbled with her key in the lock again and reached across the seat for the pad, struggling not to drop everything else in the process and to keep her feet from slipping out from under her on the frosty asphalt.

'Hi, Princess!' Gordon called, beaming. He was sitting on the porch with his puppy in his lap, a cigarette in his hand, and butts scattered around his feet. She didn't see the usual paper bag. His thin trousers and sweater were pockmarked with burns; his suspenders were twisted over a dirty undershirt; a toe or two stuck through his tattered slippers. 'I missed you since yesterday.'

'Morning, Gordon. Aren't you cold?'

'Nah. I sure do like my dog.'

'I do, too.' She hastened up the walk. 'Who's here?'

'Big shots.'

'Surveyors? Health Department surveyors?'

'They didn't say who they was to me. Just walked right in like they owned the joint.'

'Shit,' said Rebecca, not quite under her breath, and Gordon chuckled appreciatively.

'Do you think my dog's pretty?'

'*Yes*, Gordon,' she snapped, then was instantly sorry for her impatience and tried to soften it with, 'I think he's beautiful.'

'He thinks the same about you.'

'Tell him thanks.' Working one hand free, she managed to open the door, then stopped and looked back at Gordon. 'Listen, old buddy, could you do me a favor? Could you spruce up a little? Shower and shave and put on that sexy shirt I bought you and find pants that don't have quite so many holes and put on real shoes. And if you're going to be outside, please wear a coat so they don't think we're abusing you, okay?'

'Sure, Princess.' He saluted. 'Anything for my Princess.'

'I guess you'd better make your pup stay outside today, too.'

'It's cold!' he protested, hugging the squealing pup.

'He has a house. He'll be fine.'

'He stays with me,' Gordon said, lower lip comically stuck out but brow furrowed dangerously.

'Come on. We're being surveyed. Help me out here.'

'Fuck 'em,' he said, thick-tongued. 'This ain't *their* home, man.'

Holiday decorations were no match for the overall bright white institutional feel of the place, and Rebecca would have found that depressing, even tragic, if she'd had time to register it. But the spots of color and good cheer – paper snowflakes, red velvet bows on evergreen wreaths, walnuts for some obscure reason painted and glued to look like strawberries – could be said to suggest a certain perkiness. Rebecca wound her way through another Cub Scout troop lining up in the hall, one of the onslaught of carolling groups that Colleen had to start scheduling right after Thanksgiving in order to fit them all in before the Christmas holidays were over.

'I don't know what I was thinking of,' Colleen greeted her, frazzled, hair wilder than ever and hands full of decorations and wrapping paper. 'Trying to combine the Christmas party and Beatrice's birthday party. It was her idea – she said she was a Christmas baby and her birthday was always part of Christmas, and I thought it would be easier. Hah. I am losing my mind here. No doubt about it. Save me a bed.'

'No problem there,' Rebecca said wryly, and Colleen laughed. 'You didn't expect to have to deal with the Health Department at the same time. Have they been giving you a hard time?'

Colleen patted her shoulder with the back of a hand full of bows. 'Not bad. Don't worry about it. Go enjoy yourself. Dance. The band's pretty good. It's Mark from housekeeping and some of his buddies. They call themselves Making the Mark. I don't know, but I think that's supposed to be suggestive. There's nothing you can do about the Health Department anyway. They'll find whatever they find.'

The band began 'Sentimental Journey,' and Gordon

pulled her onto the dance floor. He smelled, but only faintly, of booze. 'How do I look, Princess?'

'Better.'

He pushed her away a little and scowled down at her. 'I changed just for you.'

'You look terrific, Gordon. Thank you.' His red velour shirt, stained and stretched out of shape, puffed out over his belly and didn't quite reach the top of his pants, but it was better than anything else she'd seen him wear. His shoes had no laces, but they also had no large holes. Rebecca meant to give him a quick hug; he held her too close.

Over his shoulder she saw Ernest Lindgren moving among the crowd, clipboard in one hand and a plastic cup of Christmas punch in the other. She should go talk to him.

But Gordon, sensing that he was about to lose her attention, led her in a sudden intricate series of turns and dips and whispered in her ear, 'You're sweet, Princess.'

'I bet you say that to all the girls.'

'Love me?'

'Sure.'

He looked at her gravely. 'Do you really? Love me?'

She stood on tiptoe and kissed his whiskered cheek. 'You know I do.'

After a moment his big odoriferous body moved in time to the music again, but his face was baby-solemn and his feet shuffled worriedly. 'How come the big shots are here all the time, Princess? Is it because of my dog?'

Firmly, she said, 'Your dog is fine.'

He nodded. When the music stopped he wouldn't let her go until Colleen called him to try on the Santa Claus suit.

Catching sight of her parents on the other side of the lobby, she detoured to say hello. They looked like Jack Spratt and his wife, her father wispy, her mother big and solid. Her father was staring at the mural, lost, she supposed, among the colors and forms of it, or in some other reality it might or might not have occasioned. 'Merry Christmas,' she said to them both.

Her mother hardly answered, a curt 'Merry Christmas' all she could bring herself to say.

Her father's attention swung ponderously in her direction, missed, passed over her, traveled back. 'Thank you very much,' he said, gentlemanly, speaking to a stranger. 'I wish you the same.'

'Qué Sera Sera,' the band began, and Rebecca was dangerously moved. Someone used to sing that song to her; could it have been her father? The impulse to ask him to dance with her – hold him in her arms, sing to him – was strong, but she was afraid of such tenderness between them, couldn't do it. 'Can I get you some punch?' she hastily asked her mother instead.

'No, thank you. We'll have lunch soon.' Rebecca nodded, relieved and disappointed, and moved away.

The nursing surveyor, a small grim-faced woman named Odette McAleer, sat behind the Wing 1 nurses' station, with Diane standing stiffly beside her. 'Good morning, Odette,' Rebecca greeted her, trying for geniality.

Without looking up Odette slid her billfold across the desk for Rebecca to see her state ID. 'Morning.'

'Are they taking good care of you? Are you finding everything you need? Can I get you a cup of coffee?' To her own ears Rebecca sounded obsequious.

'You don't need to be taking care of us. You need to be

taking care of the patients. Which you're not.'

'I beg your pardon?'

The surveyor shook her head in obvious distaste. She turned all the way around in her chair to inspect the clock on the wall. 'I must say I am surprised to see you here so early. I wasn't expecting you before ten or ten-thirty.'

'What?' Rebecca looked at Diane, who met her gaze.

The surveyor had turned back to the charts and continued flipping through pages and making notes as she talked. 'You do understand that regulations require a full-time administrator.'

'Odette, I was here until after eleven last night and on the phone about this place in the middle of the night.' Rebecca was furious.

'And look at that.' The surveyor indicated Trudy going by in her wheelchair like a model on a runway, waving and smiling and throwing kisses. Trudy wore a brilliant green kimono splashed with huge cerise flowers, and her face scintillated with makeup, vivid spots of rouge on her cheeks, lipstick extending inches beyond the outlines of her mouth. 'It's disgraceful to allow her to look like that. These people have the right to be treated with dignity.'

'She does it herself,' Rebecca began.

'Your job is to take care of her. She looks ridiculous.' The old woman slowly passed the nurses' station, smiling and waving in slow motion, and Rebecca couldn't tell whether she'd heard or not. The surveyor's eyes followed her until she had turned the corner. Then McAleer shrugged and went back to her charts.

Dismissed, Rebecca went into the bookkeeper's office for her usual morning cup of coffee from the pot behind the desk and her usual very detailed account from Sandy of what to expect from the day, from the month, and from life itself. 'Rebecca!' The instant she came into the office Sandy was on her feet, pouring coffee, stirring in cream. Rebecca would have liked to be pleased by all this solicitousness; instead, it never failed to bring her guard up. 'Am I glad to see you!'

'Why?' Rebecca asked warily.

'The survey team showed up at eight o'clock this morning and nobody knew where you were.'

'I was at home. In bed.' Rebecca took a sip of coffee before she added, unwillingly, 'I was here late again last night and on the phone in the middle of the night, so I decided to sleep in a little.'

'Shut the door,' Sandy said in a stage whisper.

Rebecca got up and shut the door.

'You'll never guess what just happened.'

'Lord.'

Sandy loved a good story. She sat down on the edge of her desk. 'You know how Petra and I always split Cokes? Well, she just gave me some with Thorazine in it.'

Rebecca's eyes widened. 'Jesus, Sandy, how do you feel?'

'A little foggy. I didn't get much. You can taste it, you know. She said you always say it's good for *her*.'

'Are you sure you're all right? Did you call your doctor?'

'I'm fine.' Sandy laughed merrily. 'Maybe I'm even better than normal now, huh?'

Rebecca passed a cold hand over her eyes. 'Do me a favor, Sandy. Don't mention this to the surveyors.' Saying that made her feel tacky, but she waited for Sandy's assent.

Ernest Lindgren came in without knocking. 'There you are, Rebecca,' he said cordially, but his tone was brittle. To Sandy, 'I could sure use another cup of that good coffee, if you don't mind. And, Rebecca, I need your policy book.'

Sandy rushed to pour him another cup of coffee, stirring in sugar and cream as if she had been waiting on him a long time. Rebecca groaned. 'The policy book is at the printer's. We've been working on it for months, and I had somebody in your office review it, and it's supposed to be ready today. Sandy, would you go get it?'

'Sure. I can always do this work at home,' Sandy said without a trace of sarcasm, demurely handing the surveyor his coffee and smiling up at him.

'You don't need to do that.' Rebecca knew this was not the response Sandy wanted. 'This is supposed to be a forty-hour-a-week job.'

Lindgren gave a huge sigh. 'You mean that's the only copy of the policy book you have?'

'It's being printed. We're getting five complete copies,' Rebecca said watchfully.

'And what does the facility run on while that book is being printed?' Luckily, he didn't appear to expect a reply. He took his coffee and went away.

'Poor Ernie,' Sandy sighed. 'You heard about his daughter.' Rebecca shook her head. Sandy nodded knowingly. 'She disappeared. About a month ago. Not a sign.'

'Oh, God.'

'Poor Ernie. I don't see how he can work. I guess we take his mind off his own troubles.' She giggled.

Ernest Lindgren saw his daughter everywhere. On a street corner on his way to The Tides this morning; he'd had to go around the block and pull over and talk to the young woman, who'd been downright hostile, to make sure it wasn't Kim. In the window of a passing city bus last night, late, when he'd been out all but hopelessly searching for her, as had become his nighttime habit. He'd flagged the bus down, and it had been empty except for the sympathetic driver, a young woman who, fleetingly, he'd thought might be his daughter in imperfect disguise. In the background crowd of a local TV news shot; the station had finally provided him with the name of the photographer, but the man had not been very cooperative. So far, all his sightings had been false, but he couldn't afford to ignore any of them, because he knew as much about where Kim was as anyone, which was nothing.

So now, when he heard her voice in the dining room of The Tides, he didn't think twice about investigating. It wasn't Kim, of course; the figure he was sure he saw turned out to be only a blur of reflections from windows and overhead lights off floor and tabletops and stainless-steel fixtures. He wasn't even disappointed anymore. In a way, he welcomed the deceptions, since they gave him something to do for Kim. Now that he was in the area, he flipped his survey sheet to the Food Services section and started his part of the inspection there. Already he could tell that this was going to be a long day, and that, for him, was just as well.

It was Beatrice Quinn's ninetieth birthday, and she was giving things away. Her granddaughter Mary Alice had brought items from her house as instructed. It had made her teary to pack up her grandmother's things, and she'd had to rent a U-Haul, but she was relieved that, finally, the house would be closed up and there'd be no more talk of going home. No need, either, for the chemical or physical restraints legally allowed by the mental health workers' determination of her incompetence; Mary Alice would have hated to see her grandmother sedated or tied down, but it would have been better than having her trying to go home all the time.

Beatrice reached out a hand in no particular direction and held up a shoebox. The lid slipped off and a few curled photographs fluttered out. 'These are pictures of my family,' she announced. 'Colleen. Mary Alice. Come here, girls.'

The Activity Director made her way through the crowd, and the granddaughter moved closer, looking anxious and already hurt.

'Some of these pictures are to stay in the family,' Beatrice told them. 'Some of them are to stay here. We'll frame them and put them up on the walls, don't you know. I always thought that big wedding picture of Great-Aunt Nan and Great-Uncle Charles would look fine over the fireplace there.'

Colleen frowned. 'But, Beatrice, what about everybody else?'

'We talked about it at Resident Council, little lady,' shouted Dexter. 'Don't you worry your pretty little head about it. We're all for it. Some of us don't have family, let alone family pictures.'

'But they won't mean anything to anybody else,' Colleen persisted.

'Sure they will. Not what they mean to her, maybe, but I'm ninety-two years old and I bet I can come up with something.'

'This lamp is for Mr Marek.' Beatrice indicated a rickety floor lamp with a stained satiny shade and a tassle on the pull cord. 'For all the nights he stays up so late, don't you know. It was a wedding present to Mr Quinn and myself, so you treat it with respect, you hear me, Mr Marek?' Rebecca thought the old voice, already rough with age, broke.

'Are you sure you want to part with that?' Mary Alice asked.

Beatrice looked at her. 'It's only a lamp, my dear.'

Gordon had obviously been drinking since Rebecca had danced with him; her heart sank as she watched him prance around the piles and boxes of Beatrice's belongings, snapping his fingers and singing. He stopped more or less in front of Beatrice, bent unsteadily, and nuzzled her ear. Her small white hands went up to either side of his dark head and she held him there for a moment, saying something to him that no one else could hear. When she let him go he almost fell, but steadied himself enough to bow to her. Head cocked, he fingered the ridged brass pole of his lamp as if calling a tune out of it, then carried it off, weaving, the cord trailing dangerously between his feet.

Two men Rebecca hadn't seen before appeared at the edge of the crowded room. Black, conservatively dressed, one with a briefcase. More surveyors, Rebecca thought tiredly, and didn't get up to go to them although she should have. She saw Lisa greet them, then turn to scan the room. Rebecca hoped they were not looking for her, but if they were she wouldn't be hard to find.

When Sandy burst breathlessly into the conference room, arms laden with policy book pages in white sacks from the copy place, Ernest Lindgren was standing at the windows that looked out over the back field. His hands were clasped behind him; she could see how hard the fingers were gripping each other. His shoulders were tense, and he seemed to be staring at something. Sandy stood on tiptoe for a minute to see if she could see what it was, but the empty field looked the same as it always did, desolate, neglected and sort of a mess, scooped out in the middle.

She dropped the copies onto the table, careful not to

spill them or mix them up, and said to him in her most cheerful voice, which was pretty cheerful, 'Here you go, Ernie. Better you than me. Can I bring you another cup of coffee? Looks to me like you'll need it.'

He didn't seem to hear her at first. Worrying about his missing daughter, she guessed; poor Ernie. If it was her, she'd be just beside herself. She marveled that he was so calm. She repeated her offer, and this time he shook his head. 'Not right now, thanks.'

Now Sandy didn't know what to do. Was she supposed to stay and go through the policies with him? Wasn't that Rebecca's job? Should she offer him a Coke or something? Thinking about Petra's Thorazine, she put a hand over her mouth to keep from chuckling aloud. That had been kind of an adventure, actually, a great story, especially since nothing bad had happened. She was really tempted to tell it to Ernie. He wasn't a bad guy. She bet he'd think it was funny.

She stood there uncertainly for a minute longer, then said, 'Call me if you need anything. Coffee or anything.' He might have nodded. Sandy shrugged and left. She had work to do, and she wouldn't mind going to the party for a little while.

Lindgren stirred himself. He'd caught a glimpse of movement out the window, but when he'd got up from the chair where he'd been waiting, with growing impatience, for the policies, which should have been bound in an orderly fashion for him to review, he'd been able to see nothing in the field outside. He could not imagine why approval had ever been given to construct a long-term care facility on the shores of a lake in the first place, and he could not imagine why the owners didn't do something with that unkempt field. This girl, this Rebecca, was way over her head. Kim, in any of her manifestations, was not out there, though he had thought she was. Sighing, he slid a stack of pages out of the nearest sack, and set to work.

Something was different about the mural.

Rebecca stood and wended her way among people, packages, chairs to the back wall of the lobby where the mural, her first major project at The Tides and still a source of considerable pride, was the first thing you saw when you came in the front door. Something had changed about it, and before she got there she had realized what it was.

Someone had painted tiny faces here and there among the other designs, versions of the same face, round, blue-eyed, with shoulder-length blonde curls. One of the faces slid, disembodied, down the lightning bolt Paul had scrawled in yellow paint. Another had been superimposed onto one of Beatrice's impressionistic flowers. Another peeked out from between two points of the biggest of Petra's stars.

She put her fingertips to the wall, drew them across the new paint. It was still tacky. Then she saw that it was not only faces; other body parts, too, had been added – hands with long pearl-pink and crimson and bright black polished nails; legs with pretty rounded knees, some bare and some with fancy stockinged designs; graceful mounds that could only be breasts with brown areoles at their peaked centers.

'Looks just like you, Princess.' Rebecca swung around, ready to be incensed, certain Gordon was being lewd. But he was admiring one of the perfect little faces, this one at the heart of the rayed sun Bob had slopped into the high corner, and when she followed his gaze she was shocked by how much it did, in fact, resemble photographs of herself, although she couldn't have said for sure that it looked like *her* because, outside of mirrors and photos, she had no real sense of what she looked like. 'Who did this?'

'I don't know. Wasn't me. I thought you knew.'

'How come you're not Santa Claus? You haven't backed out, have you?'

'Suit's too tight. She's gotta sew it.'

Rebecca patted Gordon's belly. 'Poor Colleen. Just what she needs.'

'Dad?'

Gordon didn't respond to the hesitant voice from beside him; just another communication that didn't concern him. But Rebecca looked past him and saw the two black men she'd thought were more surveyors, with Lisa smiling and reaching for Gordon's arm.

'Gordon,' the social worker fairly crowed. 'Look who came to see you.'

Ponderously Gordon turned his bulk in their direction. He was beaming at the prospect of company and saying, 'Hi, there,' before he had seen who it was. When he did, though, he just said, 'Hi, there,' again, with no change in inflection or emphasis.

'Dad, it's Robert and James.'

'Your sons,' Lisa added helpfully.

'Hi, there,' Gordon repeated.

Rebecca saw Dan stride into the lobby, followed by Odette McAleer, and for the first time noticed that the party was blocking a fire exit. Readying her notebook, McAleer said to Dan, 'You know, just once, I'd like to find this place looking like a nursing home.'

'It's her birthday, little lady,' Dexter hollered. 'She's giving things away. She's not but ninety, nothing but a kid. Me, I'm ninety-two years old. Do you believe that?'

'I hope,' said McAleer, 'a lawyer has been consulted.'

Beatrice hadn't seen them. She was thumbing through a stack of magazines and books in her lap. At her feet were half a dozen more boxes, their sides bulging with *Saturday Evening Posts*, *Reader's Digests*, comic books. 'From my comic-book phase, don't you know. We'll put all of these in our library.'

'We don't have a library,' Colleen pointed out.

'Then,' said Beatrice, 'it's high time we did.'

'Beatrice,' said Colleen, 'these old comic books are worth a fortune. You should sell them to a collector.'

'Nonsense.' Beatrice squinted straight at the visitors by the door, and Rebecca wondered if she'd known they were there all along. 'It's my birthday. On your birthday you may give anything to anyone you choose, and they may not refuse. Because you're giving of yourself, don't you know.'

'It's highly improper,' Odette McAleer declared, 'for a facility or any of its employees to accept a gift from a resident. The regulations specifically prohibit gratuities.'

'Hell, little lady, they ain't gratuities,' Dexter informed her. 'They ain't even what you'd call gifts. She's putting her house in order.'

The pages of the policy book had not been collated, and Ernest Lindgren could not make head or tail of it. He'd managed to find a few policies – *Infection Control: Nursing* wasn't in bad shape, but the *Personnel Policies* section, as far as he could determine, needed a lot of work, and he couldn't find *Admission and Discharge* at all. He was close to giving up and declaring the entire Policies and Procedures Condition out of compliance when his daughter Kim appeared at the window.

He capped his pen and inserted it into the holder in his inside pocket. He closed his notebook and put it into his briefcase. He locked the case. He stood up. 'Kim?' he said aloud, to fix her there. She floated in the window, beckoned to him, receded.

In all likelihood, she was not actually there. He would discover a nursing-home patient outside the window, or no one at all. But he would investigate. Searching for Kim was in his basic nature by now. He found the back door unlocked, a safety violation but to his personal advantage at the moment, and let himself out.

Dan said grimly, 'Odette wants to show us something,' and Rebecca accompanied them into Dexter's room.

'Look at this, Dan. You know better than this.' McAleer was striding around the room, back straight and face set, fists in the pockets of her suit jacket. Somehow, the fact that she wasn't taking notes now seemed ominous. 'Take a look at those windows. You can barely see through them.'

'I can see through them fine, little lady,' Dexter protested from the doorway. 'I'm ninety-two years old and I can see through them just fine. Got a birdfeeder out there, see it? Birds come. Jays.'

'Dexter,' Rebecca asked him in a daring undertone, 'when are you going to be ninety-three?'

'Next month, little lady, the fifth of the month.'

'Good.' He looked baffled. Rebecca just shook her head.

McAleer went into the bathroom. Dan followed her and Dexter motioned impatiently for Rebecca to push him in, too. 'Look at this. Clothes all over the floor. An open toothpaste tube on the sink. A dirty washcloth wadded up on the back of the toilet. This is against any commonsense standards of cleanliness, let alone infection-control regulations.'

'I can't reach things if they put them away,' Dexter

shouted. 'If they put things away like that I have to get somebody to help me all the time.' Nobody acknowledged that he'd spoken.

McAleer pushed past him to get out of the bathroom. 'Look at the accumulation of dust on the horizontal surfaces. This room hasn't been thoroughly cleaned in weeks. I'm surprised at you, Dan. We have had our differences, but I never expected to find one of your facilities in this shape.' She ran her hand along the window sill, peered with disgust at the dust on her fingers, and wiped it off on the sleeve of Dan's custom-tailored white shirt.

Ernest Lindgren was a big, bulky man, and he had arthritis in both knees, so when the lake-bed slope began he was almost at once in considerable pain. It was cold, and he'd left his topcoat on the back of the chair in the conference room, there not having been a coat-rack, but he was still wearing his black wool stocking cap, which he often didn't take off indoors because his bald head got cold easily. He hadn't seen or heard his daughter since he'd come out here, and he told himself this was probably another false lead.

But he had a feeling this time that he hadn't had before, an intuition as strong and specific as a personal message. Kim was somewhere close by.

He hadn't spent much time with any of his children since the divorce when Kim was – what? – nine or ten years old. Two weeks in the summer, until they'd started having better things to do; every other Christmas, until they'd wanted to stay home with their friends. His life had been uncomplicated, unburdensome, not noticeably lonely but flat. In a way that took him by surprise, he felt closer to this vanished daughter than when the distance between them had been more ordinary; his desperation and determination to find her allowed her more points of entry.

As slowly and painfully he let himself down the incline, he actually could feel her inside him, begging him, daring him on. It might not even be Kim poking around in there; he knew full well that she was probably as distant as she'd ever been, as unwilling to supply him with substance.

But the scent of her rose perfume filled his head, made him giddy. He'd had no way of knowing Kim was wearing rose perfume these days, but it seemed to suit her. It lapped up around him like a rising tide, coming to meet him rather than insisting that he enter it. It took him in. It was not Kim.

At the end of Wing 2, the Life Safety Code surveyor was busy sawing a hole in the ceiling. Rebecca gaped. 'Just checking to see if your fire wall goes all the way up through the attic,' he called.

'As far as I know nobody's ever asked about fire walls before.'

'This is the first time I've surveyed here,' he answered with satisfaction. 'Regulations require that the fire wall go all the way to the roof. There's no access hole, so I'm making one.'

Rebecca stood helplessly as plaster dust spattered down around her, pocking the high finish on the floor. The saw stopped.

'Well,' said the surveyor, climbing down and dusting off his hands. 'It's just as I thought. Your fire wall stops at the ceiling. You'll have to rectify that throughout the building.' He nodded pleasantly to her and went off to write it up, folding the ladder against the wall but leaving the pile of debris on the floor and the gaping hole in the ceiling.

'Are you aware,' demanded Odette McAleer without prelude, rounding the corner from the Wing 1 corridor with Dan in her wake, 'that you have dog feces in this building?'

'No, I wasn't. Where?'

'In the soiled utility room. Fecal material is a rich breeding ground for all kinds of bacteria. I'm sure you're aware of that.'

Rebecca's face was hot. 'I'm sorry. I'll get a house-keeper on it right away.' She did not look at Dan. 'The puppy belongs to one of our residents.'

'The puppy must go.'

Rebecca started to protest, but Sandy's urgent call came over the intercom. 'Rebecca to the basement stat, please. Rebecca to the basement stat.'

She stood at the top of the basement stairs with the Environmental and Life Safety surveyors behind her and stared in horror at the three-inch-deep water covering the basement floor. A plastic sack of Styrofoam cups floated past, and the water seemed to be rising. 'My God!' she breathed. 'Where's it coming from?'

'Somebody called me here a few minutes ago,' the Life Safety surveyor told her. 'A woman. Asked for me by name, I understand. Told me to go look in the basement and then hung up. It was the strangest thing.'

'You know we'll have to run tests on this water to make sure it's not contaminated,' the Environmental Specialist was telling her. 'You know you can't use anything stored down here until we get the results of the tests. You know—'

But Rebecca had seen something on the other side of the dim basement, and she stripped off her shoes and socks and waded into the cold water. Voices burbled in protest behind her, Dan's among them, but she ignored them. Almost as soon as she stepped into it, the water receded, so that she was walking on exposed wet concrete. Cold traveled up through the soles of her feet, making her ankles and shins ache.

Dave half-sat, half-lay against the basement wall. The rough rectangle of his face, between shaggy dark hair and dark beard, was slack. His eyes seemed to be on her, but when she came close, crouched in front of him, spoke his name, she saw that they were utterly vacant. He was breathing. She took his forearm where it lay across his thigh; the flesh below the rolled-up sleeve of the blue-plaid flannel shirt was very slightly warm, and there was a fluttering pulse, but he did not respond to the pressure of her hand. O.D., she thought.

But in the seconds before the others got to her, she saw movement and a flash of variegated color farther back in the corner behind Dave; she smelled the alluring scent of roses; she heard her name, and Rebecca was fleetingly, fiercely tempted to stay down there, to answer, 'Yes!' and not to summon the others at all.

Chapter 13

Faye was bored.

Faye had often been bored, but she never let it last long. More than anything, she loathed being bored. It was her right to be amused. When Faye got bored, she got dangerous.

She knew what to do to keep herself amused. Arrange herself, get herself together, put on her face, get dressed. She didn't have patience for anything drawn-out, but there were a few things she had to do to get ready, and sometimes the preparations themselves turned out to be fun.

To keep herself occupied while she was getting ready, Faye sang a little song, danced a little dance, flitted in and out of people's lives even though she wasn't much interested. It was the flitting that she liked, and the way heads and hearts turned.

Practically anyplace could be her playground, but The Tides was handy, all these pocked and disintegrating personalities under one roof like candies in a box, here and there somebody wide open and ready for her to move in. They couldn't hold her interest for long, but they would do as distractions while she got ready for her big play. Just the thought of it animated her, which she knew added to her charm.

She didn't waste time fretting over the ones she couldn't get into. Petra Carrasco, for instance, who was shut up tight and full to bursting. Alexander Booth; she'd thought he'd be an easy mark, and she'd thought she had him. His loss.

She zipped into Beatrice Quinn and whispered inside her head that she could go home any time she pleased, even if she didn't know where home was anymore, even if there was no home. She made up fantasies for Abby Wilkins that showed her the zany things you could do with a man whose body had no feeling. She grabbed Trudy Belker's hand and helped her paint a lipstick grin like a rictus, like a slashed throat, from one ear to the other.

It passed the time. It built up her strength. But she was restless and bored, and she wouldn't wait much longer.

Ira Goldberg, on his way to a business meeting, stopped by his daughter's house. Danny had said she was behaving strangely, even for her, and Ira thought he ought to assess her condition himself, he was her father and a physician, but he did not want to. He was afraid.

Naomi, well on her urgent way to The Tides without knowing why, was not at home to his knock. Ira had a key; he let himself in. It appeared that she had not been at her home all day; Danny had said as much, nice home though it was. Something about her empty house disturbed her father in a profound, hidden way, as if at the back of his soul.

When he left he locked the door again carefully, went back three times to make sure it was locked, not to be the one responsible for allowing intruders in. The last time, he left the Cadillac running in the street while he hurried back up the steps and down one more time, which was asking for trouble but none in that form came. Slightly short of breath, not a good sign in a man his age but what could you expect, Ira sat behind the wheel to collect himself, and could not escape the linked series of things he unwillingly knew. He knew where Naomi would be. He knew he had time before his meeting. He knew it was his duty to go to her, and that he would, and that he did not want to. He did not want to encounter whatever was wrong with Naomi. He did not want to go into a nursing home more than his usual two times a year.

'Good morning!' he called to the girl who was much too young and naive and unmanageable to run a facility. He did not know what Danny saw in her, or maybe he did. 'I hope you enjoyed your holidays?'

For a split second, Rebecca actually didn't understand the reference. She'd worked Christmas, for it was one of the loneliest days of a lonely year for many of her residents, and staffing was skeletal. New Year's Eve she and Kurt had been home together, but she'd spent the evening at the kitchen table doing year-end reports for the Health Department, Medicaid, Medicare, and the management company while Kurt watched TV. At midnight he wandered out, kissed the top of her head, and went to bed before she could rouse herself to respond in more than a cursory way. She hadn't meant to be rude.

She'd worked all night, and before dawn – no snow, nothing to mask the harsh outlines of the New Year except the blur of her own agitation and fatigue, no sense of anything new but only of processes begun long ago steadily gathering momentum – she'd driven out to The Tides. She'd hardly known what she was doing. She'd parked at the far western edge of the field and stepped in as if she were plunging into the sea.

When the other surveyors had declared themselves

finished for the day – they'd be back tomorrow; they had much more to do – Ernest Lindgren had not been among them. His topcoat had still been in the conference room, draped over the back of a chair with its sleeves brushing the floor, and his briefcase against the wall. The uncollated pages of the policy book he'd removed from their sacks had by this time drifted across the table, some of them onto the seats of chairs or, further, onto the floor. His notes were plainly visible; he'd written *Condition Out of Compliance*, his small neat cursive suggesting no more emphasis than any other comment, less than halfway down the survey report form. Seeing that, before McAleer turned the form over and slid it into her own briefcase, Rebecca had felt her stomach burn.

Lindgren appeared to have left the facility. Sandy paged him half a dozen times, and there was a minimal search. The Life Safety Inspector walked around outside, went a short distance down into the field, shouted, found nothing.

Eyes gleaming with knowledge she was not supposed to have, Sandy said to the nursing surveyor, 'You don't suppose he went off looking for his daughter?'

McAleer regarded her impassively. 'That seems unlikely.'

'I don't know,' Sandy said eagerly. 'I don't know, Odette; if it was me I wouldn't be doing a thing else, would you?' The surveyor did not reply. Sandy said, hopefully, 'Poor Ernie,' but this got no response, either.

There'd been calls back to the main office, consultations among the surveyors, and finally they'd all left, Odette McAleer driving alone in one of the state cars. When they'd returned the next morning, another administrative surveyor had been on the team. Sandy, of course, had asked about Ernie, and had been told, somewhat grudgingly, that a Missing Person Report had been filed.

As the New Year's sun had begun to glisten behind the cityscape to the east, a cold clear yellow, setting The Tides in featureless relief, Rebecca had crunched across frosty weeds and frozen uneven ground until she'd felt the downward tug of the old lake-bed. Shadows still shimmered in the bowl like a nest of venomous scarves, a strange metallic gray, and Rebecca had been intensely reluctant to go into them even as she hadn't been able to stop herself.

The serpentine scarves wound around her legs. The shadows rose and then fell back. The ground gave way, or her feet skidded out from under her, and she cried out as she slid down the slope.

Her right hand, scrabbling for purchase, encountered something rough and wet, and when she snatched her hand away the object came with it. It smelled of wet wool and roses. It was Ernest Lindgren's stocking cap.

Reflexively, she flung the thing away from her. It sailed cumbersomely into the deeper, writhing, dancing shadows farther down the slope, in what she hoped, as she went down after it, was the bottom of the lake-bed. It took her a long time to get to it and longer to crawl back out of the depression, slippery as its sides were from frost and frozen mud.

She was dirty and wet and cold, shaken, when she got back to her car, and the cap beside her on the seat was actively repulsive, but she'd done what she'd presumed to be her duty and taken it to the police station to turn it in. They hadn't seemed to know at first what she was talking about, and she'd wondered if a Missing Person Report hadn't been filed after all, but finally the Sergeant on duty had apparently found something in his records, because he'd taken the cap from her.

She'd spent much of the rest of New Year's Day working outside the facility, bagging up trash, sweeping the porch, scrubbing with almost total lack of effect at the water marks on the side of the building, which in some places were waist-high now. Sometime in the cold afternoon, Kurt had showed up, and she'd agreed to go home, where she'd taken a hot bath and gone to bed and slept soundly until the next morning when it was time to go back to work.

'Happy New Year,' she said now to Ira Goldberg in return, but he had seen his daughter coming into the facility just behind him and had turned to intercept her.

Naomi was thinking: Unless you looked closely you would barely recognize them as human. If you got close enough, their humanness assaulted you – their odor, their bones, their fear.

Nobody wanted to get that close. Not examiners, or experimenters, or caretakers, or chroniclers, or visitors, or loved ones, or executioners. Not those who remembered or those who had only to look a little ahead.

It seemed to Naomi that they didn't even want to look at each other: Myra's eyes had been flat and glazed; Paul's spasms prevented him from focusing on anything; her father's eyes were, at this very moment and ever since she had first looked for them, hooded in shadow and shame.

She got her father another cup of coffee from the spotted stainless-steel urn and set it in front of him, plastic on plastic making a dull click. He sat in the overlapping discs of light from the overhead fixtures, his pipe sending trails of smoke up over his smoky hair, his wrists thin past the sleeves of his suit coat. She looked away lest she glimpse the labeled white flesh of his forearm.

She'd never known what numbers his were. She

dropped her gaze to her own anonymous arm, traced numbers there. Numbers that had pretended to identify but had in fact leached identity away. 'Papa,' she said.

He drew on his pipe. He was letting his coffee get cold. 'Naomi,' he said, acknowledging her by name, and her heart swelled painfully in gratitude. 'Daughter,' acknowledging her by rank.

It would not be enough. Naomi drained more coffee into her own cup; there was very little left in the urn, and it trickled thick and bitter. Her stomach churned at the sight and odor of it, and she was remembering Myra, murdering Myra, though nothing in this moment was reminiscent of either victim or act. Briefly she closed her eyes. There would be no more coffee for her father now because she'd taken the last of it for herself.

'You don't look good, Naomi.' To her relief he was sipping his coffee now. 'Your mother worries. Your husband worries.'

'I'm all right. I'm just tired.'

'You don't sleep good?' His white eyebrows jumped. 'I give you something.'

'No. Papa, it's all right. There's just so much to be done here.' She spread her hands to indicate the dining room and the whole of The Tides, then, feeling exposed, folded her hands back in against her waist.

'A person must sleep.'

'I have dreams, Papa.'

He lowered his eyebrows, drank his coffee, waited for her to go on, for his own sake hoped she would not.

'I have dreams when I'm awake, too,' she said. 'I hear things. I see things. Smell things.' She raised her hands to her face. Behind her eyes she saw bony faces with the flesh stretched taut or the skin draping like cloth, smelled human urine and feces deep in the pores of her skin. She brought her head up and said again, helplessly, 'Please, Papa, I have dreams. But I can't reach them.'

'I give you something,' he said reasonably. 'To make you sleep.'

'She died,' Naomi said. 'I was sitting right beside her and she died and I didn't even know it. No passage. Nothing to mark her passage.' But there had been. A clear passage. An instrument she couldn't deny. She was lying to her father, still, and she couldn't help it.

'You should not be in this place. Your husband should never have allowed it. It is a place of living death.' He lit his pipe again and she watched him, his fingers, his twitching eyebrows, and heard the moaning of the hungry, the weeping and gagging of the sick, the silence of the troughs of the dead. She swallowed hard and waited for her father to say more.

When he did not, she said, 'But you own it. It belongs to you.'

'I came to America after the war. After – the war. To New York City I came, and there was a rabbi, a German Jew. And he said to me, "Lipkowitz owns places to keep the old and the sick, he makes a living, you go there." So I came here. Later I think this rabbi said to people, "Goldberg makes a living. You go there." ' He smiled, then was saying before he had stopped smiling, so that the smile took on a ghoulish aspect, 'When we are no longer here to bear witness, our dead can rest in peace. We know who they were.'

Naomi did not understand him. She bowed her head before him, as she always had. Just this morning – she did not know why the image should rise before her now, in her father's presence – the flesh on Myra Larsen's hip had flaked away like the wood of a rotten stump; it was black, and it stank. They cut off her dead flesh with scissors. Myra screamed, fought with foolish arms and legs. They overpowered her with little effort, did what they had come to do, and left her alone again.

Ira leaned forward out of the overhead light, and for a moment his daughter was afraid of him, too. 'Come work in my office. There I take care of children. Little ones. There we have hope. This other is unclean. You can do nothing here.'

Teeth. Piles of teeth. Sets of grinning teeth on shelves gathering dust. Insects crawling between broken teeth. Flecks of gold in the sunshine. Gaping mouths: pink gums, gray gums, bloody holes and stumps where the teeth should be.

'People suffer here,' she offered.

Bodies everywhere. The stench of bodies. Nakedness shamed. White buttocks spread and closed. Red hands and gray thighs and the yellow soles of feet. Bellies bulging and collapsing. Parts of bodies no longer there: hands and arms and feet and breasts somewhere, rotting, freezing, sliding back into the earth that ought to have been poisoned by all the suffering but was in fact fertilized. Water rising, receding again, depositing some of what had been suspended in it, exposing layers.

Her father scoffed. 'Three meals a day, a warm bed, a roof over their head – this is human suffering? People like you to take care of them?' He relit his pipe; his eyebrows were working dangerously. 'This is not human suffering.'

'You own it,' she said again, knowing that there was something here. 'You make money from it.'

He drew on his pipe. Surely by now, she thought in anguish, his coffee was cold. His eyes glistened with tears.

She was the cause of her father's torment, and for the first time in her life she was able actually to imagine him dirty, starving, cold. Immersed in human filth. Surviving.

'Tell me,' she said, boldly laying her hands on his arm, feeling for his numbers as if they had been Braille, 'Papa, tell me about the camps.' But he could not.

Faye was almost ready, and she had to do *something* to keep from losing her mind, she couldn't abide just hanging around anymore. So she took Marshall for a walk.

He wouldn't have known where to go without her, but she led him, flitting, singing, and (foolishly, he knew; he remembered always telling himself – and to no avail then, either – that he was being foolish when it came to Faye) he trusted her.

'Trust' was an odd word to use in regard to Faye, but the truth was that Marshall had always trusted her. Not to behave well. Not to be reliable or even predictable. Not because of anything trustworthy she did or anything dishonorable she refrained from doing, but because Faye herself inspired him to trust, drew trust out of him, a leap of faith, an expression of himself in relation to her rather than the other way around.

'Come with me, Marshall,' she'd cajoled in that sweet and awful wordless way of hers, and he went – with many second thoughts, to be sure, but he went with her nonetheless. (I'm sorry, Billie, but I had no choice.) His walker clicked erratically on the tiles and his feet still shuffled, but sure and apace, down the long shimmering white hall, around the corner, past the nurses sitting behind the high desk who didn't look up, and out the door. Just like that. He would never have done it on his own. But Faye was with him.

Faye.

Horror geysered through him, nausea, sexual arousal. He had suffered losing Faye, and yet he was not free of her. He had found Billie, who had saved him half a lifetime ago, a steady and reliable woman if there ever was one, a woman he suspected he loved more than he knew, and here he was, following Faye again, and for years he had believed Faye to be safely and tragically dead. Though, of course, he'd never had any evidence; he'd never seen her body or even her grave.

He couldn't quite locate her now. He looked around. He didn't know where he was. He remembered exactly how she used to look, to sound, to feel; that is, his memory was exact and minutely detailed, though it might not really have represented Faye as she'd ever existed beyond his impressions of her.

In his exquisitely clear memory, she was something of a shape-changer: a sprite, a succubus. Fine blonde hair, almost ashen, then red-gold, then blue-black; singing to him lullabies and love songs, shrieking curses, promising, breaking promises, changing reality. Scarves, ribbons, all manner of fluttering things; scarves, makeup, and masks, all manner of things to disguise.

He felt the caress of her hand on his member, the slap of her hand hard across his face. He smelled and – most appalling, most wonderful of all – *tasted* her: sweet, bitter, foul.

'Faye.'

Marshall walked a few steps, ran a few steps, fell. Onto cold ground and wet grass in a place he didn't know, a curved place. Into Faye's arms.

In the parking lot of The Tides, closer and closer to the busy street, Faye rolled Marshall in her whispery arms and told him in the rustle of cold grass and weeds, the *shush* and screech of traffic on wet pavement, the scrabbling of his hands and knees in the gravel and trash at the curb as he tried to get away from her, tried to follow fast enough where she led, 'You are so handsome, Marshall, my handsome man, my lover, you are my best lover.'

He knew not to believe her. He knew she was just talking. He knew she talked like this, kissed him like this, charmed and hurt him in just this combination, because she wanted something. But he had never found it possible to begrudge Faye anything she wanted. His heart was fluttering with love and horror and fear. 'Billie!' he cried, but Billie didn't come. He was lost. Faye was the only one who knew where he was. He was alone with Faye.

He had long ago lost his walker, and when he tried to pull himself upright by clinging to a bus bench, his hands weren't strong enough to clutch the rough cement and wood, and he fell. A car and then another car went by, very close. He felt snow.

'You know,' Faye breathed in his ear, sending chills along his spine, 'I always loved you best.'

'What do you want, Faye?' he cried out. Although his face was in an icy puddle and he could hardly breathe, he could see her, swirls of pretty colors, graceful motion. 'What do you want from me now?'

'I want my daughter.'

'No. She's not yours.'

'I'm going to take my daughter. I need her. I can't live without her anymore.'

'No!'

She left him. Because he had refused her, Faye had left him, and now he was utterly alone in a place he had never been before. Scraped and muddy, his pants stiff with snow and frozen urine, he'd managed to hoist himself up onto the bench, where he sat with his hands clasped tightly between his knees and his head down, trying to think. He was on his way to work, he knew, although he didn't understand why he wasn't carrying a lunch-box or why he wasn't absolutely sure which bus to take; he'd gone this way to work hundreds of times or more.

He heard a bus coming and was flooded with relief. Looking up, squinting, finally making out its slightly frightening gray hulk with stiletto headlights, he lit upon a strategy whose cleverness and resourcefulness gratified him. If this bus stopped here, for him, he would know that it was the right bus, and he would not have to admit that he'd forgotten where he was going. Forgotten who he was for a while there, if truth be told, but he wouldn't have to tell that, either.

The bus stopped. The door opened with a sound unlike the sound doors commonly made when they opened, causing him to fear for a few moments that he'd made some other sort of mistake here (perhaps this was not even a bus).

Marshall lifted his head to smile at the driver, couldn't locate a driver in the dimness at the top of the steps, would not get on a contraption like this. Someone called, 'This is a No. 15, sir. Is that the bus you want?'

Sure then that it was, Marshall got to his feet by pushing off against the pylon of the bench, and then couldn't figure out how to get from there to the bus steps. Frozen in place by fear and confusion, not to mention arthritis, he couldn't think what to say.

'Faye,' he said, and then, more plausibly, 'Billie?'

'Can I help you, sir?' called the driver.

'No,' Marshall said. 'No, thank you,' in a stronger voice. 'I'm just waiting for my wife.'

The driver hesitated. Then she pulled the doors shut and eased the bus back into traffic. While she was waiting at the next red light, she radioed in about the lost old man. She doubted they'd do anything about it, but at least she'd done her duty.

The sleet grew colder and more dense. There were colors in it, red and green and orange from traffic lights, powder blue and pink and lavender and cold silver gray from Faye. Moonlight, he guessed, from behind thick cloud cover, was low, more cloudlight than moonlight, and amber streetlights were coming apart in fluttering bits. Light of all sorts reflected off the moisture on the pavement, wriggling, oozing. Marshall was lost in all the light. Faye hinted at her presence, teased, but would not reveal herself to him now (he had lost her once before and he would be losing her for the rest of his life), and he couldn't find Billie anywhere. He was lost. Nobody knew where he was. Except Faye.

Chapter 14

Gordon threw a rock at Petra, didn't even come close. She grinned at him, stretching her toothless mouth practically from ear to ear. 'Hey, big boy,' she rasped to him, 'there's red ants nesting in my rectum, did you know that?' and Gordon recognized it as an invitation.

He was tempted, but he was too upset, and she disgusted him. Crazy old whore. Shouldn't let whores like that live here with decent people. Shouldn't let whores like that live, period. Sidearm, he threw a pine branch at her. It hit her in the face, and she giggled, but she did turn back, giving up on him for now. Gordon scowled. Maybe he'd been a fool not to take some pussy when he had a chance. It'd been a long time, man. But she kept telling everybody and his brother that there was a nest of red ants down there. How did he know there wasn't?

Anyhow, nooky was the last thing he wanted now. He wanted his puppy. They took his dog. That nurse bitch took his pup away from him. The boss-lady wasn't around. He needed her. He needed to get his dog back.

That was not going to happen. He didn't even know what they'd done with his dog, pink tongue, fat little belly, white ring like a doughnut on top of his head. Gordon had been just about ready to settle on a name. He'd been just about ready to name his puppy Doughnut. Now he couldn't. Once you lost something in this life you couldn't very well name it and you never got it back.

He lumbered down the sidewalk to the street and stopped, turned around to look at the building. Goddamn nursing home. Goddamn prison. He could set it on fire. That'd show 'em. He could punch somebody out. He could kill somebody.

Gordon ground at the tears in his eyes with the dirty knuckles of both big fists and lurched out into the middle of Elm Street, muttering, stumbling and weaving. Anybody watching him would have thought he was drunk, but it was the nineteenth of the month and his check hadn't come yet and Gordon was flat-out sober.

He was filled, though, with something wilder than booze, crazier, a lot more powerful. Rage, for one thing. They took his dog. Raging loneliness. And Faye.

Petra yelled after him, 'Pussy!' Hugging herself with bare arms and the empty sleeves of her filthy pink lace-trimmed cardigan worn over her shoulders and buttoned crooked at the neck, she spun to go back into the building and collided with Beatrice Quinn coming out.

'Oh, my dear,' Beatrice said pleasantly, distractedly. 'I hope I didn't hurt you.'

Petra spat, 'Cunt!'

Beatrice had not heard that word before, but it was clear from the woman's inflection that it was not nice. She smiled firmly and used the bulging paper sacks in her arms to wedge herself past Petra without actually coming into contact with her. 'Excuse me,' she said, minding her manners, but it was not a request.

It was much colder outside than Beatrice had anticipated, but she certainly couldn't go back for a sweater. The porch was unoccupied, thank goodness. Careful not to slip on the damp concrete, she made her way down the ramp, new since this girl had been in charge and Beatrice was grateful, for steps would have been difficult under the present circumstances. There was mist in the air, not quite rain, not quite snow, but her hair and shoulders were getting damp, which wasn't good for her health, and it wouldn't be long before her paper sacks began to weaken. Beatrice was aghast at how many details she had overlooked, never mind how many details she had thought of, repeatedly.

If she'd been able to talk to Dexter about it, he'd have helped her remember things. Even if he hadn't approved of what she was doing, he'd have helped her. But Dexter was gone. They'd taken him away, and it was partly her fault because she'd tattled on him about his hoard of candy, or maybe she ought to have told earlier and then he wouldn't have made himself sick. They wouldn't say so, but she knew she would never see him again.

She stepped along the sidewalk as carefully as she could considering that she didn't have a hand free to grasp the rail. She kept a lookout for cars. Excitement threatened to make her giddy; she calmed herself. Beatrice Quinn was going home, and this time she was taking no chances.

Marshall Emig was going home, too. He didn't know where home was, or even what it was, but he slogged along through cold drizzle that stopped and started and stopped again, between cars that didn't stop, around corners and around corners again. He was driven by a strong if vaguely organized conviction that he would recognize home when he came upon it or it would recognize him. Sometimes he was terrified. Right now, a moment with nothing behind or ahead of it, he was terrified.

A name came to him, and he called it aloud, cupping unsteady hands around unsteady mouth. 'Billie!'

He didn't really expect an answer, but one came. 'No, honey. It's Faye.'

Marshall stopped in his tracks. 'I don't want anything to do with you, Faye,' he announced, not for the first time, to the shimmer of rainwater and memory that presented itself to him. 'You've been out of my life for a long time. That's the way I like it. I thought you were dead. Go away.'

Dancing with Faye. He remembered dancing with Faye. He was dancing with Faye, her long lithe arms lightly around his neck, her hands cupping the back of his head, now and then bringing his head down to kiss him. He was standing alone then – on the dancefloor, on the beach, in their bedroom with the bedclothes still scattered on the floor, on a dark street in dark sleet – and he was watching Faye dance. Faye dancing was beauty and sadness, beauty and truth.

Faye took more and more shape: her ash-blonde hair, her rose perfume, the skin in the hollows of her neck and even on her hands and her heels so soft he was afraid to touch it for fear his touch would roughen it and yet couldn't touch it enough. She danced around him, teasing, pulling her scarves across his face and across his groin, inviting him to dance with her but never showing him how. She'd danced like that in their tiny brown kitchenette, sending off rainbows, irradiating the place, and then she'd left.

As if to the rhythm of music, although he knew perfectly well there was no music, Marshall couldn't help but move his feet. There was impatient noise from somewhere behind him, a car horn, somebody shouting, and he moved too quickly to the inside edge of the sidewalk to get out of the way. He fell. Faye, of course, didn't help him up. She didn't even stay. She flitted over him, more substantial than the mist, kissed the top of his head, and was gone. He'd told her to leave. He wanted nothing more than for her to be gone. He missed her terribly. Missed whom? Was aware only of missing *somebody*, missing *everybody*, of being lost, nobody in the world knowing where he was. He curled up on the pavement, which was warm.

Rebecca and her mother were not far away, but neither they nor Marshall knew that. Rebecca said, 'Was he wearing his I.D. bracelet?'

'I don't know.'

Rebecca didn't say anything. But, peering through the mist on the window, which refracted multicolored globules and streaks of light – traffic lights, headlights and tail-lights, signs, maybe flashlights, maybe searchlights, blue running lights from a cop car she considered hailing to help them look for her father – she allowed herself to roll her eyes in exasperation.

'I should have checked,' her mother snapped. 'It's my fault.'

'It's not your fault,' Rebecca said, not entirely meaning it. 'Hopefully the staff will have checked. Hopefully if somebody finds him they'll think to look at the bracelet.'

Billie leaned forward and pointed and said, 'There!' then, 'Oh. No.' And sat back. Rebecca looked where she had pointed and saw the man she'd mistaken for Marshall, an old man, to be sure, but much taller and sturdier, striding along confidently, probably enjoying his walk, probably knowing exactly where he was going. She couldn't believe her mother had thought that was her father, even for a second, even with the mounting pressure of needing to find him. Trick of the light, trick of the desperate imagination, but that was no excuse: As if they could pull any old man out of the twilight, rescue any old man whether he needed rescuing or not, and he would be her father, they would have done their duty by her father. How could you be married to a man for all these years and ever mistake somebody else for him? You'd think that marriage, of all things, would make you sure who somebody was.

The windshield wipers spread liquid light across her field of vision, and suddenly she remembered. Lost in the woods behind the house she'd grown up in, mist like this, dripping colors and colorlessness like this, lost, waiting for someone to come for her, waiting for her mother. That part of the memory was distinct: she was waiting for her mother. Only her mother would do.

Taking a corner onto a busy street, fervently hoping he hadn't wandered all the way over here, Rebecca impulsively asked her mother in the dark seat next to her, 'Did I get lost in the woods when I was little? In rain like this? Did you find me?'

Something about the ensuing pause was an alert. 'You used to go down into the woods a lot,' her mother finally answered, and something about the non-responsiveness of the reply made Rebecca press.

'I remember all sorts of pretty colors, like gauze. I remember you finding me.' Being found was a warm memory, and she smiled sideways at her mother, inviting companionship.

'Your father came after you,' her mother said curtly. 'Every time. Your father always came after you. You always were your daddy's girl.'

'But I remember waiting for you,' Rebecca persisted, unwilling to give up on the possibility of shared tenderness.

Her mother seemed put out, defensive. 'I don't see how you could remember anything about it at all. You stopped going down there when you were three years old.'

'I *remember*,' Rebecca insisted, wistful, confused. On the streetcorner diagonally across the intersection was a bent figure, but she knew right away that it was not her father, and her mother didn't even comment.

For some time now, Beatrice Quinn had hardly had a sense of herself except as someone who was going home. She didn't live far from The Tides, and she was quite certain of the route. But she hadn't counted on snow and rain. This was a semi-arid climate, for heaven's sake; it hardly ever rained like this, from low clouds sinking ever lower, a clammy drizzle. All the lights and other landmarks looked different in the rain, and they would confuse her if she didn't keep her wits about her. The rain would slow her down. She crossed Elm Street at the bottom of the hill, having noticed on previous trips that there was no crosswalk for many long blocks. It was all right; there were no cars.

But that man from the nursing home was behind her. There was no reason to think he was following her; she knew he often went out to the liquor store – in fact, she'd had him bring her a tiny bottle of brandy once or twice. Beatrice had felt a trifle guilty about that, a tad adventurous, a woman her age sneaking brandy, but she would not think about brandy or about this man or about the rain. She would not think about anything but going home, for that was who she was: a woman, an old woman, on her way home. Satisfaction from that image of herself filled her, warmer than brandy, much steadier.

A woman was with the man. A younger woman, by the looks and sound of her. Beatrice wondered – dangerously, for it was such a distraction – whether he had a daughter. She'd never thought of him as a family man. The woman had a light step, and Beatrice could hear her laugh. It ought to have been a happy sound, but it made her shiver. She turned off 12th Avenue at Ford Street, and the familiarity of the neighborhood swelled in a way most gratifying. She was definitely on her way home. Behind her, that man and that young woman turned onto Ford Street, too, and they were coming faster, catching up. There was no liquor store down here. The woman's laughter trilled, pretty waves over a deadly undertow. Beatrice kept her mind on what she was about.

'Where do you think he might be trying to go, Mom?'

'Oh heavens, who knows?' Billie gestured in expansive frustration.

'If we could just think the way he might be thinking—'

'Becky, be realistic. Your father doesn't think anymore, not the way he used to, not the way you and I think. Not normal thoughts.'

Rebecca's mother had stopped looking out the windows, didn't seem now even to be making an effort to search. Old anger attached itself to this new affront, and Rebecca bit back sharper words than she spoke. 'Maybe it has something to do with this Faye person,' she suggested deliberately. 'Where would he go if he was trying to find Faye?'

Without hesitation her mother said, 'To hell.' It was such an uncharacteristic thing for her to say that Rebecca guffawed. 'Faye's dead,' her mother added flatly.

'Did you know her?'

'I wouldn't go so far as to say I knew her. I don't think

your father *knew* her. I was in her company a few times, a few times more than was to my liking.'

'So she was still alive and around here when you and Daddy were married?' No answer. 'And when I was born?'

'Yes.' Her mother shifted in her seat, managing to turn herself even more thoroughly away from Rebecca while still facing nominally forward. 'Why are you wasting time talking about that woman? We're supposed to be looking for your father.'

Rebecca had a sense, though, that her mother could be pushed a little farther, and, suddenly, there was more she wanted to know. 'I take it you didn't like Faye very much.'

Her mother snorted. 'That woman was the closest thing to a demon I ever want to meet in this world.'

'Wow,' Rebecca commented mildly. 'That's pretty strong stuff.'

'She would do anything to anybody to get what she wanted. And what she wanted never amounted to anything – some trinket, some bauble, a ring, a scarf for her hair. She was especially vain about her pretty blonde curls.' That was clearly the end of a sentence, but Billie's tone didn't lower for the period; instead, she seemed to cut herself off, as if she'd had more to say but thought better of it, as if she'd already said too much.

Rebecca put her hand to her own blonde curls. 'Besides being blonde, what did she look like?'

'Small. Like a fairy.' Her mother snarled the word, an apparent quote from Marshall or from Faye herself. 'Perfect skin. Perfect figure. Perfect nails. Perfect clothes. She spent a lot of time and effort and your father's money on appearance. Appearance was *real* important to her.'

'What did Dad see in her? Just that she was pretty?' Then, taking a chance, 'He loved her, right?'

Silence. Then, to Rebecca's astonishment, her mother said quietly, 'I loved her, too.'

Rebecca took her eyes off the street long enough to glance sharply at her mother's face. Directly illuminated at that moment by a wash of blurry amber from a streetlight, it did not seem like the face of anybody she knew. 'You did? I thought you hated her. I thought you said she was evil, a demon from hell.'

Another silence. Rebecca turned another corner onto another blank street, empty sidewalk. Then her mother said, 'Once Faye got lost in the woods. She was gone all night. I don't know why she went out there in the first place. Maybe she was meeting somebody. Maybe she was just wandering. I was the one who found her. For a long time before I found her, I could hear her singing and crying. Then I came around a bend in the path and down a steep little hill, and there was a pond, the same color as all the green leaves around it so you could hardly tell it was water except by the way it moved—' Here Billie made flowing, rising and falling motions with her hands, like the tide '—and there she was, naked, dancing in the water, singing and crying. When she saw me she came running. She threw herself into my arms, wet and small, voluptuous, not like a child, not like a grown woman, either.' Billie paused for breath. 'That's why I loved her. That's why your father loved her, too.'

Rebecca was afraid to say anything.

Now Billie made an impatient sweep of the dashboard with the flat of her hand, knocked a map onto the floor. 'I do not want to talk about Faye. What's the point in talking about Faye?'

'I – I thought it might give us a clue as to where Dad could have thought he was going.'

'Oh, good heavens, there's no telling.'

'Why was all this such a big secret?'

'Becky, what did I say?'

For now, Rebecca gave up. Stiff with trepidation, she slowed for a heap in the road, which turned out to be a soggy cardboard box, and then, hating the randomness of all this, just kept going.

The lady with Gordon talked to him about his dog. He didn't know her, didn't know how she knew about his dog, but he was used to that – man, when you lived in a goddamn nursing home, people came and went all the time and you didn't know them from Adam and they knew everything about you, or thought they did. She had a voice like dark molasses, like a trumpet in a blue smoky club, working on him just like that molasses trumpet until it was coming from the inside of him out.

'Love,' she whispered, crooned, and wailed, high and sweet as that trumpet could be played, higher, low in the basement low in his groin. 'You loved that little dog, and he loved you. They had no right to take him away.'

'No right,' Gordon agreed, heartbroken like singing back the blues. 'I loved that pup they had no right no right no right,' like scat.

The lady had on some kind of filmy thing that sometimes looked purple and sometimes looked pink and sometimes had mean silver shot through it, and he could see her body. He could see her boobs. She meant him to see them. He could see her pussy. He wasn't wearing underwear, and his hard-on pushed against the inside of his zipper, hurting a little, itching, goading him.

'They hurt you,' the lady told him. 'They screwed you. So you get to hurt somebody back.' Gordon had been hurt and screwed over a lot of times in his life and he'd never had any urge to hurt anybody back, but this message came from inside him and Gordon knew it was the truth.

'That little blonde boss-lady cunt,' he muttered. 'Rebecca. Princess.'

But the word came to him like a cymbal riffed in his inner ear, making him wince and hold his head. 'No.' And then, 'She's mine.'

Now Gordon realized he was following the crooked-walking old lady with the splitting paper sacks, was closing the distance between them even though he hated being rushed, man, don't rush me! Trudging through the rain, holding his dick in one hand while the other one he stuck out to the side for balance, he was starting to get a glimmer of why.

For Marshall, everything glimmered. His vision and hearing glimmered; the nerve-endings at the surface of his skin glimmered. His memory glimmered. Faye and Billie and Rebecca and his mother all glimmered, in and out of each other, gauzy layers, superimpositions and double exposures, auras. His body shivered, glimmered, tingled. His mind glimmered in and out of consciousness, back and forth through exceedingly permeable boundaries between dimensions of experience, carrying with it his ideas of who he himself might be.

Billie said, 'It's so hard to see.'

Rebecca said, 'I'll stop at that phone booth and call the facility. Maybe they've heard from the police.'

Billie said grimly, 'The police. To think it's come to that.'

Beatrice said, 'Oh, good evening, Mr Marek. Not a very nice evening for a walk, is it?' She was nervous. Any minute she was likely to drop her things in a puddle. Her hip ached. She had to admit she wasn't absolutely certain where her home was from here. And she didn't like the looks or the odor of this man. 'Are you giving that cute puppy of yours a nice long walk?' she asked pleasantly, then saw that he didn't have the puppy with him, then saw that he was touching himself in a decidedly obscene manner, then felt him grab her shoulder and tear the sacks out of her hands. 'Oh,' she said.

Ebullient girlish laughter danced out of Gordon's mouth as he pushed Beatrice Quinn into the ditch beside the railroad tracks and went down after her. A soft, insistent grasp brought his arm down, and he covered almost the whole of Beatrice's face with the flat of one hand. One of her paper bags had landed upside down right beside him, and he looked and saw silky underthings and a dried bouquet of flowers he'd brought her one time; remembering those flowers, remembering the nice brass lamp with the tassles on the shade, he tried to stop, tried to pull himself away and even to help the old lady up. He was sorry. He was sorry she fell. He could help her. He wanted to go home, too.

She lay on her back crooked, bent to her left, just the same way she walked. When Faye guided him hard and mean and laughing between Beatrice's legs, they were crooked, too.

Hanging up the phone and folding the glass doors awkwardly outward to extract herself from the booth, Rebecca heard the strange laughter. But she was intensely preoccupied now with worry for her father and with the news Sandy had relayed to her from The Tides. Both Gordon and Beatrice were missing. Something was wrong with the furnace, and Jerry, the new maintenance man, wasn't answering his pager. The intake worker from the Mental Health Center had called twice since five o'clock, wanting a decision tonight as to whether they'd readmit Mickey Schipp. Dexter had gone into a diabetic coma and been rushed to the hospital; Diane had told Sandy to be sure to tell Rebecca that, given the amount of sweets he'd been allowed to consume, this had been inevitable. The laughter didn't mean anything to her, and it scarcely registered.

Waiting in the car with the window rolled down, Billie was getting cold and wet. It was worth it, though, if she might catch sight of Marshall, if he might just be wandering around out here in the cold somewhere and not with Faye. She was just chiding herself that that was silly, that wasn't possible, when she heard the laughter and froze.

Marshall heard it, too, and it wasn't a surprise; he'd been hearing Faye's mean, musical laughter off and on for much of his life. But now a determination settled over him. He must fight Faye off. He must destroy her. He must protect Rebecca.

The enormity of what he was called to do energized him. Shaking with passion, he set off again. The firm surfaces he'd been walking on disintegrated, and after a while it came to him that he must have left the street and the sidewalk. That seemed a foolhardy thing to have done, a glorious thing, but he didn't think he'd done it; it had been done to him.

He must hurry.

Why was it that he must hurry? Marshall attempted to slow himself in order to ascertain whether, in fact, he was required to hurry. But the headlong (literally; his head was stretched out long ahead of his body and even longer ahead of his stumbling feet) rush in which he found himself was taking place well outside his control. Hurry.

The ground suddenly sloped downward, and he slid. First on his feet, soles slick, then on his hands and knees, belly, face, down into a depression full of Faye's fragrance and Faye's laughter, not a very deep depression but one from which he could not imagine escape.

Chapter 15

'No! No! Don't send me away to die!'

The cry – vibrant as a sustained high note, horrifyingly full-bodied – came from Viviana Pierce's room. Viviana Pierce, who had been trying to die ever since Rebecca had known her, quietly and with such dignity that the people who loved her could take pride in the manner of her dying.

Now something had gone wrong. 'I want to die! You know I want to die! Why won't you let me die?' Sitting by her father's bedside in the room across the hall, Rebecca looked up sharply, half-rose, then as if there were hands at her shoulders, sank back onto the hard vinyl-covered chair, which was too low and had angular arms parallel and perpendicular to the bedrails to suggest a cage.

She didn't know whether it was her place to go find out what was wrong in Viviana's room or to stay here with her father. Her mother was here, on the other side of the bed, which was on the other side of the small room, not looking at her, not looking at him. Did her mother's presence, the fact that he would not be alone and probably wouldn't know anyway who was here with him, mean it was all right for her to leave? Nursing staff were on duty to care for Viviana; Diane was here to take charge. And there was always, night or day, at least one family member in attendance. Did that absolve Rebecca of responsibility, or merely alter the nature of it from the professional end of the spectrum toward the personal?

There were innumerable things she had to do. Departmental mid-month budget reports were stacked on her desk; she'd instituted this system to get a better handle on expenses, and it seemed to be having some impact, but it wouldn't work if she didn't study them and get her comments back to the department heads quickly, and at this point she didn't even know whether all the reports had been turned in. She had an appointment with a hospital discharge planner this afternoon, to solicit admissions to The Tides; she wasn't going to make it and hadn't called to reschedule. Tomorrow was Kurt's birthday; her total lack of gift ideas – if truth be told, her total lack of interest – was, in theory, appalling.

She would far rather worry about all of that than think about any of a host of other, terrible things toward which her thoughts kept swinging. Beatrice, found this morning raped and strangled off the entrance ramp to the highway, half-obscured by her belongings from two tattered paper sacks, more than a mile away from The Tides in the opposite direction from her home. Gordon, still missing; he would have had no identification on him, so they might never know what had happened to him, and nobody knew even his sons' names – Lisa thought she'd heard them say John and some other common name when they'd showed up at the Christmas party, but she couldn't be sure – let alone how or whether to contact them. Rebecca missed Gordon and Beatrice acutely, and guilt filled her like a marijuana haze, a nasty high, warping everything out of true.

And her father. She and her mother had searched for him well into the night, until finally Billie's objections to being driven home had subsided to pale exhausted protests, easy to override. Rebecca had been torn, an increasingly commonplace experience; she hadn't wanted to leave her mother alone, but she'd been frantic to find her father. Hating to impose, she'd called Kurt for help, but he hadn't answered the phone and, curiously relieved, she'd had to settle for leaving a message on the machine telling him there was an emergency and she'd be late.

For a long time then, hours, she'd driven and walked almost aimlessly, having no way of guessing where he might be, gradually losing track of where she'd already looked and how long ago, crazed by the recurring image – which came to seem emblematic of her life as a whole, and of human life in general – that her path might be intersecting with her father's and intersecting again without her knowing he was anywhere nearby and, certainly, without him ever perceiving or recognizing her.

Well after midnight, the sleet had stopped and the temperature had perceptibly started to rise. Spring, she'd thought, extraordinarily moved; the advent or the premonition of spring. As she got out of her car behind The Tides again, she'd even taken off her coat and left it on the seat.

Abruptly, then, the randomness and hopelessness of her search for her father had dissolved, and she'd known where he was, as if she'd been informed. She'd looked there earlier in this endless evening, and she would never know whether she'd overlooked him or whether he'd come there after she'd left, been deposited there. Either possibility was too awful to contemplate for long and made no difference anyway, for there he was now at the bottom of the dry lake-bed, lit from all sides as if by vibrating variegated stage lights, and he was not alone.

Rebecca couldn't tell how long she'd stood on the rim of the bowl, mesmerized. Fervently she hoped that it had been no more than a few seconds, and that her delay hadn't allowed more harm to come to her father, but there was the persistent suspicion that a long and hurtful span of time had passed before she could rouse herself to go in after him.

He was naked from the waist down. Rebecca could hardly bear to see him, and couldn't tear her eyes away. His thighs were no bigger than his calves except for the flesh that drooped behind them like something sewn on, and his buttocks strained and contracted and puffed out as if they had no underlying form or structure, as if they were being roughly kneaded. His genitals stood out in relief against the soft pallor of the rest of his flesh. He was moaning, pleasure and horror and pain all plausible sources of the chilling arrhythmic noises, or maybe just awe.

Rebecca had tugged off her high-heeled boots and scrambled down the incline. She knew the depression was shallow, but almost at once she lost perception of anything above or around it; she knew it was dry, filled in with weeds and urban debris she'd been meaning to have cleaned out, but she was submerged in light and odor so thick they should have had tactile properties, too, should have been wet and viscous on her skin.

Her father moaned again. She pushed toward him, through the assaultive smell of roses that must be adhering to her. Her father's arms were curved around a form she couldn't quite see, but the volume of air and light it displaced was substantial. Her father's parted lips were pursed in a lingering kiss and his tongue glinted out between them. His penis was erect.

'Dad!' Rebecca started to cover his nakedness with her clothed body but was flung away. The back of her head hit the ground hard. Dazed, she struggled to clear her senses.

Then she heard her father roar, 'No! Faye! I won't allow you to have her!' and he was pulling her by the wrists up out of the depression and stumbling with her toward the back door of The Tides.

His strength had horrified her, so obviously born of desperation and of a love for her that defined him now, defined her, too, beyond the particulars of who they were. She'd glanced back once and seen pulsing pastel light in pursuit of them like a monstrous incoming tide, but the back door had not been locked, as it was supposed to be, and she and her father had rushed inside, where he'd collapsed and she'd shouted for help.

Now, at her father's bedside in broad sunny daylight, with budget reports needing to be attended to and Viviana Pierce trying to die across the hall, Rebecca watched his face. But she was thinking about Faye. Dementia could produce powerful fantasies, but she'd seen and smelled and heard things last night, too, and even now she felt things – a pressure in the air, a lightness that in itself should not have been sinister but radiated intense danger.

She looked across at her mother. The ceiling lights were too bright, of course, their illumination flat and graying, practically shadowless. Billie Emig looked stalwart and unapproachable in the other mustard-colored chair, just like Rebecca's, hard arms and awkwardly angled back; the rectangles made by the aluminum bedrails streaked her bulky shoulder, her thick cheek. Her hand on the vertical crosspiece didn't seem to be trembling; that might be because she was clutching the rail so hard, or she might really be as calm as she appeared to be.

Her wedding ring glinted, the ring Rebecca must have seen on her mother's hand countless times every day of her childhood and had never really noticed, didn't know what its pattern was or whether there was an inscription. Only one of countless things she didn't know about her mother, it suddenly appalled her.

Seized by a desire to make contact with Billie, she thought what to say. She might try a statement of empathy, which she could offer sincerely to any other resident's family member but could not quite bring herself to say to her mother about her father: 'It must be hard for you to see him like this.' Most people responded warmly, correctly inferring that she cared about them. If her mother thought so, it would be true, but not entirely so, and the possibilities made Rebecca squirm. If her mother thought she was being a professional instead of a daughter, that would be true, too, but not entirely so.

She could just ask straight out about Faye.

'Faye.'

Somebody had spoken the name aloud. Rebecca was sure she herself had not, but her mother was still staring straight ahead, face lined and drooping in the harsh light, and gave no sign of having said anything. Rebecca leaned forward to look again into her father's face.

His eyes were open. When she moved into his line of vision, his eyes focused on her, and she saw in their wet feverish surfaces her own reflections on a swirling variegated background. Her father's lips moved, and she thought he was saying, 'Faye.' But when she bent closer she heard nothing; his lips kept moving, opening and closing very slightly, twitching in minuscule tics and tremors, the top gum coming down to touch the edge of the bottom lip again and again. She felt the faint intake and outrush of his breath on her own lips, but there were no words.

Rebecca found herself glancing behind her and overhead for the source of the filmy pastel colors that had framed her in her father's eyes. The fluorescent lights had bluish auras, but that was all.

The commotion across the hall in Viviana's room coalesced into shrieks, and something crashed onto the floor. 'I want to die here! Please! Leave me alone!'

Rebecca was on her feet and out into the hall. A small crowd had gathered. Steeling herself, she pushed past Petra, who was clutching the crossed arms of her pink sweater with her own crossed hands and muttering. The man in the flannel shirt was Viviana's grandson, but he was well out of the way.

The scene inside the room was a physical shock. Viviana lay on the floor with bedclothes scattered around her, one thin leg tangled in a sheet and caught on the edge of the bed. She was covered with blood. The sheets were wet and spotted dull red. With both hands she was clutching the gray metal frame of the bed, which hardly rattled although she must have been using all her strength.

Diane was kneeling over her. For a split second it seemed to Rebecca that Diane's stance was threatening, and instinctively she started forward to come to Viviana's aid. But then she saw the look on the nurse's face. 'Diane, what's going on?'

'She's hemorrhaging.' Diane glanced up, brushed a lock of damp dark hair out of her face and then lowered her gaze and her hands again as if to grapple with the frail, bleeding old woman on the floor. She grasped Viviana's wrists but did not seem to be exerting any real pressure. 'The ambulance is on its way.'

'I don't want to go to the hospital!' Viviana wailed, kicking with her free leg as Diane tried to remove her fingers from the bed frame. Blood spread around them, dark red and shiny on the shiny gray and white tiles.

Viviana's nightgown, spattered and torn, was up around her hips. Diane reached to pull it down and the old woman twisted away from her as if the nurse were causing her pain. 'Viviana, you listen to me,' Diane commanded. 'You have to go to the hospital. You're losing a great deal of blood.'

'Nana,' said the grandson, who had come back into the room but was keeping himself on the periphery of the drama, not to overstep his role or second-guess the professionals. 'Nana, please,' but it was unclear what he was pleading with his grandmother to do.

'I think,' said Rebecca, 'we should discuss this.'

Diane sank back on her heels and looked at Rebecca, keeping one hand on the back of the struggling old woman. 'What do you want, a committee meeting? Rebecca, she'll bleed to death if she doesn't get to the hospital immediately. This is a nursing decision.'

'It's not only a nursing decision,' Rebecca began.

'I want to die! Can't you people understand that? I want to die!'

Diane's white uniform was speckled with Viviana's blood and with dust from the floor. She put her hands on the old woman's shoulders and bent to look into her eyes. 'Viviana, I can't let you die like this.'

Rebecca forced herself to step into the room. 'Diane.'

Diane was fussing over Viviana, efficiently, as if there were no doubt in her mind about what she should do.

Viviana lay still now, eyes closed, toothless mouth open, obviously exhausted. But she still gripped the frame of the bed. Without looking up, Diane said to Rebecca, 'I'm a nurse. I won't let someone bleed to death in front of me without trying to save her life. That's what I'm trained to do. That's why I'm a nurse.'

'You were willing to let her starve herself to death.'

'That was different. Calmer. Passive. Not an emergency. This is a medical emergency, and I have to intervene.'

Viviana was crying almost silently now, but she would not let Diane loosen her grip. Blood still flowed – from between the old woman's legs, Rebecca could now see – and Diane's white shoes were flecked with it. Rebecca struggled with sudden nausea and her vision blurred violet, evidence of her own blood rushing to her head.

Then her vision cleared, even assumed a hyper-clarity, as though she were looking through a high-powered lens that concentrated on the small bright sphere where Viviana's hands were wrapped around the aluminum post of the bedframe. Other fingers were among hers, working hers free. Not Diane's; Diane had risen, was talking to the grandson by the door. No one else was in the room. But Rebecca clearly saw long strong fingers with painted nails twist and scratch and claw at Viviana's fingers until, one by one in awful surrender, they let go.

The ambulance pulled up outside, its siren ceasing mid-wail. Two attendants with a stretcher raced in the side door. One of them picked up the old woman from the floor, as unresisting now as if she were already dead. He laid her more or less flat on the stretcher, where the other attendant covered her to the neck. Rebecca looked for blood on the white sheet, but before it could appear Viviana was whisked away, Diane following to provide the information necessary for hospitalization and the grandson hastening to his car.

Haltingly, Rebecca joined the hushed little group of residents and staff outside Viviana's room. Shirley was in tears. Rebecca went to her, started to put an arm around her, but the aide pulled angrily away. 'How could you just let that happen? You didn't think it was right, but you just stood there and let it happen!'

Rebecca shook her head. 'It wasn't up to me—'

'You're the administrator! You're the boss! Everything is up to you!'

Rebecca could scarcely think. 'I didn't know what was right,' she started to say, but stopped, pressed her back against the wall, took deep breaths that hurt and made her sick.

Florence spoke up. 'I think Diane was right. You can't just let somebody bleed to death right in front of you.'

'She's been wanting to die for a long time,' Shirley said fiercely. 'This was her chance, and we took it away from her.'

Florence smiled. 'Believe me, she'll have other chances.'

Tillie and her crew had already arrived and were hard at work cleaning the blood from the floor, stripping the bed, purging from the room any sign of the struggle – life-and-death, certainly, but bewilderingly inverted. Purging, too, apparently, any residue of the disembodied fingers Rebecca had seen; there was no sign, either, of anything that could account for such an illusion.

Abby went to the linen closet for clean towels. She was shaky and upset, not wanting to talk to anybody about the awful thing that had just happened to Viviana, whatever it was, whether it was bleeding to death or not being allowed to bleed to death. Wanting, actually, to talk to Alex about it, but she could never talk to Alex about anything again. She'd hit him, and she deserved to lose her job at least, and even if she didn't lose her job she couldn't face him, couldn't ever take care of him anymore. That made her feel terrible.

She'd been on her way to give Paul a shower when she'd heard the screams from Viviana's room, and she wished now she'd just gone about her business and left Diane and the others to handle things. That was their job, not hers. Because she'd been there and watched the whole thing, stood by and witnessed it all, somehow Abby felt she had to decide what was the right thing to do. She didn't *know* what was right. What had happened wasn't right, but she didn't know what anybody should have done different. She told herself to just quit thinking about it. She had enough things on her mind.

Paul loved his shower. He asked for a shower a dozen times a day, and Maxine and some of the others said it was because he liked to get naked with girls. Abby thought maybe that was at least partly true, and so what if it was? Or maybe Paul just liked the feel of the warm water on his skin, the soapy washcloth, her hands. Colleen was talking to a massage school about the students doing internships at The Tides, and Abby thought that was a terrific idea; maybe they'd have time to do her, too. She didn't get touched enough, and neither did people in a nursing home, and neither, she suspected, did most people in the world. It seemed to her that one of the ways you knew who you were was when other people touched you, but it was never enough for anybody.

Except Alex. She didn't want to be thinking about Alex, but she knew she had to. Alex got touched pretty much whenever he asked for it, and he asked for it a lot, and as far as she knew he couldn't feel a thing below his neck. They touched his face as part of his daily care routine, shaved him and put on aftershave, brushed his teeth and wiped away the foam. He also directed them, especially her, to touch the rest of his body, bathing and drying and oiling and powdering and moving his limbs in his exact range of motion exercises, and he acted as if it felt good.

Now, reaching up to shampoo Paul's hair, she laughed along with him and promised herself that she'd touch her girls more. Maybe those massage students would teach her how to do it. 'Okay, kid,' she said to Paul, 'turn around and I'll do your back.'

If you gave him time, Paul could do this part by himself. Usually they couldn't give him time because they had so many other showers to give, but today Abby stood still with soap and washcloth at the ready and let him get himself turned around the way he wanted. First he braced both hands on her shoulders, hard. Then he took his left hand off and pressed it against the slippery tile wall and moved his right hand from her left shoulder to her right. He stood like that for a minute, grinning, making sounds. Then he took his right hand off her right shoulder, moved his left hand to the corner of the shower stall, put his right hand where his left had been, and in this way turned his upper body all the way around. But his feet still pointed sideways and he was twisted at the waist. One foot at a time, he turned step by step to his left until he was fully facing the back wall and his bent shoulders, long back, droopy butt were toward her and under her hands.

'Good,' she called to him over the clatter of the water. 'Now here comes the best part.' Paul's snort of assent and anticipation echoed.

By 'the best part' she'd meant getting his back scrubbed.

She wished they had one of those long-handled bath brushes; the bristles would feel really good, and he might even be able to use it himself. Diane would think that was a stupid idea, but Rebecca and Colleen and Lisa wouldn't; she'd bring it up in Paul's care conference. When she told Paul, 'Here comes the best part,' that was what she meant.

But all of a sudden her hands were around in front of him and she was rubbing his private parts with the washcloth and then with her bare fingers and Paul was hooting in obvious surprise and pleasure.

Horrified, Abby snatched her hands back and retreated out of the shower stall. She turned the water off. Paul kept standing there with his back to her, waiting for more, or maybe just not able to turn around fast enough to suit her now. Mortified, she was furious with him; although she knew he couldn't possibly have made her do that, it really did seem to her that it hadn't been her idea, that somebody had pushed her hands there, that she would never have done something like that on her own.

She started to dry him off, not very well and too roughly. When he realized that his shower was prematurely over and she wasn't going to touch him anymore anywhere, he got himself turned partway around, and she saw that he had a huge hard-on.

Disgust made her even rougher then, and a couple of times he almost fell; once, she almost did. By the time she got him more or less dried off and more or less dressed – clothes on him, anyway, but his shirt buttoned wrong and the collar not turned down neatly the way he liked it, and she didn't bother with his hair – he was as upset as she was, hollering and swinging at her, and she had to call for Maxine to come help her get him into his chair and restrained.

When they finally had Paul tied down so he couldn't hurt himself or anybody else, Maxine stood back, panting. 'So what got into him?' When Abby didn't answer, the other aide cuffed her arm in what was supposed to be a friendly way. 'Hey, girl, you can't let 'em get to you, you know?'

Barely able to keep from screaming at her and hitting her back, Abby did hiss venomously, 'Shut up, Maxine, okay? You think you know everything. Just shut up, okay?'

Maxine raised her hands in mock self-defense and backed off, pretending to be afraid of her, which made her even madder. 'Hey, hey, what got into *you*?' But she did go away, leaving the door to Paul's room open behind her.

Abby stood looking down at Paul. He was all twisted up, one leg half over the other, head off to one side, but he was still glaring and yelling. Through his thin yellow pants she couldn't help but see that he still had a hard-on. Meaning to calm him, to apologize to him (not for touching him in his private place; already she was starting not to be sure that had really happened, but for being impatient with him), meaning to make friends again, she knelt in front of him, holding on to the arms of his chair. 'Hey, Paul, come on. We're buddies, aren't we? Don't be mad at me.'

Abby was enveloped by a prickly warmth. It descended on her from above and behind, and as she felt it wrap itself around her like scratchy thin cloth, she saw Paul's eyes widen and his mouth stretch wide.

She felt breath on her hair, heard a teasing little song, caught a whiff of rose perfume that would have been overpowering if it had lasted more than a split second, and then saw her own hand come to rest on Paul's crotch. She tried to pull it away. Her brain sent frantic messages to her arm and hand to pull away, to *stop it*, but the messages were ignored. Instead, her fingers started working Paul's zipper, and in the process the backs of her knuckles massaged his penis. Paul, still crooked in the chair, had stopped yelling, and now his breath was coming short and fast.

'Everything okay, Abby?' came Florence's voice from the doorway behind her. 'Need any help?'

Hoping she hadn't jumped, although her heart did and she thought she was going to pass out, Abby answered right away, even before the strange soft grip on her hand was loosened and the itching along her bare arms and legs had quit. 'Oh, sure, we're okay, aren't we, Paul? I'm just trying to get his pants zipped and his shirt buttoned right.'

The older aide was suspicious of something. 'Maxine said he was giving you a hard time. That's not like Paul.'

'It was my fault.' Abby was allowed now to stand up, but she kept her back to Florence. 'I've got a lot on my mind right now, and I lost my patience with him in the shower. You know how much he likes his shower. I was just trying to tell him I'm sorry, but I guess he's going to be mad at me for a while.'

'He doesn't hold a grudge, do you, Pauly?' Florence came in then and smoothed Paul's hair, got a comb from the bedside stand and wet it under the faucet and made a part on the left, the way he liked it. At first Paul kept watching Abby, but it didn't take long for him to shift his gaze to Florence, who was crooning about how handsome he was – and actually, Abby found herself thinking, he was.

'Thanks, Flo,' Abby said miserably, and stumbled out of the room. Lights were on all up and down the hall, bells dinging. Intensely relieved to know what to do, she set about her job.

It took Rebecca the rest of the day to go through the mid-month budget reports, not because there was such a wealth of information – they were cursory at best, and Diane hadn't even submitted one for nursing, which accounted for by far the largest share of the facility's budget – but because she couldn't keep her mind on them and because other things kept happening. Wanting to concentrate on numbers, she thought of these things as interruptions, intrusions, distractions, but they were not. They were the life of the nursing home, going on. She'd have ignored it all if she could, but her attention was demanded.

The hospital called to say that Viviana's hemorrhaging had been stopped and she was stabilized; Diane reported this with undisguised satisfaction. Rebecca didn't know whether to be glad or not. She didn't know what to say to Diane, how to explain the shame she felt, whether Diane ought to be feeling it, too.

The new maintenance man, the third since what Dave's wife had told her, with curious reluctance, had been a stroke, informed Colleen he was quitting, going to California tomorrow, had just needed this job long enough to fix up his truck. Rebecca tried to take some comfort in the few things he'd fixed while he'd been at The Tides, but the prospect of hiring someone else was too daunting even to contemplate. Maybe she could persuade Kurt to work for her weekends; he was handy around the house. Thinking of Kurt made her think again about his birthday, with no more enthusiasm or persistence than before.

Suppliers called. Those whose accounts receivable were

thirty days past due tended to be relatively civil, unless this wasn't the first time; those who'd been owed money for ninety or a hundred and twenty days were increasingly nasty. Rebecca wrote a few checks. They would clear, but the management fee wouldn't. She didn't know what Dan would say to that, and it was hard to care.

She found a note in her box from Lisa: '*The county put Dexter in another facility where they'll control his spending money so he can't buy candy. He just called me crying to see why he can't come home. Can you believe this?*' Numb, Rebecca went through the motions of putting in a call to the caseworker, but it was just as well that she was out of the office until next week.

It was evening before she got back to her father's room. Her mother wasn't there; it struck Rebecca as odd and oddly sad that she didn't know where her mother was. Her father still lay on his back, board-stiff, but he was conscious, and when he saw her he gave a little yelp of, she was sure, fear. 'Dad, it's me, Becky. What's wrong?'

She reached to touch his cheek and he jerked his head away with shocking alacrity. His eyes bulged and he was breathing hard. He lifted one hand and waved it fiercely. 'Get out of here!'

Hurt despite everything she knew about dementia, Rebecca said gently, 'I love you, Dad,' and the words all but glowed between them. She could not remember the last time she had said that to either of her parents; she could not remember the last time she had felt it. She was feeling it now.

'I love you, too,' he said easily, 'and I don't want to see you hurt. Becky, you have to listen to me. You can't be here. She'll get you.'

'Who, Dad?' She never knew whether to remind a

confused person what consensual reality was or to play into the fantasy on the grounds that it was real for him and elicited genuine emotion. So she did both. 'Who's after me, Dad? Nobody's after me.'

'Faye!' he croaked.

Rebecca hesitated. Then she caught his hand, stopping its frantic motion in the air, and held it between hers, even interlaced her fingers with his. Wedging herself between one of the ungiving chairs and the equally hard bedrail, she bent as close to him as she dared. 'Tell me about Faye, Dad. Tell me about Faye.'

'Faye,' he said very clearly, 'is your mother, and she wants you back.'

Chapter 16

'He's senile,' Billie insisted. She wouldn't look at Rebecca, but that was not uncommon and couldn't be considered a clue as to the state of her mind or the content of what she was or was not saying. 'He's confused. You can't believe a thing he says.'

'Then you tell me.'

'There's nothing to tell.'

The question clamoring to be asked was, of course: *Why did he say she was my mother?* But she could not ask it.

They had walked together across the ragged field behind the nursing home to the weedy lake-bed where Rebecca had found her father – where he had been, she was convinced, one way or another in Faye's embrace. It was one of the first mild spring days, and there had been so little snow this winter that there wasn't much melt, so sitting outside for a short while would have been pleasant if not for this between them.

The fact that they were here together, alone, not quite looking at each other but on opposite sides of one of the worse-for-wear picnic tables still scattered around the field, marked this as an occasion of significance. Neither of them was in the habit of making such personal overtures. In fact, neither of them had made this one.

Neither had said to the other, 'We need to talk.' Neither had suggested or agreed to the walk to this peculiar space. But here they were, and secrets wove them together, braided them apart.

Rebecca remembered a place not at all like this, a leafy and piney wood, and it must have been a rainy day instead of a sunny one because needles of stormy light, wands of cloud had hung down among the trees. A place not at all like this place, a time not at all like this time, but something was causing her to remember.

She realized what it was: the presence of secrets, something, someone secret. Waiting for someone secret in a wood. Someone who never came.

'How are things with Kurt?'

It was a strange thing to ask under the circumstances. It was also so unlike her mother to ask such a thing that Rebecca's mind went blank and her mouth wordlessly opened and shut. Her father had greeted Kurt, the few times he'd been in his company, alternately like a long-lost relative whose identity he couldn't quite pinpoint but who was indisputably somebody important, and like a complete stranger with no significance whatsoever. Her mother, unfailingly polite to Kurt's face, had hardly ever mentioned him otherwise. Maybe she didn't approve of their living together, but that was sheer speculation; actually Rebecca had no idea what her mother's moral stance on that or any other subject might be.

What could be the import of such a query now? Was it small talk, a conversational gambit intended to divert from the numerous difficult topics at hand? Or was it leading somewhere?

'Fine,' she could say, and leave it at that. Or she could add some detail that pretended to be revealing but really obfuscated: 'We don't see each other very often, we're both so busy,' or 'He fenced-in the back yard last weekend so now he can get the dog he's been wanting.'

'Not good,' she found herself confessing. 'It's not a very close relationship. We don't seem to have – I don't know, to have found each other.' Suddenly, surprisingly, the barrenness of it struck her, brought tears to her eyes.

'You shouldn't settle for that,' her mother declared. 'There's more to life than that.'

'Mom,' Rebecca dared to ask, 'have you been happy with Dad?'

The answer was emphatic. 'Yes. Very.'

'But what about Faye?' There. The name was said. Whether or not her mother had meant to be leading up to Faye, they were in her presence now.

'More than once over the years she did her best to come between us,' Billie said in a rush, and Rebecca sat back, hugging herself, trying to be ready for whatever onslaught was to come, 'but we were stronger than she was. Stronger than she expected. Now Marshall's – losing himself, and she sees her chance. I should have known.'

'I thought you said she was dead.'

'Nobody knows what happened to her. At least, *I* don't know. Maybe your father knows. Knew. We heard rumors that she was dead. He said she was dead.'

'Rumors from whom?'

'From people who knew her. People whose lives she ruined, or tried to. People who still loved her. Not very many people ever could stop loving Faye.'

'How did she die?'

'We heard more than one story, but they all had something to do with those ridiculous scarves of hers. The end got caught in the wheels of a carnival ride and strangled her. A man, or a woman – ' Billie snorted ' – she'd jilted stuffed it down her throat. Some underworld character she was involved with soaked it in something and held it over her nose and mouth till she suffocated.'

'Wow,' was all Rebecca could think to say.

Below them, under the lip of the dry lake-bowl where neither of them could yet see it, a glitter crept toward them. There was no substance to it, no core around which its sparkles and colors were organized, but it had speed and energy, vivacity and magnetism, and it knew what it wanted.

'You said she was evil,' Rebecca said, carefully advancing the discussion. 'That's not just because Dad loved her before he loved you.' Speaking of her parents' love caused her discomfort, and she hastened ahead. 'You had other reasons?'

'Yes.'

Rebecca waited. When it became clear that her mother wasn't going to elaborate, she took another risk. 'If you could tell me something about her, maybe we could figure out why Dad's so afraid of her now.'

'I know why he's afraid. I'm afraid, too. Faye always was somebody worth being afraid of.'

'Tell me.'

'She always went for weakness,' Billie said. 'She'd make friends with somebody when they were down and out in one way or another, convince them she was the best thing that ever happened to them and they'd just love her, they'd do anything for her, and she'd just kind of take them over, use them up, and then when she got bored she'd leave them.'

'Did she do that to you?'

Her mother stiffened. 'Me? No. Before she met your

father, and even after she was with him, she tried to be my friend, but I saw right through her. She never got anywhere with me. Not really.'

Remembering the story about her mother rescuing Faye in the wood, Rebecca wondered about this. But she let it go.

'But I saw what she did to other people. I kept my distance.'

Rebecca craved detail, yearned to fully imagine this Faye. 'Give me an example.'

Her mother hesitated, then seemed to make a decision. 'There was this girl we worked with. Her husband beat her. Everybody suspected it, we saw the bruises, but she'd never talk about it, she was so afraid of him – ashamed, I don't know. I don't understand women like that. Faye got on her good side, persuaded her to confide in her, and then Faye went and got the husband in bed and told him everything the girl'd said. He killed her.'

Rebecca breathed, 'Jesus.'

Billie nodded. 'I'll always believe Faye knew exactly what she was doing. She acted shocked and horrified, cried and carried on, but I saw the look in her eyes.'

'Why would she do that?'

'For fun.'

'That's hard to believe.'

'And because she didn't have a life of her own. She didn't know who she was if she wasn't stealing pieces of other people's lives. That's what made her so appealing. It's what made her so dangerous, too.'

'Was Dad like that? Weak and vulnerable?' Sadly, it wasn't hard to imagine.

Billie nodded again. 'I guess he was a broken man. From the war, you know.'

Rebecca didn't know exactly what that meant and couldn't bring herself to ask.

'He sees her,' Billie said resentfully. 'He says she's come back, and she tells him awful things. Sometimes he thinks I'm her.' This last was particularly offensive, and obviously she could scarcely bring herself to say it. Rebecca recognized the maternal sacrifice; in some way she didn't comprehend, her mother was telling her these things for her own good.

'More and more he doesn't know who I am either. Maybe he thinks I'm Faye, too.' This time it was Rebecca who laughed ruefully and Billie who winced.

'But I don't look a thing like her!' her mother protested. 'She was smaller and prettier than I ever was. She was the kind of girl who made men *and* women turn their heads. Real nice to look at, if you didn't know what was under the surface. Like a pretty flower with poison in its heart.'

She ought to say something complimentary about her mother's appearance. It wouldn't have been hard, for Billie Emig was a pleasant-looking woman; people might not turn their heads to stare at her, but they certainly didn't turn away, either. Instead, Rebecca was driven to ask, almost meekly, 'What did she look like?' But that wasn't sufficiently to the point, and she gathered her courage. 'Could he think – do I look anything like her?'

Her mother's long silence gave her the answer, but she waited for the description that finally came. 'She had blonde curly hair – sometimes, when it wasn't red or black or silver. Marshall told me once he thought blonde was her natural color. She was small. She had big blue eyes. She always looked younger than she probably was, although she kept her age a secret, like a lot of other things.'

Rebecca's next question followed of its own accord; all she had to do was stay out of the way. 'Was she my mother, Mom?'

Billie sat very still. Rebecca heard traffic noise, her own heartbeat, a peculiar sizzling like the sound of Fourth of July sparklers setting something afire. 'She gave birth to you. I am your mother.'

'She died when I was little,' Rebecca breathed. 'Didn't she? I remember her. I remember waiting for her to come back. She couldn't come back, because she died. It wasn't her fault.' Sorrow for the woman who had died swept her, then a fiercer sorrow for the little girl waiting.

'She could have come back,' Billie told her grimly. 'She didn't die, not then. You might as well know everything. We were afraid she'd come back and steal you or hurt you, but she didn't. She was a selfish, headstrong, *evil* person, Becky, and she just flat-out left you. I wanted you. I wanted to be your mother, and I was. I am.'

There was another silence. Several times Rebecca tried to speak, but instead ran her tongue around the inside of her mouth and swallowed, taking in the bitter taste of sweet-smelling roses. At last she managed to croak, 'Am I like her?' hoping and dreading that she would be told yes.

'I don't think Faye had a self,' Billie answered slowly. 'Do you have a self, Rebecca? Do you know who you are? You're the only one who can answer that.'

Something shot across the plane of the lake bowl as if on a glossy quivering membrane of surface tension, straight for Rebecca.

Her mother didn't see it, didn't feel its seduction or its threat, didn't recognize Rebecca's choking as anything other than sobs. But she got to her daughter before Faye did, and wrapped her in her sturdy arms.

'My name is Myra Larsen and I am suffering! My name is Myra Larsen and I am suffering! Ohh! Listen to me, girlie, and you might learn something!'

Whispering, stiff as she could make herself in a chair in Myra's old room, which was still unoccupied because of The Tides' low census, Naomi Murphy reached out with one hand clawed like Myra's, then with the other, doing her best to feel the hands mittened, warm and itchy. She whispered, whispered the holy words.

'I am Joan of Arc and they are burning me at the stake! I am Joan of Arc and they are burning me at the stake! Ohh! Yes, yes, it hurts!' Nothing hurt, but Naomi had the glorious sense of being on the very brink of suffering.

Being able to shift position in the uncomfortable chair gave her to understand that she had too much freedom of movement. Not at all unsure of her footing although she wished to be, wished to collapse, she walked down the shiny, acrid-smelling corridor to the clean-linen closet, from which she took one white sheet. No one asked her about it, for she had done this before, fetched a sheet for the purpose of restraining someone, though always someone else. Excitement made her weak for a passing moment, but she held onto a shelf until the weakness waned and was replaced by strength, the promise of transcendent strength.

Back to the empty room and the imprisoning chair, Naomi folded the sheet into a strip narrow enough to go under her arms and across her chest, wide enough to bind her in place. It was too bulky to be reliable, and she wished she had a real Posey vest restraint, but they were in short supply, and the aides said sheets worked fine, never mind that sometimes the Health Department would write you up for using them.

Unable to get the sheet secured behind the chair, Naomi settled for tying it in front, but it wasn't good enough. The knot was right there under her hands and she could loosen it whenever she wanted. Almost, she gave in to despair.

Her chant this time was just slightly audible. 'My name is Myra Larsen and I don't belong here! Sit down and listen, girlie, and you might learn something! Ohh!' The pressure of the sheet over her breasts did cause a little pain, but not very much, not nearly enough. 'Ohh!'

It was lunchtime, first shift, and all the residents from this wing, the intermediate unit, were in the dining room. Staff were at the other end getting people ready for the second shift, or picking up trays for the feeders and others who couldn't leave their rooms.

Abby, unwillingly, was in Alex Booth's room, with the door closed behind her as he had instructed. She was standing all the way across the room from him, with her hands behind her back, and his head thrashed on his flat pillow as he tried to find an angle from which he could see her. 'Abby, Abby, I've got to get out of this place. So do you. Something's going on around here. It's not safe.'

'Where can you go?' Where, she almost added, can I go?

'Come home with me.'

She was afraid of him. She was afraid of herself with him. If she ran out of this room right now, he'd have no way to make her come back. 'What are you talking about?'

'Ordinarily I would require my wife's agreement. As it happens, she and the girls are in Texas, staying with her mother. Indefinitely. I think they've left me.'

'You didn't tell me.'

'You've been avoiding me.'

Abby leaned her head back against the wall and burst

into tears. 'I'm sorry, Alex! I don't know what happened! I'm sorry! I didn't mean to hurt you! I'm so sorry!'

He didn't say it was all right, he understood, although he did, fully, understand. He didn't tell her he hadn't been hurt, although he hadn't. He didn't urge her not to cry. He said, 'I haven't told anyone about that, Abby. I haven't notified the authorities.'

It was a measure of his own agitation, which he had no physical means of relieving or expressing, that he couldn't tell whether or not she'd taken his point. He couldn't afford to lose his bearings like that.

He waited only until her weeping had quieted enough that he could be heard over it. 'I have a proposition for you,' he said then, and Abby had no choice but to listen. He spoke quickly. He had given this a good deal of thought. 'Room and board for you and the girls, plus a salary we'll negotiate but certainly more than you're making here. In return, you take care of all my physical needs – you know what they are – as well as other personal services such as correspondence, driving the van, and so on.'

Abby seized on something to object to. 'I don't know how to drive a van.'

'It isn't hard,' he said gently, reprovingly. 'I'll teach you. Oh, and you'll do all the cooking and housework.'

'Kind of like a wife.' She laughed nervously through the still-falling tears and pushed herself away from the wall to go forward, not close enough to touch him but into his field of vision.

He regarded her steadily. 'In some ways. Not in all. Some things cannot be paid for.'

She blushed. 'What will Jenny say?'

'I told you. Jenny is in Texas. Indefinitely.'

'But what about when she finds out another woman is in her house?'

'Let me take care of that. What do you think of my offer?'

'I have to think about it.'

'But, Abby, do you have an objection?' He knew she didn't.

'I just need time to think about it.'

He pressed. 'We don't have much time. I don't think either one of us has much time.'

'I don't know what you're talking about,' she said feebly, but it seemed to her that somehow she did, and that scared her even more.

'Abby,' he said again, quietly, 'we need each other.'

No one was aware of Naomi in Myra Larsen's old room, in Myra Larsen's chair, assuming as much of Myra Larsen's aspect as she could fix in her mind. Naomi didn't intend to be heard, certainly did not want to be rescued. When behind her lids her vision began to fill with fuzzy pink and lavender swirls, and a carefree little song came into her ears, she thought perhaps she was losing or altering consciousness. But then, clearly, she felt hands untying the sheet, and she squirmed in protest.

'Wait,' a pretty voice crooned. 'Let me help you. I know how.'

'My name is Esther Rosen and they are taking me to the camps! My name is Esther Rosen and they are taking me to the camps! Ohh!'

The sheet had been passed under Naomi's arms, between her legs, and behind her back, where it had been pulled up snug and knotted tight. It hurt. It *hurt*. The fetid aroma of too many roses – fake, rotting – made her swoon. In her ears, in her face, somebody was giggling, a cruel and threatening sound.

'Ohh! Ohh! Sit down here by me, girlie, and you might learn something! Ohh!' Her cries were still quiet and tentative. Petra, though, was attracted by them.

Petra hadn't eaten anything for lunch because it was all poisoned, she could smell the poison and see it in the mashed potatoes and chicken and jello, they couldn't fool her. They were trying to get rid of the red ants in her rectum. If the red ants died she would die, too. Without red ants nesting in her rectum, Petra would be nobody.

She wandered into the room where Naomi was, and stopped, shifting the weight of her wiry body from one foot to the other, talking to herself, repeating without even any need for embellishment the story she had settled upon for herself. The story was about red ants in her rectum, and Naomi didn't fit into it. Petra needed a cigarette, so she left.

'I am Myra Larsen and I don't belong here! Ohh!'

It didn't hurt enough. Nothing hurt enough.

A pretty painted fingernail, long and perfectly curved, came into Naomi's eye. She yelped and her head jerked – of its own accord, its own instinct, involuntary, not because Naomi herself was trying to avoid suffering – but it was held firmly in place. The nail scratched, drew blood and tears.

Pouting crimson lips parted around pearly teeth, and the teeth bit down on Naomi's bared clawed hand. She cried out.

A weight lowered onto her, round knee in her belly, sharp little ringed fists grinding into the hollows of her shoulders. A forehead knocked into hers again and again. 'Ohh!' Naomi wailed, and there was an answering wail,

'Ohh! Ooohh!' – playful, mocking, goading.

Now the sheet was being tugged from behind, twisting and tightening as if ratcheted. Naomi's arms were pulled wide at the sockets. Her thighs were spread. Still the sheet was tightened, a hard strip now, sharpened by the pressure. It sawed up under her skirt and through her underwear into her vaginal fissure. She screamed.

Scraping trays, Shirley looked up. Myra Larsen, she thought tiredly. Doesn't she ever quit? And then remembered with a start that Myra Larsen was dead. 'Who *is* that?' she remarked to the orderly beside her, but he was from the pool and he wouldn't know. Shirley thought about going to check it out, but it wasn't her group and she had this whole stack of trays to scrape before she could go on break. Besides, nursing-home patients were always making noises that from anybody else would mean something. Especially at The Tides. Especially lately.

'I am Naomi Murphy! I am Naomi Murphy! Oohh!'

Chapter 17

Rebecca was standing by the dining-room window gazing out at the bowl of the lake, dimly imagining it undulating with heavy waves and creeping, pounding tides instead of clouded with the cold dust of this windy spring afternoon, when she recognized Dan's rapid footsteps behind her. Vaguely taken aback that she could identify him by nothing more substantial than the pattern and rhythm of his walk, she didn't turn.

No one else was in the dining room, but he pulled her rather roughly into a corner to demand, 'Now what?' She stared at him, uncomprehending. He shook her shoulder. 'Why is the fucking state in here again?'

'Alexander Booth filed a complaint of abuse against Abby Wilkins. And fraud against the management of The Tides.' She scarcely felt his hand and made no move to shrug it off. 'Alexander Booth is a patient.'

'I fucking know who Alex Booth is. I thought I told you no more complaints. I do not have time for this.'

A tiny tunnel of Rebecca's mind cleared, and through it she asked him anxiously, 'Oh, how's Naomi?'

Plainly, he didn't want to answer. 'Out of the hospital.'

'Is she home? Is she okay?'

'Shit, no, she's not okay. What's this about somebody

abusing Alex, for Chrissake? That's all I need.'

She meant to face him squarely but his image swam. 'I can find out about the abuse, Dan. But you'll have to tell me about the Medicaid fraud. Alleged.'

He released her and swung away. 'Get out of here.'

He was nearly out of range, badly distorted by the contrast between the glaring white corridor lights and the yellower, browner ones in the dining room, between the cube in which she stood and the interconnecting linear spaces he was entering through the small square arch, before Rebecca was able to say, 'What?'

'Get out of here. Go home.' He didn't pause or turn.

'My place is here—'

'Just go home.'

She stayed where she was, not out of defiance – though that was what Dan would think – but because she couldn't tell whether she was staying in a particular place or not. She meant to move. In fact, she scissored her legs one in front of the other and then reversed, as if in steps, toward a door. But a slippery sparkling patina had formed between her and the surface that supported and defined her, and her attempts at motion took her nowhere.

From behind the kitchen wall to her right came noises she recognized – pots clanging, food sizzling, tinny country music echoing among all the metal and tiled surfaces. But she heard no voices and was instantly, profoundly, disoriented: what could be making those sounds?

Straight ahead of her was a square hole of brilliant pulsating white light in a dimmer plane. Was she supposed to go there?

A mounded figure in a wheelchair appeared in the arch, features obscured by the bright backlight but clear in its motion, intent, and, somehow, in its identity. Trudy, it was Trudy, beckoning her madly. As if flung, Rebecca was at her side and kneeling, off-balance, clinging to the arm of the chair. Trudy, it was Trudy, unpainted mouth a sad clown's smile. 'How long can I stay here, dear heart?' was what she needed, urgently, to know.

Rebecca couldn't answer.

Already uneasy, Trudy now became seriously alarmed. She grabbed for Rebecca's shoulders and missed. 'Tell me. You have to tell me. How long can I stay here?'

Rebecca could not answer. Gauze gagged her, stuck her tongue to her teeth.

Trudy glared down at her, but the directedness of the gaze melted. She swatted haphazardly, the backs of her arthritis-swollen knuckles connecting with Rebecca's cheekbone. It was a glancing blow, but pinwheels spun behind Rebecca's eyes, she swayed, and she heard – perhaps she vocalized – a little shriek, outraged and delighted to be outraged. She straightened. Trudy wheeled away, calling to someone else, 'Dear heart! Can I ask you something? How long can I stay here?'

'As long as you like, honey,' came a loud, falsely reassuring reply – Diane, Rebecca thought. 'This is your home now.'

Dizzy, Rebecca trailed the outside of one elbow along a wall for support and guidance, with no hint, however, of where the wall would lead or what space it was dividing. Darker squares in the vast expanse of white floor tiles looked like gaping holes, but even as she made her way around them she knew they were only darker squares; her misplaced caution, then, was not only unnecessary but self-destructive, for it drew her attention away from real dangers of which, when they did come, she would have no warning, even a false one. She thought that was probably why the floor tiles had been installed in patterns like this. Someone wanted her to fall, or to think she was falling when she was not.

The handrail pressed into her flank. She could feel it wobbling, and made a distant mental note to add it to her repair list.

Then both the handrail and the wall vanished. She must be crossing an open doorway. She proceeded carefully.

From a long distance away – disproportionately small, blurred around the edges, then huge and sweet-sour-smelling and much too close – Marshall Emig materialized. Her father, and of course he hadn't materialized; he had been there all along, all her life, the same man now as when she had been born, but vastly changed and never the man she'd thought him to be. Something in her rose to him in a way not her own, giddy, purposeful, like a lover no longer required to bide her time.

Dimly she wanted Kurt. But Kurt had left her long ago, although he might at this moment or any moment be in the house they shared.

She thought to get out of her father's way, duck into a room, turn her back and hope he wouldn't notice her. He might well not. She thought to open her arms to him. He was carrying his walker poised as if looking for something to set it over. His downcast gaze slid along the floor just ahead of his feet shuffling among the dark gaping holes that could have tripped him or swallowed him up if they'd been real.

He kept coming toward her. She thought he wasn't going to stop and wondered who would pass through whom. With an abruptness that threatened his balance

and hers, his gaze rose to her face and he cried out, raised
the walker, struck her with it and captured her among its
metal legs. 'Leave us alone! Go back where you came
from! Leave my daughter alone!'

Rebecca said, 'Dad, I *am* your daughter. I'm Rebecca,'
but his look of furious horror intensified as if at an utterly
shameless gambit, and then she wasn't sure.

'Marshall, it's okay.' Abby put her arm around
Rebecca's father's waist, which was something Rebecca
could bring herself to do only when she thought of him as
a resident of The Tides and not as her father. 'Come on,
come with me, let's go eat dinner.'

He turned to her pleadingly. 'I have to protect Becky.
I'm her father. I have to take care of my daughter.'

'Your daughter's fine. See? Right here, she is. Becky's
fine.' Gesturing toward Rebecca for Marshall's sake, Abby
– unintentionally, Rebecca was sure – brushed and then
grasped her wrist.

Something in Rebecca flared like a Roman candle, cold
vivid fire, and she swung around to look hard into the
younger woman's eyes. She expected to encounter their
characteristic limpid brown and to be able easily to stare
her down. Instead, Abby's eyes blazed.

Marshall was looking from one to the other of the
young women, torso jerking, face crazed. At some point he
had started whispering, 'Faye! Faye! Faye! Faye!' with
each turn of his head, and the staccato cries became
louder and more rapid: 'Faye! Faye! Faye!'

'Hey.' Dan Murphy stepped between Rebecca and
Abby, breaking the hold. 'You can't be talking to her in the
middle of an abuse investigation. Jesus, don't you know
better than that?'

Abby looked at Dan. 'Abuse?' Then she turned her

bewildered gaze to Rebecca, where she was more likely to find an explanation. 'What's he talking about? Who abused who?'

'Get the hell *out* of here,' Dan said in a vicious undertone to Rebecca. 'You're just making this shit worse.'

Fighting with only partial success the urge to laugh, Rebecca squirmed out from under his towering bulk and nearly skipped down the hall, past Petra tugging at McAleer's gray sleeve. 'Cigarettes,' she hissed. 'Hey, lady, give me two cigarettes and I'll let you see my red ants.'

Rebecca was nearly running by the time she reached the door. If she went out this way an alarm would go off, and, imagining all those people running around looking for her, she could hardly wait. All but giggling, on the verge of tears, she pressed down on the bar, but was brought up short by a shrill proclamation. 'I am no one! I am no oné! Ohhh!'

Rebecca clamped a hand over her mouth, but the cries did not stop so she must not be the one making them. Albeit loud and harsh, they were emotionless, as though produced by a parrot that had blundered upon truth.

'Ohh! I am no one!'

Rebecca backed into the room where Naomi lay, flat on her back, limbs contracted and torso rigid as if she were restrained in bed although she was not. The last Rebecca had known, Naomi had been in a private psych hospital. She had not known they had admitted her to The Tides; the possibility would never have occurred to her, and she could not fathom how it had been accomplished. 'What are you doing here?' she asked her softly.

Naomi met her gaze on common, shifting ground. 'I am no one,' Naomi said to her. 'Sit down here beside me, girlie, and you might learn something.'

She grasped her hand. One or both of them whispered, 'I am no one. I am no one. Ohh.' But she could not stay here.

Her perceptions were dismembered, one quite discrete from another with spaces in between. Here was a metal bar across the undersides of her fingers. Then, here was open space, cool air. Then, here was a flash of sunny slick red, set apart from the gray day. Then, here was her car, a hollowed mound, prepared to transport her from one place to another place. Then, here was the rumble and vibration of the engine, the gasoline smell.

Her house was empty. So empty she was afraid to go in. Kurt, of course, was at work, this being a weekday afternoon, but she'd expected that, counted on it. The emptiness of the house had less to do with his absence from it than with her own. Huddled in her car at the curb in front of the small brick house she knew to be the place she lived, she could not go in; she would be swallowed up.

It didn't take long, even in rush hour, to get across town to her parents' house. A tan and white split-level in a development now well-established, this was the house she'd grown up in; there were no woods here. Surely there was no red oilcloth. She didn't have a key, of course, and even if her mother were at home rather than at The Tides, Rebecca had no place here.

Spring dusk was falling as she returned to The Tides, coming up on it from the west. One or another of its back windows flashed peach-colored, suggesting an aborted signal. Between her and the building stretched the vacant field, with the lake-bed sunk far enough below the plane of the slanting light that it wasn't really visible. Rebecca didn't want to go down there. She was afraid she would.

She locked the car doors and backed away, and was not pursued.

Here was a red light. She stopped. There was a restaurant sign. A horn honked. She went on. She checked into a motel a dozen blocks away from The Tides, cheap enough that she could cover it with the cash in her wallet. Without even thinking about it, she concocted an alias. The room had a phone, from which she called Kurt, got the answering machine, left a message that something had come up at work and she wouldn't be home tonight, realized without amusement or distress that he might well think she was having an affair.

There was, however, no room service. She considered. Her hunger was not sufficient to drive her out of the room now that she was safely in it, and her thirst she could slake, if not satisfy, with rusty-tasting water from the sink. She lay on the bed. The ceiling had no marks on it. The picture on the wall was mostly green. She was cold, felt exposed. She got under the bedspread. A few disjointed dream images surfaced, swept back out to sea.

In the morning, her first organized, conscious thought was that she could go back to her place now, find out what had happened during her exile, be with people she knew. Relief bordered on joy. Cursorily she combed her hair, had to look in a mirror to put on makeup but successfully kept her gaze focused on the specific feature being altered – lips pinked, lashes darkened, lids tinted lavender. As she dressed, it crossed her mind to wonder whether people would remark on the fact that she was wearing the same clothes as yesterday; she herself wouldn't have noticed if she hadn't taken them from the back of a chair. She'd get something to eat at the facility; if she was lucky, they'd be baking cinnamon rolls. Once she'd had a cup of coffee and mints from the roll in her desk drawer, no one would be able to tell that she hadn't brushed her teeth. She was ready, trembling a little.

The early morning was bright gray; she squinted and her eyes watered, and objects caught in peripheral vision had auras of storm gray and lavender. She hadn't thought to warm up her car, and the engine was sluggish, all but coasting out of the motel parking lot, stalling out at the first red light. It had rained in the night and partially frozen, or snowed and already started to thaw. The streets were slushy, viscous waves fanning out from her tires. Runoff in the gutters whorled in oily rainbows. The closer she got to The Tides, the closer together and more connected her thoughts became, and the clearer her understanding that this was who she was: the administrator of The Tides Nursing Center, going to work.

Even before she unlocked her office and deposited her coat, briefcase, and purse, she went to check on her father. He was up, ready for breakfast, a sheet wrapped around his chest and under his arms to knot behind the chair. He seemed relaxed, even contented. His hands rested in his lap. His gaze lifted to her face and he smiled gently. 'Good morning,' he said, glad to see her, whether he knew who she was or not.

She leaned to kiss him. His cheek was whiskery against her lips; obviously they hadn't got around to shaving him yet. Maybe she'd have a chance later this morning to come back and do it herself. She'd like that. 'Good morning,' she said to him. Then, 'Good morning, Marshall.' Calling him by his given name sent a little shock through her, not altogether unpleasant.

On her way out of her father's room she caught sight of Dan Murphy in the room across the hall, at his wife's bedside. She hesitated, then went in. 'How is she?' she asked, quietly although Naomi's eyes were open.

'No change.'

'Do they know yet what – what happened?'

'Rebecca.' He used her name like a weapon. 'We need to talk.'

She was supposed to have confirmed with the roofing company that they'd start work this week. She half-turned. 'Wait till I call—'

'We're having visitors today,' he said.

'Another survey.' She sighed and shook her head. She looked at him, though he wasn't quite in focus. 'Another complaint?'

'A Notice of Summary Closure.'

'What's that?'

'They believe there's sufficient danger to the health and safety of the residents in this facility that they're taking action to close it. Summarily. Without a hearing.'

'That's bullshit.'

'Rebecca.' He placed his hand flat on the bedside stand. There was no noise, yet the effect was of a resounding slap and she jumped. 'Rebecca, listen to me now. It's over.'

'You mean The Tides will be closed today? Just like that?'

'No.' He took the step or two to the window. 'I just got back from a breakfast meeting at Lou's with some people from Health and Social Services and from the Fraud Unit. We were able to strike a deal.'

He paused. Okay, she thought; I'll ask. 'What kind of deal?'

'They'll deliver the Notice of Summary Closure first thing this morning, make a show of force and intent, and the media will be informed. We'll be in court this afternoon. Alex Booth went home, and he dropped the abuse thing, so all they have is the fraud, and they don't really have that. So they'll settle for a compromise.' He gave his signature mirthless bark of laughter. 'Or a sacrifice, depending on your point of view.'

This is not as hard for him as it should be, she thought, not yet quite conscious that she knew what was happening. She concentrated on the part she could grasp. 'Alex went home?'

Dan went on as if she hadn't spoken. 'The price for saving The Tides is you.'

She nodded. She moved as far away from him as she could in the small room and nodded again, more shocked than she should have been. 'And you agreed to this.'

He shrugged. 'Buys us a little time.'

'When do you want me out?'

'Today.' She stared at him. 'Now. Before they get here. I told them you'd be gone. Besides, babe—'

'Do not call me babe!' She was halfway across the room toward him. Naomi stirred.

'It'll be harder on everybody to draw out the goodbyes. Just go. You'll have a month's severance.'

'Can we afford that?' she began automatically, and stopped. Dan said nothing. He wasn't exactly meeting her gaze – which, in any case, would have been hard to meet, since it was skittering, fading in and out – but he wasn't looking away, either, and she thought somehow he ought to be.

'Ohh!' Naomi breathed.

'Rebecca,' said Dan at the window. 'They're here.'

'My things,' she said helplessly.

'We'll get them to you.'

Just inside the front door, the administrative surveyor

who'd taken Ernest Lindgren's place was already reading aloud in a preacher's voice the Notice of Summary Closure of The Tides Nursing Center. Petra was pacing in front of him, hunched over inside her knotted pink sweater, muttering about the red ants that just this morning had started to colonize her heart. Diane and Sandy stood together in the door of Sandy's office, and Rebecca wondered dully that they were in so early.

Keeping her head down and her hands up as if to fend off attackers, although nobody approached her, she pushed her way outside through nothing in the least resistant. Went off the porch, across the parking lot toward her car. Veered into Elm Street as if thinking to leave on foot. Stopped. Came back.

Sneaking, like a fugitive or a spy, she went around the end of the building. The water mark on the brick was as tall and as wide as her shadow. A few weeds in the field were starting to green at the tips, making the space look complex and unstable. The lake must sometimes have been bigger than it was now, sometimes smaller. Clear in the flat morning light were scalloped markings across the ground and through the air, undulating variations in color and texture and growing patterns where tides waxed and waned. Rebecca made her way to the depression and stood there, edged to the very rim, wavering, balance off, thinking how easy it would be just to slide down.

Inside the building, Marshall – restrained in a chair now so he wouldn't wander or fall, contemplative throughout the long hours since they'd lifted him out of bed – suddenly writhed and bellowed. Those staff and residents who weren't busy with breakfast and baths and morning meds, which had to be taken care of no matter what happened next, were preoccupied with the Health

Department and television cameras, and no one was anywhere near him.

Marshall managed to work the knotted sheet around so that his arms were free of it, but it secured his neck and head. He roared, choked. He twisted himself sideways and the chair tipped, then toppled. The sheet pulled tight across his throat and mouth, a gag, a noose. 'Faye,' he called, but no one hearing him would have understood what he was trying to say.

Except Naomi. Across the hall, Naomi sat up, then pushed herself to her feet. She stood a few moments with her eyes closed and her head down, getting her bearings, then walked out of the room.

The side door was mere steps away, and she leaned on the bar to push it open. An alarm was supposed to sound, but the apparatus was not functioning, and the door jerked open and swung shut without attracting anyone's attention.

Naomi breathed, 'Ohh!' as the prickling, swelling, demanding sensation inside her took form and voice. 'I am Faye! I am Faye!' That was not quite true, not quite, though it wanted to be. 'Listen to me, girlie, and you might learn something!'

In a ferocious undertone, lying on the hard shiny white floor with the chair on his back and the sheet over his nose and mouth and around his straining throat (not understanding and not needing to understand what was under him or on top of him or why his movements were impeded), Marshall was talking to himself, talking to Faye, talking to Rebecca, exhorting himself to hurry, to find a way, telling her no, pledging himself to her, saying be careful be careful, saying no. He managed to get up onto his hands and knees, the chair on his back like the cracked shell of a turtle, the sheet pressing painfully into his Adam's apple. He managed to crawl.

Just outside, stepping into her own crisp shadow as it emerged from the long low shadow of the building, Naomi experimentally began a soft wail. 'I am Faye and they took my baby away! I am Faye and they won't give me back my baby! Ohh!' This, Naomi perceived, was still not authentic suffering, but it was leading somewhere.

Marshall collapsed.

Billie had come to feed him his breakfast, not minding so much this morning, tentatively entertaining the possibility that it might be bearable to define herself as the wife of a demented man. Seeing the reporters and cameras, avoiding them, at first she had thought Colleen was finally getting press coverage for some sort of special activity, and wasn't that nice? But then she'd spotted the long sheet of paper tacked to the front door and had gone over to read it: *Notice of Summary Closure.* Even though it was written in bureaucratese, its meaning was plain enough. They were going to close this home. She would have to find someplace else for Marshall. She couldn't trust Rebecca to help her, either, for the paper said, for the world to see, that Rebecca wasn't a good nursing-home administrator after all. That hurt. She tried to think of a way that it might not be true, but surely the Health Department of all people knew what they were talking about. Rebecca would lose her job. This job meant everything to her. Billie never had understood that; how could working in a nursing home matter that much? But it scared her, how much it mattered to Rebecca.

Billie looked around, not wanting to. All these people would have to find another place. That made her mad, at her daughter and at the Health Department and at she didn't know who all.

She didn't see Rebecca. That worried her. Rebecca would be devastated, even if she had gotten herself into this mess. Billie's impulse was to find her, go to her, but she held it sternly in check. What was there to say?

So she went instead to her husband's room and found him on the floor with the chair tied to his back, arms and legs squirming. She said just his name, 'Marshall!' which didn't come close to saying what she meant but she couldn't imagine what would.

She got him free, even though he thought she was Faye and tried to fight her off. When he realized who she was, he called for Faye, tried to chase after Faye, crawling, until the girls came in and they could get him into bed with the siderails up. Shirley kept telling her it was all right but it wasn't all right; Billie couldn't look her in the eye. She was afraid he'd try to crawl out over the rails. Just the thought of it made her sick. But he seemed to have settled down now. He just lay there flat on his back staring at the ceiling. Billie had to stop herself from reaching over and shutting his eyes.

Instead, grunting, she cranked up the head of his bed and tried to feed him his breakfast. He wouldn't eat a bite. He just wouldn't open his mouth. Finally she gave up and put the full tray in the hall for them to collect and went back and hoisted herself up on the bed beside Marshall and they just sat there. She didn't think he knew her anymore. In a sweet, unnerving, surprising way, though, she knew him.

The window of Marshall's room was closed against the cool spring air, curtains drawn against the light although the room was fluorescent bright inside, and so Billie didn't see the pale fog settling over the empty lake-bed and fluttering out of it like layers of gauzy scarves. She didn't hear Naomi keening softly to herself as she set off into the tidal field: 'I am Faye and they took my child away! I am Faye and they won't give my baby back to me! Ohh! Sit right here beside me, girlie, listen to me and you might learn something. I am Faye! Ohh!'

Chapter 18

Petra knew about the fog. Ants liked fog, she was told, especially red ants, especially fog that had all different colors in it like this. Muttering, hugging herself with the flat arms of her grimy pink sweater, she went out into the many-legged fog.

'She cannot be allowed outside in this weather,' Odette McAleer said sternly to Dan. 'Especially without a coat. Accepted standards of patient care require clothing appropriate to weather conditions if patients are permitted outside the facility.'

'Go get her,' Dan snapped in Maxine's direction.

Maxine restrained herself from coming back with, 'Go get her yourself.' But she did protest, 'She won't come in if she doesn't want to. Or she'll go right back out again.'

'Go *get* her,' Dan snarled and, dismissing her, pushed his way behind the nurses' station where Diane, Sandy, and Health Department officials were preparing discharge plans for all the patients of The Tides to present to the court this afternoon, although they would likely not be put into effect.

Maxine waited, barely, until Dan's back was turned before mouthing obscenities at him. Then she went out the front door and around the end of the building in search of Petra. It was chillier out here than she'd expected, and cloudy, clouds scudding across a paler cloud cover, a front or something coming in. She shivered and swore. She didn't know where Petra was and she didn't care. Damned if she was going to freeze her ass off out here. She let herself in the north door without noticing anything unusual outside other than the weather.

Wind was picking up. The fog floated and whipped to meet Rebecca, laying a cushion between her feet and the field she was crossing, then tugging it away so that she stumbled. Swaddling her like a baby's receiving blanket, soft and warm, then swishing like a cold veil across her exposed flesh.

Inside The Tides, the lights flickered more and more harsh and bright as the light outside dimmed, and the ambience of the place took on qualities suggestive of a winter afternoon although it was an early morning in spring. Sandy, pouring coffee for one of the Health Department team, remarked on what peculiar weather they were having today, teased that it must be some sort of sign, but he, irritated at having to be out here monitoring the routine activities of this facility when he had work of his own to do at the office and the damn place wasn't going to be shut down anyway, everybody knew that, didn't respond to any of Sandy's conversational gambits. Sandy thought that was rude, and her feelings were a little hurt.

Billie had dozed off beside her husband in his narrow bed. Shirley found her there and, smiling fondly, sadly, didn't disturb her. No harm in leaving her there for a few minutes; she'd have to face reality soon enough. Shirley turned off the overhead light and shut the door most of the way, rendering Marshall's room dim and nearly hidden from casual view.

Wide awake, Marshall lay still a while longer, listening, getting ready. Sometimes he knew precisely what he was preparing for. Sometimes he knew only the preparation. Finally, he eased himself over the siderails without making much noise or jarring his sleeping wife enough to alert her to his intent.

He knew he wouldn't accomplish his mission on his own two feet. He might very well not anyway, but at the moment he was calm and clear-headed, and he would use any means at his disposal to increase his odds of success.

A wheelchair sat beside the bed. One corner of the privacy curtain draped across the back of it, and Marshall understood how easy it would be not to recognize what this thing was. How easy it would be, too, to be afraid.

But the bewilderment and the possibility of fear faded. Grasping the bedrail with both hands, he shuffled in sideways strides as long and smooth as he could make them, two, three, four, and Billie stirred but didn't wake to stop or confuse him. He leaned on the chair. It rolled, and his choice was either to resist it or to go along. Like bringing a car out of an icy spin, he acted counter-intuitively and went into the dangerous motion instead of against it, wrested his other hand off the relatively stable bedrail and for a few long seconds was moorless in space and time, then got himself turned around and sank into the slung seat.

He needed to pause then, to take some deep breaths and reorient himself as much as possible. But there was no time for that. He was missing some information about his environment, to be sure, but he had enough to go on.

Walking his feet between the front wheels of the chair and pushing at the big back wheels with the heels of his hands, he took himself out of the room into the glare of the hall. Feeling and smelling fresh air, he maneuvered toward its source. Petra, coming in, held the door open for him. She was talking, but he thought not to him. He had no wish for an actual conversation with her, but he did intend to nod a thank you at her. He might not, however, have done so, since it was necessary for him to focus his entire attention on the task at hand.

Which was monumental. Whose stakes could not have been higher. The instant he entered the fog, he saw Faye's face in it, eyes shimmering, lips stretched wide in mocking laughter. The instant the door behind him was shut and latched, he no longer lived at The Tides.

Faye could hardly control herself, but she had to, for a little while longer. She couldn't remember the last time she'd been this excited. To think this was happening now, *now*, when she'd almost come to believe her days of having real fun were gone for good. She should have known better.

Here was her daughter, here was Rebecca, coming of her own free will across the cold weedy expanse toward her. She was virtually a stranger, of course. Faye couldn't tolerate knowing very much about people; the details of other lives were so *boring*. All she knew about Rebecca, which was more than enough, was what she'd picked up from observation – close observation, mind you – these last few months, grafted onto bits and pieces of memories from the indignity of the pregnancy culminating in the outrage of the birth and from the first two or three days of her life which was all it had taken for Faye to know beyond a shadow of a doubt that this was not for her.

Rebecca looked a little the worse for wear, Faye thought. Her makeup was a disaster, and that was a terribly unflattering hairdo even when it was combed, which it wasn't at the moment. Faye could hardly wait to get her hands on that hair. Rebecca's clothes, sort of frumpy in the first place, looked as if she'd slept in them; at the very least, it was the same outfit she'd been wearing yesterday, which was disgusting.

But Rebecca was a pretty girl, her mother's daughter no matter what. This afforded Faye one of those bright, mean little spurts of triumph every bit as satisfying and addictive as a shot of whiskey had ever been. She was petite, which was useful with men. Good features. Not bad posture, and nothing wrong with the way she carried herself that a little motherly instruction couldn't fix.

Faye clasped her hands over her heart, then held out her arms. 'Ah, my darling, they can't keep us apart any longer! The sacred bond between mother and child is simply too strong!' That was lovely.

Many of the weeds in the field were higher than Rebecca's shoulders now, tangling in her hair, brushing her cheeks and under her chin, working themselves inside her clothes, inside her head. It must have been longer than she'd thought since she'd been down here; this must be spring growth. Fog made it hard to think. Fog blurred sky, ground, lake-bed, lake. The lake was full. Overflowing.

Rebecca squinted, stared. The lake was full of a substance with the consistency and rippled sheen of water but streaked with wild color and pulsing with tides of surprising strength and rapidity. There had been rain recently, but hardly this much, and the ground she was crossing to get to the lake wasn't wet; it must be some drainage oddity, or maybe only some trick of the foggy light.

The substance undulated and splashed over the edge of the depression, tongued at her. In it was a woman in a flowing gown, lavender and pink, with streaming hair the colors of the fog. Faye. Rebecca took a step backward. The woman's face was animated, pretty: enormous blue eyes with lashes thickened and curled, artfully heightened color in the cheeks, rosebud lips parted in a dazzling smile. In the silver sky above her was her face again, again and again, and in the tree, just budding like an admirer's bouquet, that was bending and tossing over the lake as if it would break, and in the surface of the lake tilting now so Rebecca could see her own face and the woman's face in it and then dipping flirtatiously away.

Billie woke up. Marshall was gone. Ponderously she struggled off the bed and scrambled for the call button on the cord, then didn't wait for help. As she hurried out into the hall, out into the fog, to catch Marshall herself, the awful suspicion nagged at her that she hadn't really been sleeping hard, that she'd known somewhere in her mind when Marshall went to Faye and she'd been just too tired and too defeated to care.

The field behind the nursing home was ugly as usual, colorless, weedy and bare, littered, generally unkempt. Somebody ought to do something with it. Billie didn't know who, now that Rebecca didn't work here anymore.

But Rebecca was out here. Billie saw her moving toward the hollow in the middle of the field where they said a lake used to be, and wondered what in the world she was doing. At almost the same time she saw Marshall careening after Rebecca in his wheelchair. As far as she could tell through the wisps of fog here and there on the ground like dust mites, the field was practically level, no slope steep enough for him to build up that much momentum, and he certainly didn't have enough strength to be pushing himself that fast. But he was speeding, hell-bent for leather through the blowing litter and scraggly weeds in pursuit of Rebecca, in pursuit of Faye.

Billie had no hope of catching up to him. Yet she had no choice but to try. She called to him, but of course he paid her no mind. She took a deep breath, stepped off the sidewalk, and started out across the field, already panting. Dust spat into her face, smelling oddly of roses, making her breath hurt in her chest. The sky was gray and lemon-yellow now, mean-looking. In a few places, an individual cloud was outlined in purple like a glimpsed breast. The wind shoved at her. A storm was coming up. Billie could taste the dangerous energy in the air.

Faye twirled. Lavender and pink billowed around Rebecca, and now the wind brought rain – perhaps not rain, for it blew horizontally off the surface of the lake. Faye cried happily, 'I've come back for you! Isn't that wonderful?'

'Who do you think you are?'

Faye let her laughter peal in delight. Her laugh was one of her best natural assets, enhanced by the ways she'd learned to use it in the years since she'd last seen Rebecca. 'Yes, yes, because of you I *know* who I am at last, and I am in your debt.' She'd said that more than a few times, to quite a range of people, in the distant and recent past, editing it each time until it was perfect. For instance, she used to say, 'And I thank you for that,' but 'in your debt' was more elegant. The declaration was so effective that it had become part of her standard repertoire. This time, though, she could add, 'I'm your mother!'

'I already have a mother.'

Faye was starting to lose patience. She did not like challenges. Things should be easy and come to her as her due. She began to frown, then thought better of it and instead formed a pretty little *moue* with her lips and made a grand dismissive motion with one hand, careful to keep her wrists gracefully bent so as to show off her long glossy nails to their best advantage. An image of herself came to her that she rather liked, so she turned both palms upward, cupped them slightly, and wiggled all her fingers toward Rebecca in a lovely, playful, insistent beckoning. 'Oh, but I'm your *real* mother. Come here!'

'You're not very real to me.'

Now Faye allowed tears to trickle from her eyes, her voice to wail and crack a little. Why was this girl being so stubborn? 'How can you treat me this way, Becky? Your own mother! After all this time . . .'

'I didn't even know you existed until Dad started talking about you, just lately.'

Faye nodded. She wasn't surprised. 'They had no right to hide us from each other! My own flesh and blood! It wasn't their secret.' Faye was weeping in earnest now, but softly, no ugly sobbing, facial contortions limited to a puckering of the mouth that she knew made her look childishly pouty and endearing but that could be easily reversed.

'Dad keeps calling you,' Rebecca said accusingly, as if that meant something. 'Since he's had Alzheimer's, he says your name and talks about you a lot. Talks to you.'

'Marshall's such a dear,' Faye cooed, smug through the trailing off of her tears. 'He always did love me so much.'

'He's been married to my mother for a long time,' Rebecca objected.

'She's not your mother! I'm your mother! Do you hear me? *I'm* your mother!' Thoroughly exasperated, Faye darted forward and managed to catch Rebecca's wrist.

'She raised me. She was there when I needed her.'

'Oh, honey, I'm not any good with kids. Really. Trust me, you were better off. But now you're all grown up, and you and I can have such *fun* together.' She rested her free hand against Rebecca's cheek, having learned a long time ago that people would allow you all sorts of liberties if you just acted as if you had the right, and that made them your accomplices.

The lake rose around them. The sky lowered. Rebecca felt no moisture, but the sensation of tides coming in and going out at split-second intervals made her skin crawl and her thoughts elide. The touch on her cheek widened and deepened to take in the entire side of her face, then pressed lightly against her mouth so that she could kiss the tender palm, for an instant stopping her breath.

Billie turned her ankle and went down hard.

Marshall was riding through Faye, the force of his trajectory spreading Faye apart, shoving aside one manifestation of Faye after another. Much of the time he couldn't exactly see or hear his daughter, but his mental image of her was a clear and steady stick figure in the miasma that was Faye, and he kept himself focused on that, headed for her, sometimes forgetting why, sometimes knowing better than he'd ever known anything who he was at this moment in his life and what he was doing here. Faye was under his wheels, turning them and keeping them from turning, propelling him forward and trying to tip him over. Faye was in his face. Faye was dancing in his mind, jumbling his thoughts like a child's blocks, mixing up his thoughts one with the others like fingerpaint. But he couldn't stop now. He was almost there.

Rebecca made a slight but definite movement into rather than away from the cradle of Faye's palm. Faye had been alert for just such an opportunity. She stepped in and took her daughter in her arms.

Faye's substantiality was both surprising and primally familiar. Rebecca didn't know what she'd expected – she wouldn't have said she'd expected anything – but she allowed, then went into, then returned the embrace as if she had no choice, and the shock of Faye's undeniable presence was shot through with relief. There was something profoundly comforting and profoundly unsettling about being pressed like this against Faye's small body, so like her own; about the intimate fall of blonde curls among her own blonde curls; about the sensation of being identified and filled in ways she hadn't even known she was missing. Rose fragrance adhered to the hollow of her neck and the insides of her wrists, taking on slightly personal qualities as it interacted with her own chemistry but still fundamentally roses, fundamentally Faye's. Silver-pink lipstick smeared onto both corners of her mouth.

Faye whispered, 'Come away with me. Let's go someplace fun.'

'I can't.'

'Sure you can. Who'd miss you here? Your boyfriend? Your boss? Your dad?' Faye laughed.

Turning, swimming in the fog and wind, spun by the cloud of minute particles off the surface of the waxing and waning lake, Rebecca looked back at The Tides. A wash of colors and shapes, one indistinguishable from the next and in no real pattern, it hovered without either foundation or roofline between the waves of ground and sky. From every blurred doorway, Faye beckoned. She lolled in every bed. The skirt and wide sleeves of her gown frothed at every opening and closing window. The stench of roses whipped in the laughter of the storm.

Hobbling on her twisted ankle, which hurt quite a bit

but so far supported her weight, Billie kept after her husband and, through him, her daughter. It didn't look to her as if anything was really going to come from this storm; there wasn't any wind to speak of, no rain or snow, and neither the fog nor the cloud cover was very dark. But it was chilly, and Marshall shouldn't be out here. He'd catch his death. Rebecca shouldn't be out here, either, for reasons not as clear in Billie's mind but equally compelling. She didn't guess she could do much about either one of them, or about Faye, either, but here she was.

After a long moment Rebecca said, 'I can't leave Mom,' astonished that she was actually considering whether she could.

'Your father's wife,' Faye said deliberately, derisively, 'is all wrapped up in your father. She won't even notice.'

'She needs me.'

Faye shook her a little. This was almost not fun anymore. 'She's got all these nurses and aides and people to help her. She doesn't need you. Why should you stay here where everything's so ugly when you could come away with me and have a good time?'

To Faye, this seemed an irresistible invitation, but Rebecca was not letting her in. She pulled away, flounced, maybe overplaying her hand but she didn't think so.

'She doesn't need you. I need you.' Every time she'd said, 'I need you' to somebody, she'd meant it, for the moment, with all her heart. She meant it now.

'What for?'

'What?' Faye had had it. 'What are you talking about?'

'What do you want with me?'

This was ridiculous. Faye wasn't about to be talked to this way. 'You want me, too,' she said petulantly. 'You do,' and then got very quiet. The silent treatment. Usually that worked. People thought they couldn't live with her, but they couldn't stand the threat of living without her, either.

Inside the building, Sandy stopped Diane as they passed each other in the hall, each on another errand for the Health Department. In a stage whisper, she remarked, 'Have you looked outside? My goodness, I don't believe I've ever seen fog like that around here. It's kind of spooky, you know?'

Petra sprinted down the hall and threw herself at Sandy from behind, wrapping her hard thin arms around the bookkeeper's neck and her hard thin thighs around her pelvis, clamping her ankles in front. Sandy staggered. Diane stepped forward to intervene. Petra's screams were gravelly and staccato, but what she was saying was clear: 'They're gone! They drowned! They washed away!'

Rebecca was descending, strata rising around her. Tides had left sediments. A scrap of brown paper from a grocery sack. A repeated refrain as if from birdsong but bluesy, woodwind. A green bottle, more than half-full of thick purple wine. Rebecca sank. A car in the woods, pretending to be hidden but not really hidden for she saw it; the acrid and strangely luscious taste of gasoline in the air as the car pulled away, and the taste of her own frantic tears.

Faye whispered, 'We can be together now.'

The smell of oilcloth warmed by hotter sun than this, through a kitchen window. The smell of roses, up very close; the taste of roses.

Faye murmured, 'That's right.'

As her feet parted the gauzy weeds and her hands the crumbling strata in which they were embedded, Rebecca thought: I have noplace else to go. Nobody expects me anywhere. Why not go with her?

Faye breathed, 'Oh, my darling, why not?'

Rebecca thought: I'm not the administrator of The Tides anymore. I'm not anybody's lover. I'm not the same person to my father from one minute to the next. I'm not my mother's daughter.

'I'll show you who you are!' Faye shrieked in delight, and pink and lavender spangles puffed toward Rebecca from all directions like a pretty mushroom cloud.

Rebecca said, 'No,' and freed herself.

'What? What did you say?'

'Go away. Nobody wants you here.'

The cloud burst apart in fury, and Faye screamed, 'You little fool! You little bitch! You'll be sorry! You'll regret this for the rest of your boring little life!'

'Leave me alone. Leave us all alone.'

Faye was beside herself, a dervish, crisscrossing streaks and stars. 'Nobody is going to keep me from what's mine. Not even you.' A bottle broke against Rebecca's shoulder, shards skittering across her skin and scratching, drawing blood, but not embedding. A long branch, just budding at half a dozen places along its shaft, flung up her skirt and whipped across the back of her leg.

'Go away!'

'Sure, Becky,' Faye hissed. 'Fine. Whatever you say,' and then, swelling, giddy and full of herself, she started toward Rebecca again.

Teetering on the viscous, shifting edge of the pit, strobed by its wild tides, Marshall reached for his daughter and caught her arm. The wind raved, and the fog spat and clawed, and Marshall tugged at his child until she stumbled backward into his lap. He wrapped his arms around her there, bent his head over her, was whispering not her name now, which he couldn't say, but wordless connectives.

Faye threw herself on them both, howling. Billie lumbered up to them, ashen-faced and dizzy, as Naomi burst out of the angry fog and cried, 'I am Faye! I am Rebecca! Let me!' and flung herself in Faye's path.

Curled in her father's lap and with her mother's sweaty hands on her back, Rebecca heard, then turned and saw the shiny bits of Faye shoot up in a sparkling fountain and then organize around Naomi as if they couldn't help themselves. Naomi spread her legs, opened her mouth, pried open her own clenched fists, and Faye went in. Glittering opaquely, Naomi's eyes rolled back in ecstasy, and the suffering coming out of her mouth, on breath stinking of roses, in words upon words upon words, was at last her own.

Faye had made a mistake.

She had expected to be in and out of Naomi on her own terms, as always, taking what she needed with no fuss or price. But she had underestimated the strength of Naomi's imagination and will. Naomi wouldn't let her go.

Faye pushed against the confines of Naomi's mind, the prison that had masqueraded as playground and feast. Naomi seized, clawed at soil that had not been nourishing or supportive in the first place and now had been further disturbed, broke apart strata to make new strata. But she would not let her go.

Faye cajoled, threatened, pleaded, sang riffs of desperate wantonness. Naomi screamed and babbled and keened. But she would not let her go.

Faye danced and fought. Faye threw herself off high places and burrowed into deep ones. Faye rose and fell with the tides. But Naomi had been waiting all her life for habitation like this, for possession and martyrdom like this, and she would never let Faye go.

DOUGLAS

HALLOWEEN
THE
MAN

CLEGG

The New England coastal town of Stonehaven has a history of nightmares—and dark secrets. When Stony Crawford becomes a pawn in a game of horror and darkness, he finds that he alone holds the key to the mystery of Stonehaven, and to the power of the unspeakable creature trapped within a summer mansion.

___4439-0 $5.50 US/$6.50 CAN

Dorchester Publishing Co., Inc.
P.O. Box 6640
Wayne, PA 19087-8640

Please add $1.75 for shipping and handling for the first book and $.50 for each book thereafter. NY, NYC, and PA residents, please add appropriate sales tax. No cash, stamps, or C.O.D.s. All orders shipped within 6 weeks via postal service book rate. Canadian orders require $2.00 extra postage and must be paid in U.S. dollars through a U.S. banking facility.

Name_____

Address_____

City_____State_____Zip_____
I have enclosed $_____ in payment for the checked book(s).
Payment <u>must</u> accompany all orders. ❏ Please send a free catalog.
CHECK OUT OUR WEBSITE! www.dorchesterpub.com

BRASS

ROBERT J. CONLEY

The ancient Cherokees know him as *Untsaiyi,* or Brass, because of his metallic skin. He is one of the old ones, the original beings who lived long before man walked the earth. And he will live forever. He cares nothing for humans, though he can take their form—or virtually any form—at will. For untold centuries the world has been free of his deadly games, but now Brass is back among us and no one who sees him will ever be the same . . . if they survive at all.

___4505-2 $5.50 US/$6.50 CAN

B|TE RICHARD LAYMON

"No one writes like Laymon, and you're going to have a good time with anything he writes."
—Dean Koontz

It's almost midnight. Cat's on the bed, facedown and naked. She's Sam's former girlfriend, the only woman he's ever loved. Sam's in the closet, with a hammer in one hand and a wooden stake in the other. Together they wait as the clock ticks down because . . . the vampire is coming. When Cat first appears at Sam's door he can't believe his eyes. He hasn't seen her in ten years, but he's never forgotten her. Not for a second. But before this night is through, Sam will enter a nightmare of blood and fear that he'll never be able to forget—no matter how hard he tries.

"Laymon is one of the best writers in the genre today."
—Cemetery Dance

___4550-8 $5.50 US/$6.50 CAN

Dorchester Publishing Co., Inc.
P.O. Box 6640
Wayne, PA 19087-8640

ATTENTION HORROR CUSTOMERS!

SPECIAL
TOLL-FREE NUMBER
1-800-481-9191

Call Monday through Friday
10 a.m. to 9 p.m.
Eastern Time
Get a free catalogue,
join the Horror Book Club,
and order books using your
Visa, MasterCard,
or Discover®

Leisure
Books